The Dragon's Threat

By Peter King

CHINA
EAST CHINA SEA
BURMA
LAOS
PHILIPPINES SEA
THAILAND
CAMBODIA
PHILIPPINES
ANDAMAN SEA
GULF OF THAILAND
MALAYSIA
MALAYSIA
NORTH PACIFIC OCEAN
INDONESIA
INDIAN OCEAN

The Dragon's Threat

Prologue

Peter Holroyd, Professor of Maritime History specializing in Ming and Qing Dynasty voyages, looked over the front page of his newspaper as he sipped a cup of tea. A small item near the bottom of the page reported the presence of Chinese warships in the South China Sea—nothing for him to get excited about. Professor Holroyd's field was China in the 1400s and 1600s, not the 21st Century. He put the newspaper aside and returned to reading grad student papers, sipping tea, and savouring warm toast thickly spread with creamy butter and marmalade.

Peter's world was an academic world, a quiet world, and ever since the accidental death of his wife and teenage daughter, a lonely world.

Over at Whitehall, though, people *were* getting excited. The phrase "Gunboat diplomacy" was resurrected in whispers. Secure electronic channels were humming. Doors were being closed. Phone calls were being made. Even the tea lady found

herself and her trolley hustled out into the corridor.
The hive had come alive with its special dance.

1

"The foreign secretary is calling, sir."

"Put him through." Holding the receiver in his left hand, the prime minister of the United Kingdom put down the cabinet paper he had been reading on a bill to limit immigration from the former British colonies and leaned back in his chair. What could not wait, he wondered, that would prompt his foreign secretary to call? Something unwelcome, no doubt. He waited, resigned to yet another distracting issue, as if the continuing fallouts of Brexit and illegal immigration weren't enough, not to mention tomorrow's likely contentious question period.

"Sorry to interrupt you, Prime Minister, but we might have a situation developing. We just got a call from the governor of Dejection Island. He reports a Chinese naval force patrolling offshore."

"Patrolling? Not simply passing by?"

"Patrolling, sir."

"And why is that of interest to us?"

"They are off Dejection Island, a tiny island in the South China Sea that belongs to us."

"Never heard of it!" The prime minister rubbed the bridge of his nose, once again thinking he should have his spectacle frames replaced.

"Few people have," the foreign secretary continued "From what I've been told, we acquired it by one of those accidents of history, but no one quite knows why we ever bothered to hold on to it."

"So, what's the problem, and what do you advise?" The PM leaned over, grabbed a cigarette, and lit it. He inhaled deeply, enjoying the flavour but wondering again how to hide this act of defiance from his wife. *That woman has the nose of a bloodhound!*

"It's in the middle of the South China Sea, which the Chinese claim is all theirs. Possibly, the ships are there because the Chinese believe the island sits in Chinese territorial waters. Given the proximity of the naval force, they may want to take it by force. I thought I'd give you a heads-up."

"Why now?"

"We're trying to find out, but it may have something to do with the Arbitration Court's decision that the Chinese have no claim to the whole South China Sea."

"Yes, quite right, but will there be a problem for us?"

"One never knows with the Chinese. They're still miffed about the Opium Wars."

"I see. Do you think we need to take any immediate action? And if so, what would an appropriate one be?"

"Not ready to suggest anything right now. We could not, for instance, send the Navy out because it's too far away, and given the situation out there, any ships of ours might cause alarm in what is already a volatile area. Besides, no one seems to think the effort would be worthwhile as I'm told it's a pretty isolated and desolate place, like Tristan da Cunha."

"Tristan da where?" The prime minister paused. "Oh, never mind! Sort it out, bury it, or lose it, will you? But try to avoid anything that might wake sleeping dogs. The last thing I need is for the press or the opposition to get more excited." He hesitated as a thought struck him. "Do we still want to keep the place?"

"Prime Minister, they're British subjects!"

"So were the Americans at one time."

For once, the foreign secretary couldn't immediately find a suitable reply. "I haven't been fully briefed yet, but I can see advantages to getting rid of it and avoiding any irritants given the current fuss over colonization and rewriting history. But there may be a hitch. The American ambassador asked if we propose to do anything about it."

"Was he indeed! Bloody Americans are always throwing sand in the works. I wonder why at this time. Keep abreast of it and let me know when you have a clearer picture."

"I'd like to put a small team together to follow developments. I have someone in mind, but I need your agreement."

"Who do you have in mind?"

"Hantington."

"Oh, yes! The father's an old friend. Yes, yes, I think he might be a sound choice."

"Thank you, Prime Minister."

*****

"Director Hsien will see you now. Please follow me."

Ron Miller, the first counsellor at the British embassy in Beijing, stood up, straightened his regimental tie, pulled out a little more cuff on his sleeves, and buttoned his jacket. Grabbing his briefcase, he followed the elderly, grim-faced woman to the door behind which he would find the

Foreign Ministry representative of the People's Republic of China.

Once inside the office, he faced a man sitting at a polished desk who looked up at him expressionlessly and said nothing. Two more men stood by the desk.

The office was roomy and painted in subtle light green. A picture of the president hung behind the desk, flanked by a Chinese flag. The walls were half-panelled in rosewood, and a thick patterned carpet covered much of the floor. To one side was a leather sofa facing a small coffee table with a flower arrangement. Three armchairs had been placed in front of the table opposite the sofa. A large mural depicting the Summer Palace partly covered the upper part of the wall to the right, giving the room a less business-like atmosphere.

Windows on one side of the room opened toward the Forbidden City. On clear days, the golden roofs of the ancient palace would have gleamed in the sun, but not today. A grey haze covered Beijing and hid any view, leaving a depressing impression. The Chinese Environment Office announced the pollution index was 250 ppm. However, the American embassy posted 720, and Miller believed the latter.

All three men facing him wore dark business suits and open-necked white shirts. Their unsmiling expressions were hardly welcoming, but they held a hint of curiosity and even disdain.

Miller thought he sensed tension but could not think why there should be. Unusual, he thought, but he had no choice but to wait.

"So good of you to come, Mr. Miller." The man behind the desk stood up. "Please be seated." He indicated the sofa. "I'm Hsien Fu Ling, and these are my associates, Li Wu Fen and Liu Hao Wen." The associates acknowledged their introductions with nods.

Miller sat on the sofa, pulled at the crease in his blue pinstripe suit trousers, and waited. He was slightly amused that sitting on the couch meant he had to look up at his hosts. No question who was going to try to dominate the conduct of the meeting.

"Forgive me for asking you to wait, but first, would you care for some tea?" At this question, a secretary came in and placed teacups on the table. Delicately spooning some tea leaves from a caddy, she poured hot water into the cups and put a small lid on each. After folding and placing a small white serviette beside each cup, she left the room.

Miller looked at his cup, admiring the delicate porcelain with its painted designs of gilded flowers and dragons, but did not reach out for it.

"Thank you for your kind invitation, Director Hsien, but perhaps we could come to the point of the meeting?"

A look of irritation crossed Hsien's face at such a breach of Chinese etiquette, but he got up, went to an armchair, and sat down, flanked by his associates.

"Of course, Mr. Miller, we do not wish to keep you from your important and, I dare say, pressing duties any longer than necessary." He paused to let the implied sarcasm sink in. "We received Her Majesty's Government note expressing concern over the presence of Chinese warships in the South China Sea near the so-claimed British colony of Dejection Island. We note Her Majesty's Government requests the government of the People's Republic of China to clarify the significance of the presence of these ships." Hsien paused and looked at Miller in silence.

"Significance?" he queried. "We do not recognize the existence of a British colony there, so of what concern are Chinese warships to Her Majesty's Government?

He waited for a reply, and when Miller remained silent, Hsien continued, "Has there been any sign to suggest that the ships are engaged in activities other than in China's peaceful interests?"

"Director Hsien, surely you are aware that Britain has long claimed Dejection Island as a British colony in the South China Sea. Because of that colony, colonial territorial waters clearly affect any nearby maritime activities. Her Majesty's Government would like assurances from the People's Republic of China that China will respect the colony's sovereignty over those waters."

"Mr. Miller, let me say that Britain claiming territory does not mean it belongs to Britain." Hsien reached for his tea and sipped delicately, holding the lid on top to keep the tea leaves in.

"Excuse me, Director, but the island is inhabited by people who have been and voted to remain British subjects."

Hsien looked at Miller with an expression that suggested a mixture of amusement and pity. Finally, Hsien leaned forward. "But you seem to forget our warships are off its coasts." After a moment, Hsien leaned back and continued. "But rest assured their presence should only be taken as a normal naval exercise by Chinese ships in Chinese territorial waters."

Miller was taken aback. He looked down at his shiny black brogues, gathering his thoughts. It sounds *to me like the gloves are most definitely coming off now. I think I just heard the opening salvo of gunboat diplomacy. This is way above my pay level. Still, it could get messy, and I doubt I'll be able to escape scot-free.*

"The South China Sea is Chinese territorial waters," Hsien repeated. "As I'm sure you know, although several nations dispute that fact, the Permanent Court of Arbitration has ruled to support their disputations. However, my government is concerned about the court's fairness and does not accept that ruling. Thus, we do not recognize any sovereignty other than our own." Hsien paused and waited for Miller's reaction.

Because Miller did not reply, Hsien took another sip and then continued. "Given my government's position, any activity China might be undertaking in that area will be to protect Chinese interests. Of course, we know the British and other claimed interests, such as the Americans. The American policy on the South China Sea is unacceptable to us, but we hope to encourage them to change their aims. We prefer they stay out of Chinese and Asian affairs."

Miller decided that some tea would be nice after all. Following Hsien's example, he struggled out of the couch and took a sip, holding the lid in place.

He looked up at Hsien. "Well, yes, Director Hsien, I understand, but given the island's status as a British colony, its policies hardly concern China. Britain is only interested in keeping its peaceful and cordial relationship with the People's Republic of China. As to American policies, Britain has no say in that matter. Why not go straight to the Americans?"

Hsien looked at Miller in silence before replying. "The Americans have been most uncooperative. We do not believe further discussions with them will help. However, may I understand that Britain will cooperate with China in preventing American or any other nation's activities and or expansions into the area?" Hsien carefully put his cup back on the table.

"I'm unable to give you any assurances on future British policies or the actions of other sovereign nations other than to repeat that we wish to avoid any disruption of our current friendly relationship."

"Excellent. But in the light of the British claim to the sovereignty of this island, we wondered why Britain did not appear before the Arbitration Court. To express concerns over the presence of Chinese warships, even if unfounded, seems late. However, in a spirit of cooperation, we would prefer to understand the British position before any misunderstandings occur."

"I'm unaware Britain had any reason to appear before the court. But, as you must realize, I'm unfamiliar with the British government's position on that matter." Miller heard one of the men say something in Chinese and understood he had just been dismissed as an administrative lackey. Miller hid his knowledge of Mandarin and bridled at the insult but held his anger.

"Yes, we understand that, but we would like Her Majesty's Government to address the issue." Hsien's tone suggested this was not a request for Her Majesty's Government to refuse.

"I apologize, but I was not aware there is an issue." Miller assumed a look of innocent bewilderment.

"But surely you understand that we are puzzled why, after the return of Hong Kong, Britain persists in its false claim to this island."

"False claim? But Director Hsien, you know that Britain has owned that island since the late eighteenth century, correct? As far as I know, China has never disputed that claim."

"Perhaps not, but that does not mean China accepts the continuation of an unfounded claim over Chinese territory," Hsien said.

"And as I pointed out, British subjects who have been there continually for some two hundred years live on that island," Miller replied.

"I'm sure alternative habitats are available to them, habitats that are not subject to dispute." Hsien paused for Miller to consider this suggestion before continuing. "Alternatively, they could remain on the island and apply for Chinese citizenship."

Miller took several moments to decide that Hsien had progressed beyond the territorial waters argument and now claimed the British colony belonged to China.

"Our concern is that Britain illegally holds on to this island as both an insult to China and to assist American expansionist aims or to support other interfering interests that could cause us irritations." Hsien's tone hardened.

"Ah! Yes, I can see how you might come to that conclusion! However, I repeat my assurance that Britain has no desire to disrupt its friendly relations with the People's Republic."

"That is most reassuring! I feel certain we can resolve the matter in a mutually cooperative manner." Miller had little doubt what cooperation would entail, but Hsien went on. "We apologize for the delay in bringing this matter up. Despite the delay, we are most interested in coming to a speedy resolution of the problem." He paused to let Miller consider to what problem Hsien could be referring.

Hsien continued, "As I'm sure your government understands, we are fully prepared to assume our rightful occupation of the island and are taking steps to do so quickly but peacefully. The presence of

Chinese warships should not be taken as an indication of China's intentions. The ownership issue may be just an administrative inconsistency requiring nothing more than paperwork that everyone would like to reduce."

Miller looked at Hsien. *Well, now, the significance of the warships needs no further explanation. The pundits in Whitehall will be pleased—or more probably not pleased at all. I'm not sure of the next step.*

"You said an administrative inconsistency?" Miller improvised.

"At the time England claimed the island, it was already Chinese. Our records show China never ceded its claim to the island; therefore, the English claim was illegal. We suggest addressing the issue now. We hope to do so amicably and cooperatively."

"But if your records show that the island is yours, why not produce them to justify your claim?"

"We intend to do so. At the proper time."

"Ah! Yes, I see. When might the time be appropriate?"

"When it is convenient."

"Ah! Yes, I can understand the problem. Does the People's Republic have any suggestions to give to Her Majesty's Government?"

"Come now, Mr. Miller! The People's Republic never makes suggestions to other sovereign states. We prefer to come to a mutual agreement." Hsien smiled, but Miller did not take it as a friendly gesture.

"Would I be correct that changing the status quo would be a convenient suggestion? A suggestion that could be in the best interests of both our governments and, more specifically, would prevent unfortunate and distressing consequences?"

Miller looked askance at his host, but Hsien smiled. "Mr. Miller, my superiors express the hope that Her Majesty's Government will act quickly and not disappoint them. To do otherwise could prove irritating."

With Chinese warships on hand, I doubt the irritation will last very long. With that thought, Miller took his leave and hurried back to his embassy.

2

The phone rang, and Peter Holroyd flopped down the graduate student's paper he had just started reading.

"Hello?"

"Peter, the old boys are having a pub crawl tomorrow evening. Corky's decided to marry again before he goes overseas, and we're sending him off. Care to join us?"

"Are you serious? I thought he was happy being footloose and fancy-free. Whatever changed his mind?"

"No idea, but he's terribly smitten, or so he says. Absolutely certain he's found the right woman this time."

"Who's the lucky maiden?"

"No idea, but rumours are she's not much of a maiden anymore, though she is terribly rich and upper class."

"That probably explains a lot. Poor girl: I hope she knows what she's in for. What's planned?"

"We meet at six p.m. at the Crown and Headsman. After that, we're moving to that club in Soho for a stag, and I wouldn't count on getting home early."

"A stag? With all the trimmings?"

"Oh, very much so. Bring that video if you've still got it."

"I've got it, and I'll bring it, though I think Corky will go batshit crazy. Super, I'll be there." With that, he smiled and hung up. He hadn't had a good booze-up for quite some time, and he suddenly realized he relished the idea of a boisterous night out with his former classmates.

In general, he abhorred social occasions with their meaningless exchanges of work or social successes, golf scores, and holidays in ghastly tourist traps. Holroyd liked the quiet routine of his academic life and preferred the company of books to most people. The parameters of professionalism largely dictated his social life; however, he did enjoy getting together with some of his school chums when freely flowing beer led to carefree and even boisterous camaraderie, to use quaint phrases.

He sat back and let the familiar coziness of his untidy home help him recover from the intrusion. The foliage of trees in front of the house mellowed the light through the windows of his darkly panelled study-cum-living-room. Valuable *objets d'art* and paintings decorated his Georgian-style flat. An aspidistra, the sole product of his indifferent horticultural skills, struggled to survive despite his ministrations or lack thereof. Maybe it needed more light and tender loving care.

He looked over at one corner of the desk where four photographs in silver frames had been placed. One showed Julia, his late wife, in an elegant evening gown. Another showed Alice, his deceased daughter, age eight, playing on the beach near Port of Spain. Two showed all three of them together. In one of them, Holroyd and his wife accompanied Alice, age ten, in a pink tutu after she got into Madame Svetlana's ballet school.

The last showed Holroyd, Julia, and Alice after Julia was conferred her doctorate in psychology. His wife's traditional hooded medieval regalia glowed next to his tailored grey suit and the blue of their daughter's dress. Seeing them still brought a lump to his throat and tears to his eyes.

Two years later, almost to the very day, he still missed them as much as he did the day that a drunk driver ran them down. The closet still contained Julia's two coats, and Alice's windbreaker emblazoned with a Mickey Mouse logo. A pair of Julia's walking shoes, a jumble of Alice's sneakers, and a discarded backpack with another Walt Disney motif cluttered the floor.

Perhaps it would have been better for him to throw this old junk away, but he lacked the will to close that chapter of his life. He missed the sound of Alice's laughter and Julia's warm touch, and he irrationally hoped that, by some miracle, they would return to him. Sometimes, he wondered whether he sought to dull his pain by limiting his contacts with the outside world and immersing himself in his work.

Today would have been Alice's twelfth birthday. He and Julia had always celebrated her birthday by taking Alice to a meal at Wheeler's Oyster Bar off Leicester Square. Joy, hugs, and laughter always marked the occasion. Now, he was alone.

To add insult to injury, that venerable institution had gone out of business after 150 years, the victim of some shyster developer or financier's greed. That left Bentley's Oyster Bar near Piccadilly Circus. Nice, but not the same. Regardless, he preserved the annual ritual by dining there.

He sighed and picked up the paper he had been studying when the phone rang again. This time, the dean's secretary delivered a peremptory summons to meet with the university's administration.

"Damn these pencil pushers," he grumbled, "always interrupting work for some trifling detail and scrapping my morning's agenda." He hoped this meeting wouldn't interfere with his remembrance ritual. His mood soured at the possibility.

What occasioned the call? Perhaps this is about getting my tenure, although that's not due to be discussed for another couple of months. One other possible reason could be my recently published paper on the voyages of the Ming Dynasty Admiral Zheng He.

In his paper, he supported the popular writer Gavin Menzies, who contended that the Chinese and not Columbus had discovered America.

During the early 15th Century, *Zheng He* set sail with a massive Armada that reached East Africa but according to Menzies components of that fleet sailed East and reached the Atlantic Coast of North America decades before Columbus.

Many historians, especially in America, refused to accept this version of the discovery, claiming that it was founded on conjecture rather than fact.

Although Holroyd admitted the paper was controversial, he was satisfied that it was sound, and the university had backed him up. Given this support, he could not find a satisfactory reason for the sudden summons. *Oh well, I'll find out soon enough.*

Peeved, he called his graduate students to postpone the seminar planned for that day and got ready to go out.

He quickly checked himself in the mirror by the door, inspecting his reflection, which showed a chirpy face with laughter lines at his mouth and eyes but also a trace of sadness. He wore thick-lensed glasses and a head bearing only a distant memory of hair,

He was wearing a cotton shirt that had seen better days and now hinted at a frayed collar. A faded school tie testified to an upper-middle-class education, but the knot had been carelessly tied, giving an impression of inattentiveness. It was hardly a prepossessing picture, but then, he was not out to impress anyone. He preferred his work rather than his appearance to proclaim his status.

By the time he set forth, his spirits had risen. *Can't be bad—it might even be good news, perhaps a research offer from some benefactor who has an interest in Zheng He.*

He took a notepad and ambled over the cloistered green to the administration meeting room. He stopped to enjoy the undergraduate students sitting on the grass either actively debating whatever cause energized them that day or dreamily playing whatever cacophony passed as currently popular music. As usual, he was amused by their energy and acknowledged a couple of friendly waves.

He had a good rapport with his students and often stopped to exchange cheery banter with them, but this time he hurried on to avoid being late.

To his surprise, the dean's secretary intercepted him and requested he stop by the dean's office first.

Once inside, the dean came out from behind his desk. "Doctor Holroyd, thanks for stopping by. I wanted a quick word before you go over to the meeting. Just had the chancellor on the phone. He's concerned about the public outcry over your paper on the discovery of America. Seems some benefactors warned they would stop support unless the university acted to withdraw the paper." He stopped before assuming a conciliar tone.

"Of course, we wouldn't dream of questioning the soundness of your work, and we would prefer to continue supporting you. On the other hand, hostile reactions that could lead to funding cutbacks aren't welcomed, as you know. I wondered if you might have had any second thoughts." He paused to look at Holroyd suggestively.

"Perhaps take another look? Verify any of the facts that might be questionable?"

Holroyd was taken aback. He respected and admired the dean, but this was an outright ambush.

"Well, dean, I can understand the reactions, but I'm not sure to which facts you might be referring.

While I apologize if I ruffled any feathers, I don't quite see what I can do, short of retracting the paper."

"That might be a good decision."

"But it's not one that I'm prepared to take. The paper is sound no matter what others may say."

"Well, give it some thought, will you? There's a good chap."

"I don't think I need any thought, and—"

"I won't press you, but do take some time to think it over," the dean broke in. "I think we'd all be happier if you did." With that Holroyd was dismissed.

As he walked over to the meeting, Holroyd was shaken and mystified. *I guess I've been warned that my tenure is open to debate, but what brought that about? I've never been treated like that before. If there's a problem with my paper, someone might have the decency to tell me what it is rather than trying to blackmail me into revoking it.*

Gloomily, he entered the meeting room and noted Ian Thackerthwaite the bursar, and a couple of the department heads.

Thackerthwaite welcomed Holroyd. "So good of you to come, Doctor Holroyd. Please sit, and we can get down to business."

Holroyd had never liked Thackerthwaite, whom he thought of as a devious, snivelling toady or perhaps better as a weaselly little sycophant. *Every time I see him, I can't help thinking of Uriah Heap.*

"I think you know Professor Acheson on the university funding committee and Doctor Sanderson, the head of the Microbiology Department," Thackerthwaite continued.

Holroyd nodded but wondered why the meeting had been called. He could make sense of Thackerthwaite and Acheson being present if the matter was about funding, but why Sanderson?

He looked over the man wearing a woollen tie, a checked woollen shirt, brown corduroys, and Birkenstock sandals. *All that's missing is a briar pipe. The man can't even grow a decent beard or moustache, not that either would do much for his weak chin and sallow complexion.*

"You're probably wondering why we called this meeting, but we need to discuss an unexpected situation requiring your cooperation." Holroyd nodded as if to indicate he would be very prepared to cooperate.

"Dr. Sanderson has been offered a substantial grant to continue his innovative research. There are, however, conditions attached to that grant."

"Conditions?"

"Yes. The university has to contribute a large sum from its resources." Before Holroyd could ask anything further, Acheson spoke up. "We're going to have to move funds around."

Holroyd suddenly recognized where this was heading. *Bloody hell, I'm about to lose some or all of my funding.* He started to panic, his mind scrambling to find a defense.

"Of course, I support innovative research," Holroyd said, controlling his voice as best as he could, "but could someone please help me understand just what about Doctor Sanderson's work is so innovative?"

"I'll let Doctor Sanderson explain," Thackerthwaite said, sitting down.

Sanderson preened like a peacock showing its fan. "We can trace relationships by comparing chromosomes," he began. As he went on to deliver a lecture about his work, Holroyd's concentration was focused on his own predicament. *Where is Sanderson going with this? Don't chromosomes have something to do with colours?*

As he tried to gauge how bad things could get for him, he was momentarily distracted by the portraits of past notables mounted in gilded frames on the oak-panelled walls. He wondered what they would have made of Sanderson's utterances.

Probably, they would have quoted the Bible, dismissed claims about chromosomes as heresy, and then ended the meeting. Possibly, they might even have condemned Sanderson to the stake. Holroyd remembered the custom had been very much in favour during Bloody Mary's reign but ceased during the eighteenth century.

As he savoured the image of Sanderson consumed by purifying flames, he realized Sanderson had changed the direction of his narrative.

"As a respected expert in your field, my dear fellow," Sanderson said, addressing Holroyd directly, "I'm sure you will agree that we must further knowledge and not chew the cud of ancient history. I mean, let's consider your work. I ask you, of what use is ancient cartography in this modern-day satellite technology?" He paused to let Holroyd think about the question

Before Holroyd could answer, Sanderson went on, "You wouldn't want to stand in the way of progress and let people think of you as an impediment, would you?"

No, Holroyd did not want people to think of him as an impediment, but he wanted such a condescending dismissal of his work even less. Sanderson had displayed appallingly unprofessional behaviour. Holroyd wished he could wipe the smirk off Sanderson's face with something blunt and spiky. He liked the thought of a medieval mace or a ball and chain.

"I say, that's an outrageous comment. I demand you withdraw." Furious, he got up and looked at Sanderson. Dimly, he thought he might be shouting, but he got no further.

Thackerthwaite stood up and, in a voice that brooked no resistance, told Holroyd to sit down. There was a moment's silence before Thackerthwaite brusquely announced that Sir Harold Pastell-Whyte, the chancellor, and the Finance Committee had agreed to increase funds to genetic studies and cut back in several other areas, mostly in Holroyd's section.

"This is despicable! Why was I not consulted?"

"Doctor Holroyd," Thackerthwaite said, "the dean informed me that you were warned but refused to listen. Under the circumstances, we have no choice. The matter is no longer up for discussion."

Holroyd was dumbfounded and seething with anger. His world had been shaken and maybe had collapsed beyond retrieval. He sat back, trembling as he picked at the fraying cuff of his favourite shirt, at a loss to figure out his next move. *I guess any hope of tenure just took wings. They could tell me to resign, but I won't give up without a fight.*

He loved his university. He felt safe cocooned in his academic life and wanted to remain nestled in the studies of yesteryear's customs and traditions. Despite his colleagues' indifference to his field—and, by implication, his work—he was not ready to skulk away. *Sanderson and his sycophantic minions may have won today, but tomorrow has yet to come.*

The meeting concluded, and he walked out of the room, furious at how he had been told to expect a decrease in funding. *Why had it been necessary to announce it in such a sudden and hostile manner? Surely, I should have been consulted or at least informed privately rather than allowing Sanderson to humiliate me. Sanderson will doubtlessly triumphantly spread the word if only to emphasise the enormity of his success.*

Bloody hell! It's not only a matter of funding but also about humiliation and a warning to anyone who stirs up controversy and refuses to retract when asked to do so. So much for academic freedom.

As he walked out the door, he saw Sanderson grinning triumphally and experienced an uncharacteristic wave of pure hatred. Filled with bitterness, he decided he might as well cancel the rest of the day and just go home.

Then he realized he could still mark his daughter's birthday and, if nothing else, wash away the distaste of the morning's events with a good wine.

He was lucky to get a table and ordered half a dozen oysters on the shell. A grilled Dover sole with a glass of chilled Chablis followed the oysters. Just as he started on the fish, a shadow passed before him.

Meredith Shaw-Pepperidge, Ninth Viscount Hantington—or "Merry" to those who knew him well—stopped at Holroyd's table.

"Holroyd, old boy, haven't seen you in a while. How are you? Doing alright, are we?"

No, Holroyd thought, *I'm not doing alright, and even less so for the interruption. What is Merry doing in a place like Bentley's?*

Merry was the eldest son of an earl and wealthy, by all appearances. Holroyd imagined him frequenting the exclusive London dining venues around Mayfair, such as Bellamy's or the Bagatelle, rather than among the tourists in Piccadilly. His photograph appeared occasionally in the social news, often in the company of a coterie of young women but never a wife.

Merry and Holroyd had gone to school together. If memory served, Merry had studied classics and left with a state scholarship, but their paths diverged after that. Holroyd joined the Navy, after which he went for academics.

The only thing he knew about what Merry had done after school was a vague notion he had gone into the Foreign Office. But he couldn't remember and didn't care about Merry's job.

Sitting alone over his sole while Merry stood there in his bespoke Saville Row business suit, Holroyd felt every bit the dowdy old professor.

While Holroyd's once slim frame showed signs of flab, Merry maintained an athletic figure with no evidence of approaching middle age. He had a lean, almost chiselled face with a firm jaw, blue eyes, and a full head of blond hair. His appearance was so impressive that neither his effeminate mouth set in a permanent pout, nor his excessively pink tie could spoil it.

"Mind if I join you for a sec?" Merry continued. "I rather hoped we could have a natter."

"I..." Holroyd groaned and hoped his face did not betray his feelings. He didn't want anyone to interrupt him, least of all Merry.

"Got an interesting problem on my desk," Merry continued, seating himself as if Holroyd had invited him to do so. "I rather think you might find it right up your alley. Has to do with old Chinese voyages of discovery."

"Really? Hardly thought that was something you were interested in."

"I'm not usually, but it seems now the Chinese are making noises we don't like, and I thought you might have some useful thoughts."

"Merry, my interests in Chinese activities center on over three hundred years old events. Hardly what I would call contemporary. Thank you very much, but I'm busy now."

"Not what I hear, old boy."

Merry smiled, and Holroyd stared at him, wondering what Merry was referring to. The meeting that morning was the only thing that would have made sense, but it seemed unlikely that Merry would have known about it.

"I hear your hallowed halls of esoteric contemplation were not nice to you. Not nice at all," he said, dispelling any doubt about what he was referring to. "Unfair, I thought, but maybe there's a silver lining. Maybe I can winkle the old boy out of the doldrums, ginger him up, give him a new outlook, and so forth, what?"

Holroyd hadn't realized he was in the doldrums or needed gingering. "How very thoughtful of you, but —"

"So, tell me what's happening, old boy." Merry persisted.

"You hear wrong," Holroyd lied. "I'm taking a sabbatical. I have always wanted to travel more and extend my research field. Now seems to be an appropriate time. I might go look at some libraries that survived the Cultural Revolution in China."

"China, what? I say! Jolly good, jolly good." He paused, and Holroyd took advantage of the moment to change the topic.

"Meredith, what have you been doing with yourself? I haven't kept up with all your comings and goings."

"Oh, nothing worth mentioning. Just toiling away at a desk, trying to defend British interests, whatever they may be."

"I heard you joined the Civil Service. Still at it?"

"Yes."

"And how is it going?"

"Not too bad, thanks. Keeps the wolf from the door."

"I see. And what's new?"

"Nothing much. Just went through one of those recurring shuffles at the top and got a new man as permanent secretary. , Merry said.

"Are you involved?"

"Not really, but sometimes, when things get out of hand, one has to lend an oar. Can't leave our lords and masters between the devil and the deep blue sea, can we?"

Holroyd refrained from answering that he thought there was the precise place where to leave their lords and masters. As he thought of a suitable reply, Merry got up.

"Well, good to see you again! I really think you'll be interested in what I have to say, and I'll be in touch soon to hash out the details." His suggestion forestalled any answer Holroyd had been thinking of, and Merry disappeared into the adjoining room.

Holroyd sat looking at the door through which Merry had passed before returning to his sole. Somehow the fish did not taste as good as before, and the potatoes had turned cold. When he ordered an Eaton mess for dessert, the waiter told him the kitchen had run out of strawberries. Glumly, he confirmed it had not been one of his better days.

*****

Merry's call came the next morning. "The Athenaeum at seven? Alright with you?" Merry didn't bother to ask if Holroyd had other plans, which irritated him, especially as he had planned to go out on the town. Detecting a hesitation, Merry pressed. "I really think we should meet. I've got something that you might find interesting."

"I have an engagement, Merry and—"

"Put it off, will you?"

"Merry, I don't—"

"This is serious, old boy. Otherwise, I wouldn't press you."

Holroyd suddenly became curious. *What is this about? Out of nowhere, Merry insists on a meeting and won't take no for an answer. At the Athenaeum? Never been there, so maybe I'll see how the high and mighty live. Alright, I'll bite.*

"Athenaeum at seven? I'll be there."

He hung up and then rang to cancel his night out with the lads. His retreat was greeted with more than a few ribald comments.

The Athenaeum reserved its membership to men of letters, philosophers, artists, and other disciplines, among whom, at last count, only fifty-two had won Nobel prizes. Holroyd thought it above his rank and wondered how Merry had become a member.

On entering the marble-tiled lobby, the club porter led him to the wood-panelled bar, several elderly couples were chatting, and some lone individuals were hiding behind newspapers. Holroyd neither saw nor heard any cell phones and breathed a sigh of relief.

Merry was sitting in a corner but, on seeing Holroyd enter, rose, and greeted him with unusual warmth. "Holroyd, old boy, so good of you to come. No problems getting here, were there? Let you in, did they? Jolly good, glad you could make it. Come and sit down."

He led Holroyd over to the small table surrounded by stuffed leather chairs that probably had supported the bottoms of members celebrating the relief of Mafeking.

Holroyd looked around the room. Painted portraits hung on the walls, most depicting elderly gentlemen with mutton-chop whiskers. A few men wore the ecclesiastical garb of bishops in the Anglican Church. Looking at the expressions on their faces, Holroyd thought none of the Victorian grandees looked happy.

"Drinks, Peter? Sherry?" Merry looked over to the barman, who nodded. Holroyd noted that Merry addressed him by his Christian name and was surprised their relationship had improved so much. Merry remained quiet as the steward brought their drinks in cut glass crystal on a silver salver. "Cheers." He raised his glass, took a sip, leaned toward Holroyd, and started.

"So, tell me more about this sabbatical of yours. Not thinking of becoming a bookworm chanting ancient litanies in a monk's habit, are you?"

Taken by surprise, Holroyd looked at Merry, wondering how he had ever survived long enough to gain his degree. "Chanting in a monk's habit? What gave you that idea? To remind you, Meredith, it means I'm taking a rest from my usual occupation. It's a rest period that allows me to focus on something other than the demands of my job. Recharge the batteries."

"I see. Sounds like fun. So, you'll tootle over to jolly old China and become a bookworm. Can't say it's my cup of tea. Happy for you fellows to do those things. Looking for anything particular this time?"

"Yes. Evidence of maps and explorations drawn after the Ming Dynasty began."

"Ming? Aren't they the chaps who made plates and vases? All very expensive, I believe, and not my taste at all."

Holroyd had had enough of this. *Merry turning up in a restaurant he wouldn't frequent and taking an interest in my work—well, I could believe in one coincidence but not two. I don't know or want to know what Merry is after, but I've had enough of this small talk.* "Merry, come on," he said, "get to the point, please."

"Yes, well. We need your expertise in dealing with China in a territorial dispute. Specifically, we want you to establish who owns a small island in the South China Sea called Dejection Island. We need a recognized expert who can be relied upon to give a disinterested analysis."

"What? Ownership of Dejection Island? Where on earth is that? And anyway, I don't have qualifications for that." Holroyd was both stunned and aghast at the idea. He had no wish to engage in such a venture. He was, after all, a research professor, not a legal adjudicator, even if his field of research fitted the government's needs. He took a deep gulp from his drink.

"Look, Peter, the Chinese have warships off the island, but we don't know why they're there," Merry said, "We don't think they've arrived just to show us their pretty ships. Add to that they are doing some rather aggressive things, like grabbing people across the Hong Kong and Thai borders. All rude and unsporting acts, what? It could mean a war."

"Merry, you must be joking. You're asking me to get involved in a matter that's way out of my field," Holroyd protested, "I'm not an expert on maritime law, especially when it comes to China. My Chinese reading is adequate for what I do, but I don't think I can peruse and understand documents, certainly not legal ones.

"And if you think I can avert a war with China, you have been sadly misinformed. Sorry, chum, you've come to the wrong address." He paused. "If there's nothing else, thanks for the drinks, but I'm starved and think I'll go now." He made as if to get up.

"That's awfully unsporting of you, Peter. You might at least hear me out and see if I have something to offer. And dinner here is on me."

The prospect of dinner stayed Holroyd's intention to leave, and he settled back into his chair.

"Oh, alright," he said. "I'm all ears."

"That's better." Merry paused, took a sip from his glass, and went on, "Think for a moment, why are you going over there?"

"Vindication. The dean was unhappy about my recent paper and asked me to retract it. Damned cheek! If I retract any part, I lose my integrity, and I'm not prepared to do that. The whole thing has stained my reputation, and I want to remove it. If I don't nail the question, I may never get tenure and may even get dismissed."

"Sticky wicket, what? But I'm not clear what the question is."

"The 14th Century Chinese developed a navy far superior to anything in Europe, but they didn't focus on maritime travel other than a lot of coastal trading. One attempt at a naval invasion of Japan during the Yuan Dynasty ended in a total loss of their forces. That stopped anybody from going too far offshore again. However, during the Ming Dynasty, the Yongle emperor commissioned an admiral to explore farther afield. There's debate as to the purpose of that exploration."

Merry's eyebrows pricked up as if to say, "Go on."

"There are a few theories out there, including one in Menzies' book '1421,' published in 2002."

Merry assumed a puzzled look.

"Menzies was a lieutenant commander in the Royal Navy, and a navigator who analyzed the capabilities of Chinese Ming Dynasty vessels in the light of oceanic winds and currents. He concluded that the Chinese *could* have sailed and probably *did* sail around the world." Holroyd took another sip of his sherry.

"Based on maps available at the time, he went on to claim that the Chinese very likely arrived off the coasts of Australia and America. But there's a suggestion that the Yongle emperor, whose proper name was Zhu Di, having usurped the throne by killing his nephew, wanted to stop rumours that his nephew had survived and left the country. Zheng He was given the task of finding out if the rumours were true." He looked at Merry before going on.

"Zhu Di died before Zheng He returned from his final voyage, and Zhu Di's successors showed no interest in further explorations. The following emperors, Yongle's son and grandson, stopped further exploration and destroyed all ships, plans, and capabilities for building ships and reports of the voyages. " He paused.

"Maybe something to do with the politics of trade. It's not something I've got around to researching yet, but I'm intrigued by the real reason and the possibility of the nephew's survival."

"So, you'll look to see if you can find anything that might help you answer that question?"

"Yes."

"In other words, you're going to look for travels in that region at that time. Jolly good." Merry took another sip from his glass and looked at Holroyd for a moment, to the point where Holroyd became uncomfortable with the scrutiny.

"Anyway, Merry, what has all this got to do with you?" he asked.

"Rather curious about the Chinese."

"I didn't know it was your part ship.[1]"

"It isn't, really. But by a curious coincidence, I saw your paper on those Ming Dynasty voyages. I found it fascinating to learn what those Chinese could do. Thought it good. Sent it upstairs, and it caused quite a stir. Wanted to know all about you. Rather flattering if I may say so."

"I know full well you don't follow my work. Why would you?"

---

1 Royal Navy expression meaning "your responsibility"

"We've known each other for years. It's only natural to follow the career of an old friend, no?"

"Sorry, but I can't quite convince myself that you suddenly developed an interest in historical Chinese maritime travels or cartography. At least not enough interest to go to all this trouble."

"Fair enough, old chap. Forgive me." Merry took another swallow from his glass. "Normally we'd handle this without calling for help such as yours. But there's something else, and we'd prefer to keep officialdom out of it for as long as we can." He paused to look around to see if anyone was within earshot. There wasn't and he went on.

"Those Chinese warships are causing the Americans to growl, which you can imagine the Chinese aren't happy about. If we deal with this officially, we could end up in the middle of an argument between them or maybe have to choose sides. Not a position we want to be in, so we'd like to settle this ownership issue quietly before things escalate."

"You mean the Chinese or perhaps the Americans might grab the island? Wouldn't that be an act of war?"

"Yes, but I don't think we could do much about it. I can't see another Falklands-type operation; the Chinese are not the Argentinians. Seems rather silly to start another world war over this flyspeck on the map." Merry paused, sitting forward with a conspiratorial glance around the room. "Ever heard of HMS Steadfast?"

Holroyd shook his head.

"She was a seventy-four sent out to the Far East in the late eighteenth century to look after our interests there. Sounds rather grandiose, but the East India Company dispatched her to give muscle against the French near the East India and Dutch East India companies' trade routes." Holroyd became intrigued, and Merry continued, perhaps sensing an interest.

"The Steadfast also had been looking for pirates who kept pestering Company ships, but she ran aground on an uncharted island. The captain and several of his crew survived and, on getting ashore, claimed the place for Britain. Must have been a hellish place because they named it Dejection Island and then waited for rescue."

"Dejection Island? Can't believe that was an encouraging name! Anyway, I can't say I've ever come across it in any of my studies, but then the name might have been different earlier on."

"Yes, well, the place was off the usual trade routes, and after a few months, they went to look for help. The captain and a few of the crew set out in one of the ship's boats, leaving most of the crew on the island. Almost didn't make it before a Dutch East India man sailing from Sumatra to Holland came across them." He took another swallow from his glass.

"Dutchman couldn't or wouldn't go for the other survivors but dropped off the ones they had picked up at Dover. On returning to London, the captain reported to the Admiralty but got court-martialed for losing his ship and abandoning his crew." He stopped to look for a steward to refill the glasses.

"Poor sod got dismissed in disgrace. However, they recorded his claim to the island and made plans to send out a rescue ship. For whatever reason, they never sent one." Merry paused while the barman served the drinks. He took a sip and then continued.

"During the First Opium War, the fleet's commander transporting troops to Canton sent a frigate to look at this island the Steadfast crew had claimed. Seems the captain found survivors, so he landed a few marines, hoisted the flag, played 'God Save the King' or some such, and then went on his merry way." Merry sipped from his glass.

"No one knew why he didn't take the survivors with him. I suppose that after all the time they had been on the island, there was no incentive to leave."

"Wait a moment." Holroyd interrupted. "You said the ship went out in the late eighteenth century, so that would be about forty or more years before the First Opium War. If you count the time between the original landing of the shipwrecked crew and the visit of the frigate, many, if not all, the original survivors should have died of old age. But if the frigate's log omits anything abnormal in the settlement, I suppose that means the frigate found a thriving colony."

"Exactly." Merry beamed with pleasure at Holroyd's conclusion. Merry took another sip before he continued. "Anyway, over the years we shouldered up to our colonial obligations, what? Sent them an annual maintenance fee, gave them some infrastructure, and left them alone. Sort of like a colony of remittance men. Then came the war. " He stopped as. If lost in thought.

"The Japs overran the island, and the whole population got deported and interned in Japanese camps. We aren't sure what happened at the war's end. They misplaced many records, so we don't quite know the sequence of events. We know the population, or what remained of the original population, made its way back to the island. There's nothing in the files that covers the next few years. Still, they must have maintained contact because the Treasury resumed paying the island's pocket money or whatever the Treasury paid our former colonies." He ordered another round of drinks.

"When the Labour government dissolved the empire, lots of old fogies retired and took their knowledge with them, and the island was forgotten in the general chaos that characterized government offices at the time. More important matters to address, I guess."

It was all hard for Holroyd to believe, but stranger things had happened than an island being forgotten by a bloated, overtaxed bureaucracy. And he doubted Merry could imagine all this.

"The War Office remembered the place during the Korean War. They rebuilt the airstrip as a base for bigger planes, flew a few sorties, and then packed up and went home again. All was peaceful until the coronation when we got a call.

"A very peeved individual asked why no islanders were invited to the coronation.

"Some perfumed coxcomb at the new Commonwealth Office told the caller the British government had no colony in the South China Sea. Ruffled a few feathers that did, so we sent the silly bugger off to count sheep in the Falklands for a while. Should have been Saint Helena or Tristan da Cunha, and we would never have heard of him again. Probably won't anyway now that I think about it.

"Anyway, after everyone calmed down, we looked at the place again. Found a few hundred souls happily doing whatever a few hundred souls do on a tropical island. Wondered if there wasn't some hanky-panky going on, a lot of inbreeding. But we decided not to inquire too deeply into that. Might not like what we found. I always wondered where the women came from. Touch of the tar brush, d'ye think?"

Holroyd resented Merry's racist comments and thought not a few of his ancestors had conceived if not given birth on the wrong side of the blanket.

"Didn't eighteenth-century English warships sometimes carry women on board in those days?" Holroyd offered. "If so, that might explain how the colony survived."

"I believe they allowed women on board when ships were in homeport, but I don't recall women on board once a ship set sail. I always thought superstition said having women on board was bad luck. While listing the survivors, the Steadfast log includes no obvious women's names.

"I suppose if there had been any they could have all been whores and so not worth recording." Though Holroyd found Merry's attitude toward women insufferable, he decided it was not the time to become righteous about it, so he said nothing.

"Anyway, having satisfied ourselves that the small settlement had grown rather like the Pitcairn Islands, we went home again. That should have been the end of the matter."

"Doesn't sound exciting. Almost boring." Holroyd did not understand where all this was leading, and he wasn't sure he wanted to know.

"Could be, but then things got more complicated because of the location."

"How complicated?"

"Starting a few months ago, the Chinese have been making noises about who owns what out there. Got so far as to irritate the neighbours, who went to the Permanent Court of Arbitration. We didn't intervene, and no one else brought up the island. Anyway, the court dismissed the Chinese claim. Ruffled a few pigtails that did."

The Chinese, Holroyd thought, *haven't worn pigtails for over a hundred years*. "Are you telling me they forgot the island or at least conveniently ignored it? I mean, with all these satellites and so on, no one noted the place? What about the inhabitants?"

"Yes, well, right." Uncomfortable at the admission, Merry shifted in his chair. "Quite right. Very inconsiderate, what?"

"Oh, come off it, Merry! One doesn't just forget an island, especially not one with a history and with inhabitants. I mean, you told me that the government or at least Treasury and Defence both knew about the island."

"Yes, they did, but it wasn't their job to intervene at the Court, you see. Probably should have been the Commonwealth Office or one of the legal beagles. Regrettably, no one advised them to get involved. Very careless, really." Merry shifted in his chair and sipped from his glass. Holroyd couldn't decide whether Merry was embarrassed or feeling guilty; perhaps both.

"Good Lord! Words fail me!" Holroyd sat there for a few moments, speechless. He sighed and reached for his glass. "Anyway, I suppose you had better go on."

"Yes, well, after the Court decided against China, China wasn't too happy. There was a lull before we got a phone call from our chappie in Beijing. Seems the Chinese got all in a tizzy over the Court's decision, and some bright spark over there had another look at the map.

"He realized that Britain has this island that up to then everyone had forgotten to mention. Viewed the whole thing as a painful pimple on China's backside. Then he pointed out to his masters that the island's position rearranges all those nice lines on maps showing territorial rights. Next thing, China sent some warships into the area.

"That got the attention of our powers-that-be. Entered their tiny minds, our little island has found itself in a major territorial waters dispute. I suppose they already knew it but ignored it." He twirled his glass with its pale-coloured liquid as if admiring the light reflections from the room's lamps.

"Anyway, then someone decided we had better have another think about the place. Perhaps it dawned that they might have to do something, like make a decision, and they didn't want to get bothered. Awful thought, that was. Caused shivers up their tight little backsides." He stopped as if to give Holroyd a chance to comment.

When Holroyd remained silent, Merry continued, "China now has this idea they want the island, and if we don't roll over and give it to them, they're prepared to take it."

"And you don't want to give it up?"

"To be candid, we do. It's a financial burden on the Treasury, and we would be obliged to defend it if someone attacked it. But we don't have the forces to mount a defence there. But given that British subjects are living on the island, we can't say anything like that in public."

"Like the Falkland Islands, you mean?"

"Yes. Only the Falklands have resources, which gave us a good reason to interfere besides knocking the Argies for six."

"Why not just give the place away like we did Hong Kong?"

"Nice idea, but why would we give it to China? Might not be the best choice now. If we give the island to China, the surrounding countries like Vietnam, Malaysia, and Singapore, not to mention Taiwan, will get rather peeved at us. If we give it to one of these other countries, it will peeve China. And to make matters worse, the inhabitants voted to remain British — sort of a repeat of the Falklands scenario. And now, to add to the mess, the Americans may want to set up a base there."

"How very selfish of everyone," Holroyd said, not without a note of derision. He twirled his cut-crystal glass, admiring the reflections from the lights in the room, and waited. Merry took a deep breath before he continued.

"From Her Majesty's Government's point of view, the best solution would be if the island never belonged to Britain. Provide a graceful exit strategy, so to speak. That would follow if the Steadfast claim had no legal standing, which could happen if the Steadfast had claimed something that already belonged to someone else. The 'someone' is anyone with whom at the time we were not, or since then have not been, at war."

"Yes, I suppose that would be convenient. But we have been at war with China. Twice as I remember, in the two Opium Wars. Why didn't we settle the island's ownership then? We got Hong Kong as booty from the first war."

"Probably slipped people's minds. These things happen."

"So it would appear." Holroyd sat back. "Why can't you arrange a retrospective correction? Sort of discover an old record or whatever. Perhaps a lost page from a surrender document that has conveniently reappeared. Make a big announcement and send out apologies to all concerned. They've done it before. It happened when Clive signed a peace accord in India with a fellow named Omichund. I mean—." He was interrupted by a bark of laughter from someone engaged in a conversation on the other side of the room.

Merry waited until the noise returned to its former level before replying, "Yes, we thought of that. The Chinese say they have some such evidence but won't produce it right now. We think they're bluffing. If they have the evidence, they've lost it or, more likely, never had it. So, it's up to us to find it. But someone upstairs got it into his head we need an

independent source to discover something like that."
He paused.

"Finding a lost page to a surrender document that's almost two hundred years old won't quite do. What we need is a credible and disinterested source." He assumed a mournful look before continuing, "Dropped the whole thing on my desk, and they did. Didn't appreciate it at all. I thought they must have been suffering from lack of oxygen living in the rarefied air of the upper echelons of Whitehall." Merry reached for his glass.

"I see," Holroyd said. "So, now you want me to look over early maps, charts, or reports to see if there is anything to show the island belonged to someone else. Someone like, say, China, so the Steadfast's claim would be invalid."

"Something like that, yes."

"Merry, I told you I'm going on a sabbatical. Such a sabbatical has nothing to do with looking for lost or, perhaps better said, forgotten or ignored colonial islands. You should also know early Chinese charts are very imprecise and often only show the presence or absence of landmasses. Such maps wouldn't necessarily show a small island. Even if they did, its position likely won't bear much resemblance to modern maps."

"Yes, we understand all that, but your expertise could help fill gaps in the documentation."

"How would I know where to look? I mean, several countries border the South China Sea. How can I be certain which place to choose? If they exist, such documents could be in any of those countries."

"Yes, I know that, and you have my sympathies. But we would be happiest if you or someone like you found such charts in China. Her Majesty's Government would sleep better at night."

"Merry, you know it's not my cup of tea at all. I could look for maps, charts, or reports that refer to the place. If I find any, I could take a stab at verifying their authenticity. But to extrapolate from there to ownership is outside my area of competence. Anyway, it's not what I want to go to China for."

"But you are going to China, aren't you? So, we could find some financial support for your endeavours on our behalf. And we could offer official help, such as paying an expense allowance and smoothing official channels where necessary. Not that we could go too far in being seen to help. Might arouse people's curiosity, that could. We prefer to keep this quiet… sort of let sleeping dragons lie." He paused and looked at Holroyd.

Holroyd took a moment to think. The offer was attractive, considering he was facing a reduction in his university funding. And if this was a government operation, well, he could count on being paid. Whatever the amount, it could help in supporting his own research.

"Look, Merry, as long as everyone understands, I can't guarantee I will find what you want; I could fit it in. What you're looking for may not exist. However, I can see that our interests might overlap, so provided we agree on terms, I'm willing to have a go."

Merry shot his hand across the table and latched onto Holroyd's. "Jolly decent of you, old boy. I'll send over copies of the pertinent sections of the Steadfast's log, and anything else I think will be useful. Let me know if you need more. Shall we dine?"

Holroyd nodded. They finished their drinks and went in. He ordered the rack of lamb and the club claret, which were both delicious. To finish the meal, the waitress brought a pot of Stilton and a decanter of port. Holroyd spread the soft, creamy cheese over a water biscuit and savoured it. He followed the bite by sipping the port and letting the rich liquid swirl around his mouth.

A warm glow spread through him, and he surveyed the pot wondering whether to indulge further. *Oh, what the hell, why not?* He dug out another spoonful of cheese while the sommelier unobtrusively refilled his glass.

"Come to think further about this job you've offered, it might prove quite fun." He sipped a mouthful before taking another bite of cheese. "Shipwrecked sailors, an ignored tropical island near the East Indies, and threats of imminent war with malevolent Chinese sounds almost like something Conrad would have written about."

He chuckled and let a dreamy expression wander over his face. "Wonder if there will be an innocent Eurasian maiden in need of help?" His hand wobbled slightly, and he spilled some port on his tie. "Oops! That red doesn't suit the old-school colours." He regarded the stain with dismay.

"Steady on there. Be serious, old boy." Merry regarded Holroyd with alarm. "We're not sending you out there on some fanciful jaunt. You're going out there to do work that's vitally important to Her Majesty's Government."

"Yes, but that's what James Bond was sent out to do, and he always found a damsel in distress, or at least pretending to be in distress."

"But you're not him. Now off home with you."

*****

Once home he was preparing for bed when the phone rang. He thought of ignoring it but knew he would not relax without knowing who was disturbing his peace.

"Hello, Peter old boy," Meredith said, his irritating voice floating down the line. Holroyd groaned, regretting his urge to answer the phone. "Not disturbing you, are we?"

"Well, I was just getting into bed."

"Won't keep you then, but I wondered if you would be free for drinks tomorrow. There's someone else who's keen to help you with your research. I think you might find it of interest given what we discussed earlier. Shall we say six o'clock at the Midas? That's the gaming club just behind Brook's. Alright with that, are we?" Holroyd didn't relish another evening with Merry, but he had no other plans, and since Merry would probably pick up the tab, why not accept?

"Yes, thank you. I shall be there."

Meredith hung up without further ado, leaving Holroyd to ponder the speed with which arrangements were being made. Just as he was about to replace the receiver, he thought he heard a faint cough followed by some clicks, but he couldn't be certain. Perhaps it was just a poor connection.

Still, he couldn't help wondering what he was letting himself in for.

4

It was raining heavily by early evening, so Holroyd took a taxi straight to the club. A doorman led him to the bar, and upon entering, Merry appeared at his side.

"Hello, Peter. Good of you to come." He led Holroyd to a table near a corner where two Asian men and a Westerner were sitting.

Holroyd guessed from their evening attire that they were going to gamble later and felt underdressed in his best business suit. He was relieved that he didn't have to join in these plans, as he doubted he would have been able to keep up with either the drinking or even the smallest stakes involved.

"Peter," Merry said, "let me introduce Mr. Xiang Jin Leng, his son Deng Tan Liu, and General van Roggenback. Gentlemen, may I introduce Doctor Peter Holroyd." They nodded and sized each other up.

Holroyd noted that the father and son did not bear the same surname but remembered that Chinese children sometimes adopted the mother's name, especially if that family was more respected. "General van Roggenback has just retired from the American Air Force," Merry continued.

The general stood up and proffered his hand. He towered over Holroyd, who had the distinct feeling the general might, in his youth, have been a football linebacker. Holroyd extended his hand, which the general seized in an iron grip.

"Pleased to meet you, sir," Holroyd managed weakly.

The general exuded the insincere bonhomie that Holroyd associated with Americans who believed they were God's gift to humankind and wanted the world to know it. Merry continued with the introductions.

"Mr. Xiang has just returned from China, and his son will go up to Balliol this term."

Merry gestured toward a small balding Chinese man with a round, shiny, expressionless face that suggested wariness, nervousness, or both. He wore a bespoke evening outfit complete with patent leather shoes. Holroyd extended his hand. After a momentary hesitation, a limp and clammy touch was returned, suggesting Xiang did not shake hands often.

Looking at him, Holroyd guessed that he was in his early fifties, which meant he would have been born close to, if not during, the Cultural Revolution.

The son was tall for a Chinese man. He looked athletic, and some people might consider him handsome. Holroyd sensed a touch of irritation and even insolence in his demeanor, which suggested he was only there out of filial duty and would have preferred livelier entertainment. He gave a perfunctory nod and did not offer to shake hands. In Holroyd's opinion, Merry's gaze lingered a little too long on the boy's face.

With the introductions made and Holroyd's drink finally ordered and delivered, Merry opened the conversation. "Shall we, gentlemen?" Xiang and Roggenback nodded.

"Peter," Merry said, turning to Holroyd, "you're wondering what this is all about."

"Yes," Holroyd said, "I would say so."

"Mr. Xiang is the managing director of a large Asian corporation with branches in many parts of the word and is very influential. Does lots of things but mostly imports and exports all sorts of mining and agricultural machinery."

Holroyd nodded and hoped he looked impressed.

"The trouble is that when you have a large business with branches all over the world, you get many problems. Sometimes, you can't find and get the people you need to do things for you. Sort of problematic to find the right mix of competence and integrity when involving different races." Merry paused, looked at Xiang, and then looked at Holroyd.

"I see," Holroyd said, having no idea where this was going but trying to project an attitude of knowledge and intense curiosity. Not an easy task but likely a successful one given the way Mr. Xiang leaned forward.

"His lordship is correct, Professor Holroyd." Xiang's voice was soft, but Holroyd detected a hard tone. "We sometimes face tasks that call for extraordinary skills and discretion. Such a mix is difficult to find in an individual. When we find such a person, we are happy to pay well for his services. Very well, in fact." He paused, letting this sink in.

"His lordship assures me you are a widely acknowledged expert in Chinese historical maritime travels, maps, and cartography. Furthermore, his lordship assures me we can rely on your discretion and integrity." He paused, looking intently at Holroyd, who felt vaguely flattered but wondered at receiving so much praise.

Xiang went on, "A member of our staff has met with an indisposition, and we are looking for a replacement. We have decided that no one in the firm has the qualifications for the task, and time is of the essence. When I mentioned this to him, his lordship recommended you.'" Xiang paused as if waiting for Holroyd to react. Holroyd said nothing.

Xiang went on, "Would you be interested in undertaking a small task for my company? We require an immediate start, and time and secrecy are essential."

Holroyd hoped he had not lost his air of uncommitted interest, but he realized that shorn of all the frills, this was a recruitment drive. Then again, why did a machinery trader need his qualifications?

"Forgive me, but this is a surprise. I really don't quite see how I can be of service."

Xiang looked at Merry, who leaned further back in his chair, swirled his glass, and took a sip. "Peter, old chap, Mr. Xiang is asking you to do some research for his company." His condescending tone irritated Holroyd.

"His lordship," Xiang said, "may not have explained the matter fully, Professor Holroyd. My company is interested in getting certain rights in an area that is, shall we say, *contested* by several governments. We prefer to negotiate with a government on which we can rely. We seek assurance that any investment we may make is viable and based on stable conditions."

"I see," Holroyd said, sensing where this might be going. "Am I correct in surmising that the area in question is in the South China Sea?"

Mr. Xiang answered with only the slightest of nods.

"Any particular area?"

"Yes, a small British colony there."

"Ah! Dejection Island."

"I told you he was sharp, didn't I?" Merry said to Xiang, his mouth stretched into grin. The general settled back into his chair with a satisfied look, and Holroyd wondered why.

Xiang looked expectantly at Holroyd but with a hint of curiosity, as if he was surprised that Holroyd had so easily managed to determine the area under discussion.

"I see," Holroyd said, flattered but also miffed that Merry had not consulted him first. "Nice of his lordship."

Holroyd wondered what sort of indisposition the former staff member had met, but he did not have much time to wonder. Xiang continued, "We can offer you twenty-five thousand pounds on commencement. We will pay a further seventy-five thousand pounds upon completion and cover all expenses."

To say Holroyd was surprised would be a gross understatement. *One hundred thousand pounds plus expenses? That might be the price for an assassin in some fiction thriller, but this is not some fiction thriller, and I'm the furthest thing from an assassin.*

"That is a princely sum," he managed, his voice strangled as a waiter refilled his glass. "And just how might I be of assistance?"

Xiang smiled as if satisfied that he had hooked a particularly valuable prize. "As you may be aware, the situation is delicate, and we do not want to arouse curiosity in places from which people might try to interfere with or even stop our venture."

"Interfere or stop? Just who might want to do that?"

"Peter, old boy! The world outside your cloistered halls writhes with skullduggery. When it comes to business ventures, anything goes as long as it's not discovered." Holroyd shot Merry a look, but he continued, oblivious. "I have to say, Mr. Xiang has made you an exceptional offer that fits your plans. Can't think that you might refuse it. I know I wouldn't."

Why is Merry encouraging me? Holroyd wondered. *Xiang wants to exploit some unknown resources on Dejection Island and sensibly prefers to deal with the British government rather than the Chinese. I wonder if the preference reflects a general antipathy for the Chinese government or if there's a more specific reason.* He sipped his drink. *But given Merry's earlier description of Dejection Island, what interest could Xiang possibly have?*

He focused on Xiang. "Mr. Xiang, I have to say you are making a very attractive offer, which I would find hard to refuse. But I'm not clear on what precisely you want me to research, and without that knowledge, I hesitate to accept."

"The research will rely on historical evidence in an area in which you are an expert. Furthermore, his lordship has informed me you intend to conduct research in China." Holroyd suddenly realized *Merry's motives in hiring me are at odds with Xiang's, something of which Xiang appears to be unaware. It would be honourable to point this out to Xiang, but one hundred thousand pounds is a lot of money. I'm beginning to think this isn't such a good idea. Let's see how I can refuse gracefully.* Before he could say anything, Xiang continued

"We thought we could assist you with the trip and find ways to help in your research."

Alright, Holroyd thought, *I'll rise to the bait.* "Such as?"

"We can connect you with some valuable contacts, including ones with private collections and libraries you could not normally access." Xiang let this added offer, even more tempting than the first, hang in the air.

"Merry," the general broke in with a grunt, "may not have briefed you on my interests here. Since I retired from the Air Force, I have agreed to act as a consultant for some American interests. These interests coincide with Mr. Xiang's. We will offer you proper fees if you agree to work with us."

Holroyd was startled by the familiar reference to Merry and began to feel a mixture of irritation and curiosity but thought it was not the time to voice any disquiet. *Let's see where this leads.*

"Gentlemen, this is a generous offer—"

"Splendid!" Xiang said. "I will have my people send you the details. Meanwhile, permit me." Holroyd was taken aback, uncertain that he had committed himself, but he noticed that Merry and the general seemed relieved and even satisfied at the turn of events.

Xiang turned and spoke to Deng in Chinese. Deng left the bar, and Holroyd noted that Merry followed his departure with a puppy-like look.

After a few minutes, Deng returned with a package Xiang handed Holroyd. "With his lordship's permission, I offer a small token of my company's appreciation." Xiang smiled and handed Holroyd the wrapped parcel. "Please, not to drop it." With that, the meeting ended.

Once he arrived home, he put the kettle on and sat at the table to unwrap Xiang's parcel. He peeled away the quality wrapping paper to reveal a wooden box, the shape of which suggested a bottle was inside. Sure enough, he opened the box to discover a bottle of vintage port.

"Good Lord!" he exclaimed, lifting it from the box to confirm it was real. "A Graham's Ne Oublie 1882 Tawny!" Holroyd knew Graham's was an old family firm that reserved this vintage for family members and very special guests. "What on earth does this man want from me?"

Looking at the bottle, he suddenly thought that perhaps the task he had been engaged in would not be as straightforward as it had appeared.

Deciding it was too early to go to bed, Holroyd went over to his laptop and searched for information on his hosts but found nothing useful. Next, he retrieved his files on ancient Chinese cartography.

Chinese mapmaking traditions go back over 2,500 years and maybe even 4,000 years, but most maps covered land rather than sea areas. His files reflected his many years of research on trade patterns in the South China Sea, focused on the movements of goods along the coastal waters of China and Vietnam.

He could not find any reference to the island or offshore island settlements, but he did find references that might bear on his new project.

The Ming Dynasty cartographer Luo Hongxian had written the *Guangyutu*, a comprehensive atlas of sea transport to the southeast and southwest. Another writer, Zhang Huan, had prepared a huge atlas, the *Tushubian,* that included a detailed geography of the Ming Empire. But no island dotted around the South China Sea was labelled "Dejection Island."

Even allowing that the name probably had changed over the centuries, nothing allowed for an easy comparison with islands shown on modern maps, all of which Holroyd found extremely irritating.

He also found it difficult to accept that no voyages had taken place that might have found and established a settlement on the little island. As with explorers in the West, Chinese explorers must have wanted to know what lay beyond the horizon unless someone else reported going there. And with all the expeditions and trading in those ancient times, some ships may have passed or landed on what was now Dejection Island.

He began a general Internet search with expanded search criteria. To his great satisfaction, he discovered that in 2008, Robert Batchelor, an American researcher, found what they now called the Selden Map while visiting the Bodleian Library.

This map, unlike most Chinese maps of the time, did not show China at the centre of the world but squeezed the landmass of China into one corner, with the middle of the South China Sea as the map's central point. As a consequence, the map showed China's coastal regions and, to the east, vast areas of oceans from Java, the Moluccas, Japan, and the Philippines. To the west lay what was now Myanmar.

Also marked were the sea routes of Chinese boats sailing from Quanzhou on the Fujian coast and the ports along those routes. Near one island that might or might not be the location of Dejection Island, Holroyd noticed a red mark with an inscription, but he could not decipher its meaning. He made a note to go over Batchelor's book and perhaps write to the curator of the Bodleian Library to see if he could get a clarification.

Another independent but congruent source was a record of maritime activity out of the port of Quanzhou written in 1617 by Zhang Xie from Zhangzhou. He had compiled a compendium of maritime activities out of the port of Haicheng, Zhangzhou's port on the coast. He transformed the disordered information of maritime routes in the South China Sea into a systematic account in his book, entitled *Study of the Eastern and Western Seas* (*Dong Xi Yang Kao*).

Together, these various sources detailed navigational notes on the shoals and rocks now known to comprise the larger part of the Paracels and Spratly islands and which Holroyd later discovered lay near Dejection Island.

Holroyd wondered if Dejection Island might have had resources that would have encouraged exports and what size of settlement would have made imports worthwhile to traders. If no maps showed the island, perhaps documents, such as the financial records of customs officials and/or traders, mentioned it. However, he had no such records in any of his files. Perhaps a different approach might reveal a clue.

He dug into his inbox and recovered an old email from a colleague who referred to a late Ming or early Qing Dynasty tomb close to FujinHaiZhou, a small provincial town near China's south coast. He continued reading the email and discovered that the tomb belonged to a provincial official who had written reports of activities in local coastal waters.

When he received the email, Holroyd didn't follow up because he thought the records would be irrelevant to any of his then pursuits. Now, however, if any of the activities included a reference to Dejection Island, they might be useful in his search. Even though it might be a long shot, he decided to find out more about the discoveries in the tomb.

A Google search revealed FujinHaiZhou as a small town of some three million inhabitants. Holroyd chuckled to think of a town with a population of three million—larger than the metropolitan cities of Birmingham and Manchester—as a small provincial town.

Then Holroyd realized that even if he found any records, they would not refer to the island by that name, and he had no clue if he could link any report to his project. Still, with no definitive lead, as yet, he might as well follow up on the email.

He checked the time and realized it would be morning in Taiwan, so he called his colleague, only to venture into the frustrating domain of automated telephone inquiries. He was fortunate finally to get in touch with her. Offhand, she could not remember the records in question but promised to get back to him.

"But, Peter, what got you interested all of a sudden?"

"Oh! Something just cropped up."

"About the South China Sea? Let me guess! You've been asked to help solve the problem." She laughed.

"Not at all." Holroyd cursed himself for the lie.

"Really?" she sounded skeptical. "Okay, then. Let me get back to you."

Later, he received an email suggesting he might want to pursue his inquiries in FujinHaiZhou. The email also suggested that he should contact an old friend of hers, Pieter de Hoog, now living in Holland, who had researched the Dutch East India Company. Given that a Dutch East Indiaman had rescued the captain of the Steadfast and that the Dutch had been very active in maritime matters when the Selden Map was printed, Holroyd thought the suggestion to call de Hoog was a good one.

That evening, as he settled into bed, he realized this case threatened to be more than just a search trolling through ancient records, and he thought of the possible difficulties he might face. It was not a comforting final thought for the day.

5

The room had no windows and was soundproofed. A picture of the president and two large blank television screens hung on the walls. On one side of the president's picture stood the American flag, and on the other side, a departmental flag.

In the room's centre was a large table around which a dozen men sat, each behind a bundle of files. The men wore civilian clothes or military uniforms decorated with medals and insignia denoting high ranks. Despite the air conditioning, the room was stuffy, as could happen after a long meeting in an enclosed space.

"Okay, let's get at it. The South China Sea."

Admiral Stuyvesant looked around the table. He was a tall, thin man with a weathered face that testified to many years at sea. Looking at him, a casual observer would conclude that this man was used to command and unlikely to tolerate incompetence. And yet, beneath his exterior, one could discern humanity and a sense of humour. "What's our take on this? Who wants to open? State?"

A civilian man dressed sombrely and with a slightly mournful expression beneath his bald pate shuffled papers in the file lying open before him and then looked up.

"Not happy. We don't want the control of the South China Sea to go to Beijing, but they have a bunch of warships off the coast of a small British island out there. Our allies in the area are asking what we propose to do."

"Are we proposing anything? Do we need to do anything?"

"Nothing planned, but we might want the Brits to hang on to the place in case we want to use it for something."

"Okay! What do we know about those ships?"

"It's a small flotilla including a landing support craft, a supply vessel, and a couple of destroyer escorts. We've been monitoring its activities by satellite surveillance. The destroyers are Jiangwei II class frigates. They're multipurpose ships with ship-to-ship, AA, and ASW capabilities."

"ASW?" a civilian interrupted. "What's that?"

"Anti-submarine warfare."

"What are anti-submarine ships doing there? Do we have any submarines nearby?" the same man asked.

"No! And it's strange because rocks and small islets clutter the place, so a submarine better be very careful. We think the ships are out there on exercise or to show the flag. Rather a small exercise if that is what it is, but a lot of power just to show the flag in the middle of nowhere."

"And what do we propose to do?"

"Nothing yet. We need permission or a request for help from one of the bordering states before we can do much. So far, there have been no requests."

"We think the Chinese are going to pressure the Brits to hand over the island," another civilian broke in.

"Typical! What's your take?"

"The Brits could look for a face-saving way to solve the problem. They might or might not want to get rid of it. If they want to get rid of the place, they'd have to figure out how to do it without getting everyone pissed. If I were them, I might want to invalidate any original claim and give the island back to whoever was there first."

"Whoever?"

"Maybe Vietnam, Thailand, China, Indonesia. I suspect no one would know for sure. If they did, we would have heard about it before now."

"How would they go about finding out who was first?"

"Wasn't who on second base?"

"No, he's on third." There was subdued laughter around the table.

"As I was about to ask, where they gonna look? Can't just go knocking on doors and asking if they remember being there before the Brits."

"Why not?"

"Too obvious and too public. Besides which, how would we know if their memories are accurate?"

"So, where does this leave us?"

"Not sure we need to do anything right now. Let the Brits do some spadework first. Do any of you remember van Roggenback? He's in the private sector now. He just told us about a meeting with an academic named Holroyd who fits the description of the sort of guy the Brits might want to hire to find out if anyone owned the place before the Brits moved in."

"I see! Well, we're here to make sure we don't get caught with our pants down next time a Chinese military wannabe has a wet dream and does something stupid. Whatever we decide to do, we'll have to be careful. Showing interest could help as a big stick against Chinese expansionism but could also set off alarm bells." Stuyvesant looked around the table. "Anyone got something more to contribute?"

"Best if we could persuade the Brits to ask us to get involved."

"Anything in mind?"

"Not yet."

"Maybe we could throw sand into the works," a voice at the end of the table chimed in.

"What does that mean?"

"From what I could surmise, this Holroyd is gonna look to see if settlers existed before the Brits arrived. If I'm right, we could keep our eye on Holroyd and move in before he can complete his job."

"Move in how?"

"Put one of our guys on scene and block him. Grab the records before he gets them, take them if he gets them, or make sure he never gets them. I'm told it can be very dangerous looking for old records in some parts of the world. Many intrepid explorers have never returned from their travels." There was silence in the room.

"Nasty! Can you do it without inviting attention?"

"Who would ask questions?"

There was no answer. After a pause, Stuyvesant looked around the room. "Well, that sounds like a plan. Go ahead but keep me in the loop."

6

Deputy Director Ting looked at the schedule on the computer screen. Today would be busy. He noted the time of the afternoon's meeting of department heads and tried to guess what his role might be. One never knew with the director.

One could prepare to discuss one subject at a briefing only to find out that the subject of the meeting had shifted, leaving one unprepared and embarrassed. Gloomily, Ting understood this was a ploy the director used occasionally to prove control over his staff.

The phone on his desk rang, and he picked up the receiver. He would not ignore this caller. After a brief exchange of pleasantries, he listened with attention. The caller informed him that Xiang Jin Leng had been seen in London. Ting put the phone down and asked for his assistant, Inspector Li Wen Yao, to come in.

Li was a thin man of average height who dressed modestly and without any jewelry. Passing him on the street among millions of other office workers would have occasioned no surprise. In fact, he might almost be invisible. Only close scrutiny would reveal an intensity in his eyes, suggesting the man was not ordinary.

Ting recognized that Li possessed an aura of self-confidence, knowledge, and power that suggested that in this department, Li was more influential, perhaps even more so than Ting himself.

"Good morning, Li Wen. I have just been informed that Xiang Jin Leng was seen in a London meeting with a British government official, a retired American, and a British academic. What do we know about this meeting? Bring me up to date, please."

"I have not received the full details of this meeting."

"Perhaps your other duties have been too demanding of your time." Ting allowed the reproof to sink in.

"Then what do you know?" Ting asked. "As I remember from your last briefing, Xiang Jin Leng left China with his family before we realized he had departed."

"Yes, Deputy Director," Li replied. "He took a considerable amount of wealth and settled in Central America. From there he was reported to be working with a drug cartel in Mexico and conducting other business, often with Mainland Chinese contacts. There are whispers in the courtyards that he has maintained ties with some corrupt Party members and has access to buyers interested in gaining antiques looted from ancient tombs."

"Yes, yes, " Ting interrupted, "is that all?"

Li nodded.

"And what do you intend to do next?" asked Ting.

There was a moment's silence before Li said, "I'm curious how this extraordinary collection of individuals would help Xiang in his nefarious activities. I see some logic in meeting with a government official, but I fail to see the relevance of the others."

Ting thought for a moment before speaking. "I think you should pay more attention to Xiang."

Li nodded, understanding that Ting was about to set a trap. Well, to be forewarned was to be forearmed, and two could play that game.

"Well?" Ting frowned at Li. "Do I have to spell it out for you? What is Xiang doing and why?"

"As yet, Deputy Director, I cannot be more specific. I will keep you apprised of matters as they develop."

Ting nodded. "Your cooperation in this matter is appreciated."

"Thank you, Deputy Director."

With that Li returned to his own office. Li had been given his orders to succeed or fail. He was under no illusions and would have to tread with caution. Any mistake and he would find his head on a platter instead of the deputy director's or Xiang's.

This meeting Xiang attended is curious. Conceivably, Xiang wanted some favour from the government official and probably offered a bribe for it, and conceivably the American general was a party to giving or receiving this favour. So, maybe there was a conspiracy, but to what end? And what of this academic? Who is Holroyd? I need to pursue inquiries.

He picked up the phone to call in a favour, though he doubted the person on the other end of the line would look at it as such.

7

Holroyd rose late and looked out the window of his flat. It was still raining outside, but now it was a penetrating winter rain that drummed onto the balcony and the windows. Peering down, he saw that the street was almost empty of traffic.

A couple of cars passed by their windshield wipers struggling against the cascading water. A taxi sped by, unaware of a woman hailing it. Umbrellas hid the few pedestrians scurrying along. One exasperated individual was walking his dog, but Holroyd gathered that the experience overjoyed neither pet nor master.

He pitied anyone who had to go outside in such weather even though it was normal for England at that time of year. Today was a stay-at-home-ensconced-in-comfortable-surroundings day, and, to be honest, he felt no pressing need to go out. He was snug at home.

He turned to his desk where two bulky envelopes lay, each delivered by a special messenger. One was from Merry, and he opened it first. Inside he found an envelope and three file folders, each sealed with embossed red wax. A coat of arms on the seals showed a government department had sent the envelope and the files.

He opened the envelope containing a short note, a postage-paid self-addressed envelope, and an official-looking document. The note requested that he sign and return the enclosed form using the self-addressed envelope. Merry had added a handwritten personal postscript wishing Holroyd luck.

The official-looking document turned out to be an *Official Secrets Act* form in which, by signing, he would agree never to reveal what he was about to learn on pain of unspecified punishment as set out in the *Act* (of which he found no copy). *What on earth? Bloody bureaucratic twaddle. As if my research could possibly involve official secrets. Next, I'll be followed by spooks! Oh! I suppose I'd better sign.* Even though he wasn't sure of the consequences, he signed it and then sealed the form in the envelope.

The first file contained copies of the HMS Steadfast's log. The second, labelled "Confidential," contained information about the South China Sea case before the Permanent Court of Arbitration (PCA), and the third contained a miscellany of papers and newspaper clippings. He opened the second one first.

Studying the court proceedings, he found that the Chinese, although very concerned about the matter, had not intervened. He wondered why not. Though the Chinese must have considered the possibility of a judicial rebuff from the beginning, such a public rebuff would be an intolerable loss of face. Perhaps an *in-absentia* rejection was less insulting and could be ignored.

However, the traditional Chinese way of resolving disputes was based on long experience with corrupt or slipshod magistrates. Instead of resolution by institutional means, the Chinese preferred bilateral and separate negotiations with each interested party. Even then, those negotiations took place for appearances' sake only.

Chinese negotiators would hammer home the Chinese position that, as the Middle Kingdom, the Chinese point of view was always righteous and right. After they had established Chinese moral superiority, the details of any ultimate agreement would include concessions and sops to the losers in the form of face-saving economic aid, preferential treatment, or both.

It seemed as if other parties rejected any offer to hold bilateral negotiations and had gone to the PCA instead. Holroyd wondered why the smaller Southeast nations were banding together to tweak the dragon's tail. Although China historically avoided force, there could be no certainty the dragon would not retaliate forcibly.

Sun-Tzu, the Chinese strategist who wrote *The Art of War,* noted that the supreme art of war was to subdue the enemy without fighting. But twice in its history had China successfully solved a problem outside its borders by military means. First, under Empress Wu, when China conquered Korea, and second, when China helped stop Western incursions into North Korea.

On the other hand, during the Yuan Dynasty, when the Chinese army set out to invade Japan, a typhoon destroyed it at sea. During the early Qing Dynasty, attempts at gaining what was then Siam expired under the onslaught of Siamese troops and the challenges of the jungle. An attack on Japan in 1895 destroyed the Chinese army and navy.

Perhaps since Korea, the country had changed its attitude and was more prepared to be adversarial. However, while military invasions to conquer new territories were not China's forte, China defended its existing territories ferociously.

So, given modern China's more adversarial and even militaristic approach to territorial disputes, Holroyd wondered if China's failure to appear before the PCA and the presence of the warships off the island was an indication of China's intent to invade.

China pretty well controls the East China Sea, and if it gets to control the South China Sea, most of Taiwan's trade routes will be through Chinese waters, and Taiwan will almost be boxed in. Under those conditions, Taiwan, like the islands of St.

Pierre and Miquelon, off the Canadian coast, will probably maintain its independence only by the grace of its larger neighbour. Unlike Canada, China has not shown much indication of extending grace, and Taiwan could eventually be forced to accept China's sovereignty. Brilliant! Holroyd could appreciate Britain wanting to avoid further involvement, and he realized why Merry had invited him to provide an alternative solution to the dispute.

He had a sudden thought

Merry wants me to provide a face-saving solution. If I fail, he thinks there could be a war. Whatever possessed the man to think I could prevent a war?

He continued examining the information on the PCA proceedings and noted internal memoranda and notes detailing background information and advice on possible options. The background information was sparse and added nothing new to what he had been told.

He looked to see if anyone had done any useable research but found no reports of records or artifacts that might have indicated early settlements, and he concluded he needed to find some written evidence.

He suspected that only an administrative proclamation or an imperial writ proclaiming Chinese sovereignty over the island would have to be found. But neither of those made up a valid legal claim unless records existed of a population that agreed to the fiat.

But perhaps no writ existed, or no one knew where one such might be. *I'm beginning to see why I was asked to do the research. But this is way outside my area of competence,* Holroyd thought. *How nice of Merry to dump this in my lap!*

He turned to the second file, which contained copies of extracts from the HMS Steadfast's log. As he read through it, he again found nothing that he did not already know.

The third folder had a miscellany of internal memoranda and newspaper clippings. Some clippings foresaw bloody invasions reminiscent of the rape of Nanking. These clippings showed well-endowed but skimpily dressed blond females smiling seductively from what looked like tropical island beaches. Holroyd wondered why none of the beauties showed signs of third-degree sunburn, then decided they contributed nothing to his research.

A few clippings, obviously from better newspapers, reported that the islanders were annoyed about being ignored and objected strongly to any loss of colonial status. In sum, the memoranda and the newspaper clippings reflected Merry's comments about the island having been conveniently "ignored if not forgotten" by the powers that be.

Given little to suggest that anyone in Whitehall had seriously addressed the issues that Dejection Island presented, Holroyd realized he would be the knight in shining armour for finding a solution or the sacrificial lamb if he failed, and he relished neither role.

Inside the second package, Holroyd found a cheque for £25,000 and a note from Mr. Xiang asked that he quickly present his passport at the Chinese embassy, so it could issue the proper academic research visa. *So, the offer from Xiang is genuine!* Also enclosed was an embossed official letter from Fujinhaizhou University inviting him to come to China to conduct academic research on Ming and Qing Dynasty exploration, navigation, and cartography.

Despite this, he noted there was no ticket enclosed, but the cheque would cover that cost, and the government would honour its commitment. There was nothing from the American. *Perhaps the American payment is included in Xiang's, but that was not what I understood the arrangement to be. Perhaps the American has decided to pull back. Well, sod him, I don't need him.*

With that in mind, he calculated that with the government's support and his own resources he could afford a first-class ticket.

Still, he felt a faint stirring of unease. *Something doesn't quite add up, but what?*

8

Holroyd put down the files and decided to call the Dutch contact, Pieter de Hoog. Luckily, de Hoog was at home and answered the phone at once.

"A colleague suggested you might be able to help me with some information on Dutch East India Company (VOC) trading voyages back toward the end of the eighteenth century," Holroyd said after introducing himself and exchanging a few pleasantries.

"That is very nice of them." De Hoog's Dutch accent was strong. "It would be helpful if you could give me more precise details, such as a particular voyage or which ends of the routes are important and what cargoes were carried."

Holroyd paused to consider how much information he could safely reveal and decided to avoid any direct mention of the Steadfast or the island. "My interest focuses on Royal Navy activities that may have supported or hindered VOC ships returning to Holland between, say, 1775 and 1800. The area of interest is between Vietnam, Malaysia, and Borneo."

"That's just about at the edge of the South China Sea." De Hoog paused. "Most VOC ships sailed farther south, calling at Java, so I'm not sure there will be much to give you."

Later, De Hoog called to say there were no reports of engagements with Royal Navy ships during that time or in that area. "However, one ship, Het Goede Vrouw van Hoorn picked up some shipwrecked survivors to take back to Europe," he said.

"Unfortunately, parts of that record have been lost, so I can't tell you where these survivors came from or precisely where the rescue took place." *That could fit Merry's report of the rescue* but *doesn't help me. I hope such outcomes won't become the norm during my research.*

Holroyd considered his options for narrowing the places where he might start searching for the documents he needed. Looking over his collection of books and in his reference files, he found nothing that he thought would help.

On the other hand, one immediately available source that might prove useful was Anderson's booksellers, who had a vast knowledge of the antique books market and often sold rare books to a selection of reclusive and anonymous collectors. Holroyd had used them in the past, and perhaps they had acquired something new. He picked up the phone.

"Mister Anderson! Holroyd here. I'm following up on my earlier request and wonder if you managed to obtain a copy of Zhang Xie's 1617 book, entitled Study of the Eastern and Western Seas or Dong Xi Yang Kao."

"Doctor Holroyd! How nice to hear from you! I'm terribly sorry, but we have so far not located a copy, but I promise you I will keep looking."

Holroyd expressed his appreciation and was about to hang up, but Anderson continued. "If you have no other matter for us, I was just about to call you. We recently gained a volume on the Indonesian archipelago, written in Chinese and dated around 1680."

"Indonesian archipelago? I'm not sure that's what I'm looking for—"

"This is a rather unique situation because we have a buyer who has expressed almost desperate interest in this exceptional volume, and he proposes to come by later this afternoon." He paused. "Under normal circumstances, I would not dream of diverting a sale, but the gentleman was unknown to us and so insistent that he aroused my suspicions. I looked him up but cannot find any reference to him at all. It's so unusual that I would appreciate it if you would come around immediately to help shed some light on the matter."

Holroyd's curiosity was aroused given Anderson's insistence and reference to an "exceptional volume." He decided he could delay further research and set out.

The Anderson family's bookstore dated from the early nineteenth century. Though not as old as Hatchard's in Piccadilly or as extensive as Alibris, it catered to special-interest groups favouring a specific collection of books on eclectic and arcane subjects.

The shop was in a small alleyway off Charing Cross Road, the precise location known only to its clientele. Its neglected storefront discouraged casual shoppers from entering.

Most customers only crossed the threshold based on referrals and introductions from existing clients. However, once inside, clients met an old-world courtesy that included recognition and privileges, such as free delivery and book return guarantees.

Holroyd had been a privileged customer for over a decade and relied on them to notify him when printed material of interest became available. But with a potential sale in sight, Holroyd wondered why bring the matter to his attention and why the urgency? What had aroused Anderson's concern?

As he walked the few yards to the alleyway's entrance, he realized he was looking around to see if he was being watched or followed, only to laugh at himself for being so foolish as to think anyone would take the trouble to follow him. He was just a university professor, albeit one whose future seemed to be under a cloud.

He turned into the alleyway, passed a massage parlour, a Malaysian takeaway opening later that afternoon, and a shuttered shop, the existence of which had always remained a mystery to him.

He stopped in front of Anderson's and considered the frontage. It reminded him of the description of Dickens' Old Curiosity Shop with its grimy exterior behind which lay a treasure trove of not-so-dusty knowledge and experience.

Only in London would such an eminent establishment be neighbour to such a collection of mismatching businesses. But perhaps the fast-food and massage parlour enjoyed some form of symbiotic relationship.

Before he entered he looked up and down the alley and noted a man entering who quickly ducked into the Malaysian takeaway as Holroyd looked at him. *Strange, why duck in the takeaway when it's closed?* He entered Anderson's.

Inside the shop, the walls were lined with shelves laden with hardcover books bound in leather styles long abandoned by modern publishers. Two old-fashioned desks with leather-inlaid tops stood on opposite sides of a carpet that ran the shop's length and divided it in two.

At one desk, an elderly man who was busy writing looked up at Holroyd, peering over his glasses, and smiled a welcome before resuming his work. Mr. Anderson Senior would have fit into a nineteenth-century bookshop even better than he did now.

The man getting up from behind the other desk was younger, but there was a clear physical resemblance to the elder man. "Doctor Holroyd! How good of you to come, sir. Please, just give me a moment."

The younger Anderson went to the back of the shop, disappeared for a few moments, and then returned carrying a package in his now gloved hands. He put the package on the desk, reached into a drawer, and handed Holroyd a pair of white cotton gloves. Holroyd put them on and waited.

"My father and I bought this from what they told us was an estate sale of a deceased Japanese gentleman, living in London. We verified that the sale occurred, and that Sotheby's verified the provenance of all items sold. But we could not discover why they declined to be the auctioneers. You can imagine that with this item, we were very concerned about its authenticity." With that, he handed Holroyd the book.

Holroyd looked at the yellow silk hardcover and the 'wrapped back' Ming Dynasty binding style. With care, he opened the cover to see a heavy paper with dark red vertical lines or rulings and subject headings written in red on the outer edges of the paper.

"I thought you mentioned a Chinese book on the Indonesian archipelago, but am I correct in thinking this is an original volume of the Yongle Encyclopedia? The Yongle *Dadian*?" Holroyd looked up. "Can't be! I mean, this would be priceless."

"It is. I thought it better not to mention it as such on the phone." Anderson smiled.

"I can understand your caution. But I thought only a few exist, of which three are in the Bodleian Library."

"Yes, that was our information too, but as you can see, one more has surfaced."

"And you are sure this is genuine?" Holroyd was stunned at the enormity of what Anderson was showing him.

"All our tests say so, but then, forgeries are becoming very sophisticated."

"I have seen a copy in the Bodleian, but I never thought to handle a copy myself. What a lovely,

lovely, and unique experience. Thank you so very much." He looked lovingly at the book.

"But I confess to being puzzled. As you know, this work mostly covers subjects that are outside my area of research. As much as I appreciate the opportunity to inspect it, may I ask why you called me?" Anderson nodded and reached for a piece of paper that he had previously laid on his desk.

"We found this between the pages. Other than what appears to be directions to some location that we can't recognize, we don't know what it is. We thought perhaps you might assist us."

Holroyd reverentially laid the book on the desk and then reached for the sheet of paper proffered by Anderson. It was flimsy, but it showed outlines and coloured symbols that Holroyd did not recognize and Japanese *Hiragana* or *Katakana* writing. He felt a sudden surge of curiosity. *Why would this document be hidden in such a valuable book and by whom*?

"I don't think I've come across anything like this before, but it must have some very special significance. I may be wrong, but I think it's a map or directions or a description, but of what I do not know, and the writing is Japanese."

"That was our information. But we were hesitant to conjecture further because we thought it might not be an anomaly. Originally, we thought this came from the same period as the book, but our first tests suggest that it's much more modern. We considered getting more qualified advice, but we are reluctant to do so given that it was among the pages of the encyclopedia. So, we felt that without knowing what this paper stands for or why it came to be in the book, we could not, in honesty, proceed with a sale."

Holroyd nodded.

"We wondered if you might shed light on the question."

"It's outside my field, so I'm not sure I can be of help. Perhaps it would be better to ask someone with expertise in Japanese writing."

"That was our original reaction, but then we decided to ask you because this was found in the Dadian, which is, I believe, the time frame within your area of expertise, and if it's a map it might have something to do with travels of the time."

"Thank you for your confidence." Holroyd smiled. "Then let me make sure it's not misplaced. I'll do what I can. Can I borrow the book and the paper?"

"We have no problem with your taking the paper, but I'm sure you can understand our reluctance to part with the book unless there are proper arrangements for its safekeeping."

"Then it might be better for you to keep the book," Holroyd agreed.

"I think we might inform our potential purchaser that, regretfully, we sold the book to you, but we could also promise to inquire if you would sell. That might give you enough time to complete your investigation."

Holroyd nodded. "Perhaps you could put this into an envelope for me?"

"Just a moment if you please." Anderson accepted the paper and then went to the back of the store before returning with an envelope, which Holroyd put in his inside coat pocket. He thanked Anderson and then moved to exit the shop.

As he thought about the paper, he remembered an old colleague, Alfred Rostwick, who had been a professor specializing in Japanese history but had moved on to other venues. *I think I'll give Alfred a call and see if he can help me decipher what's on this paper.*

As Holroyd was walking out the door, an Asian man walked in, and the two almost collided. Holroyd's impression was that it was the same man who had ducked into the takeaway, but he was uncertain. Holroyd gave a quick apology and then turned into Charing Cross Road.

He decided he would take the tube part of the way home and would walk the rest of the way, thinking a breath of fresh air would do him good. As he descended into the tube station, he did not notice the Asian back at the entrance to the alleyway looking frantically up and down the street.

9

Isayo Muramori, owner and managing director of Muramori Industries, was a small, frail-looking man, and his hair, though full, had turned a silver grey. He wore an immaculate blue silk suit over a starched white shirt with a striped, maroon tie. He straightened his sleeve cuff to hide a gold-and-carved-jade cufflink. That carving was worth more than all the furnishings in the boardroom.

His appearance was deceptive because his fragility hid a ruthless and ambitious attitude driving a tenacious yearning for the traditions of the Japan of yesteryear. Losing World War II was, in his mind, a temporary setback that preparation and good planning would overcome. In this, he knew he was not alone. Many Japanese leaders sympathized with his point of view.

He was sitting behind a large, polished rosewood desk when the phone on his desk buzzed.

"Moshi, Moshi."

"Our man could not retrieve the document kept by your late uncle. It was hidden in a book that his son sold to a bookseller in London."

"Was someone sent to buy the book back?" Muramori's tone suggested a hint of possible reproof.

"Yes, Muramori san. Your cousin was to undertake the task personally."

"You said 'was.' Why?"

"Your cousin was convinced of the uselessness of further efforts."

"Do we know how he arrived at this undesirable conviction?"

"Oh, yes!"

"Oh?" Muramori allowed an expression of interest to surface.

"He leaned too far out of his tenth-floor hotel window and met with an undesirable stop on reaching the ground, thus terminating any further interest in pursuing the matter. A most unfortunate occurrence."

"Most unfortunate." Muramori agreed. "Do we know what excited his interest in looking out from his window, or was he under a sudden impression that he could fly?"

"We do not know the full circumstances of his departure from his apartment, but we suspect that someone assisted his leap into the void." By now Muramori focused his full attention on his subordinate's report.

"Assisted? By whom?"

"That, Muramori san, we do not know."

"How ill-starred. Your lack of so much information is regrettable. However, I'm sure you will make every effort to discover who assisted my cousin on his unlucky voyage of discovery. And, of course, you will pursue your efforts to recover the document." After a pause to make sure the message was understood, he continued. "Anything else to report?"

"Yes, Muramori san. Our agents informed us that the Chinaman Xiang Jin Leng and a retired American general met with a university professor named Peter Holroyd."

Muramori paused. "Of what interest is that to me?"

"You wanted us to watch the Chinaman, and in doing so we became aware of the meeting. We hope to find out if the meeting is of interest."

"Hope? Do I pay you to hope?" Muramori inquired softly.

"No, Muramori san, you pay me to produce results."

"Good, then proceed and keep me informed." Muramori hung up. The sudden demise of his cousin in London worried him. He did not regret the loss of his relative, but he wondered who might have been responsible for his death. Have other interests become players at his table?

He reflected not for the first time at the stupidity of his uncle, a former colonel in the Japanese Imperial Army. How could he have been so foolish as to hide the hidden location of gold looted from the occupied territories in that priceless book he had bought from Xiang Jin Leng?

Now that his uncle had passed away, it was reasonable that Xiang would want to recover the volume, but did that mean Xiang had arranged for the sudden departure of Muramori's cousin? That made little sense if Xiang only wanted to retrieve his book. He could have negotiated a price for its acquisition. But murder made sense if Xiang knew of the gold and thought he could get directions to its location.

But how would Xiang have known about the gold unless Muramori's uncle had told him about it? Or had someone else who had taken part in the hiding told Xiang? A Japanese soldier? A slave laborer? If Xiang knew of the gold, Muramori could foresee a competitive situation that he fully intended to win.

Privately, Muramori seethed with fury at the possibility that the Chinese might frustrate his plans to recover the treasure. He would not allow those misshapen dwarves to disturb Japan's path toward a glorious future, not again. There was no question; he could not allow anyone to interfere. Or did Xiang have another reason for wanting the book? If so, what was it?

For the moment Muramori would keep his feelings hidden behind a calm and confident demeanor. However, he thought he could expect a call from Xiang, perhaps even soon. Meanwhile, the answers to those questions could wait. Now he had to find out what this meeting was about. Perhaps this Holroyd should be carefully watched and maybe even "handled," should it prove necessary.

As instructed by Xiang, Holroyd presented his visa application at the Chinese consular section of the embassy. It was located on the side of the embassy and could be reached by entering a plain wooden door that opened into a soulless room. There were no seats, and other than some notices in English and Chinese, no wall hangings.

Several people were queuing in front of a glass-fronted cubicle in which one clerk was receiving and dispensing documents. Holroyd resigned himself to a long, boring wait, eventually reaching the front of the queue after more than an hour. The expressionless male clerk received his application, examined it, and told him to collect his passport in a week.

As instructed, a week later, he arrived to collect his passport, only for a young Chinese lady on the other side of the glass to say, "Not ready yet. Please come back in a week."

"They told me to return in a week when I presented my application last week."

"Yes, but it is not yet ready. Please come back in a week." Holroyd was taken aback.

"Is there a problem?" he asked. The clerk looked at her computer screen before answering in a toneless manner. "Please return in a week."

"But I intend to leave soon." The girl looked at him and then back at her screen, her expression unchanging.

"Just a moment, please." She got out of her chair and disappeared into a back room. After about five minutes, she reappeared, sat down, and looked at him.

"Please return in a week."

"What's the problem?"

"I'm sorry. Please return in a week." She looked past him at the next applicant. Holroyd gave in and left. As far as he could tell, he had made no errors, so why was his application delayed?

He reviewed the application in his mind, finding the letter from Fujinhaizhou University to be the only potential weakness. Although the university had a history department, nothing on the website suggested the university offered courses in maritime activities. Given the invitation, he had not questioned this detail.

When he next arrived at the visa section, they made him wait ten minutes until a dour man in an ill-fitting suit arrived and asked him to follow. The man led him into a side office where a pudgy middle-aged man sat behind a desk.

The office was bare except for the desk, a few chairs, and a hot-water carafe on a table next to the desk. The pudgy man had hung his jacket over the back of his chair and loosened his tie to reveal a shirt too small for him.

His guide motioned for Holroyd to sit in a chair before the desk while he sat farther back, next to the door. The desk was empty except for a single file folder.

The pudgy man looked at him in silence and then leaned forward to open the file, which Holroyd assumed was his. Still, without uttering a word, the pudgy man leafed through the file, carefully perusing each document. Holroyd felt uneasy but hoped it did not show. The silence continued until the pudgy man had examined the final page and looked back up at him.

"Doctor Holroyd. How good of you to come."

"Not at all. May I ask what this is about?"

'Pudge,' as Holroyd called him, looked at him impassively. After a moment's silence, he spoke. "You may ask, but I won't promise to answer until I've asked a few questions, and perhaps not then." He looked at Holroyd, who could not divine what he was thinking. "May I offer you some tea?"

Holroyd nodded and the man behind him handed him a paper cup with a few leaves floating in tepid water. He sipped it, so preoccupied with his predicament that he barely noticed its lack of flavour.

"You intend to visit the People's Republic of China. May I ask why?"

"I believe I stated the purpose of my visit in the application." Holroyd realized he had adopted a defiant tone and quickly changed course. Better, he thought, to appear humble when facing even minor officialdom.

"Yes, you did, but as you can see, I'm asking you now." Pudge looked at him.

"As I said on my application, I'm a historian who studies Ming and Qing Dynasty cartography—map making. My purpose is to do further research on the voyages of Zheng He."

"Thank you for the clarification. I would have thought the voyages of Zheng He have been fully researched." Pudge said, a note of derision in his voice. "But *cartography*," he emphasized the word to show he knew exactly what it was, "is a rather large subject, and I would appreciate it if you could be more precise."

"I'm hoping to learn more about Zheng He's reasons for some of his voyages and the trading routes of Chinese sailors during the late Ming and early Qing Dynasties."

"And how does cartography contribute to your knowledge?"

"Maps and charts may show how much Chinese explorers explored their part of the world."

"But surely, Professor, you know much about that already. What part of your knowledge needs improvement?"

"I'm particularly interested in trade routes that may have existed but about which I know little. These routes led to the south and east and could cover Indonesia and the Philippines. I intend to look for charts or maps proving that Chinese sailors had travelled in those areas."

"And why are those routes of interest to you?"

"I know little about them and wish to add to my knowledge."

"Do you have a particular interest in those routes?"

Holroyd was becoming irritated. Pudge was being unusually inquisitive and possibly obstructive. What was behind these questions? However, Holroyd doubted he would get any answers, so he stopped from letting his feelings show.

"Not yet. It's possible that my research may show something that could be worth more study. But otherwise, I have no special interest."

"I see," Pudge replied. He looked down at a paper in the folder. "And just how do you intend to look?"

"I want to visit libraries and, if possible, private collections containing originals or copies of charts or maps."

"Do you have any persons in China with whom you have been in contact about this research?"

"No."

"This is not your first visit to China, is it?"

"No. I was there as a child with my parents from 1973 to 1975."

"And why were they there?"

"My father was at Beida as an exchange professor"

"Beida? Beijing University? And what was his purpose there?"

Holroyd felt a surge of anger and was about to make a cutting reply but restrained himself. "He was teaching English."

"Why did he leave?" Pudge looked intently at Holroyd.

"As I'm sure you will understand, conditions for academic work at that time were not exactly the best, and doubly so for a foreigner."

"And in what way, Professor, do you suggest conditions were not the best? Were you not welcome? Were you not granted access to our libraries? Were you not allowed to meet with some of the best Chinese experts in your field? What was lacking for conditions not to be, as you so quaintly put it, 'the best'?"

"I think we both know about those conditions. I hardly think it proper to go over the events of those days." Pudge looked at him in silence, and Holroyd wondered if he considered the answer a criticism.

"That was during the Cultural Revolution, was it not?"

Holroyd felt an urge to make a silly remark about the extent of his knowledge but refrained from saying anything other than a simple "Yes."

"And what do you think of those events?"

"At the time, I was far too young to follow, let alone understand what was happening. Looking back, I think the whole thing was a horrible mistake."

"Why do you say so?"

"All studies stopped, and they treated eminent and qualified academics viciously. Why? For thousands of years, the Chinese held education in great esteem. It all went up in smoke to the cheering of young men and women who were destroying their future. I could not understand how a culture as rich and historic as the Chinese could have fallen so far."

"Yes, and the government has acknowledged it will never happen again."

"That is bolting the stable door after the horse has left. They could have avoided it if people studied their history. Dynasties may change, but no revolution has ever achieved its aims. I don't think the Cultural Revolution did anything more than destabilize a society that has survived for millennia. And…" He was about to add, "they did some barbaric acts," but stopped when he realized that he was running into a minefield.

"Yes?"

"Oh! I was about to remark that they destroyed many cultural items of value. Many of those items would have been invaluable for doing research. But then, that was one of the purposes of the whole thing, wasn't it?" Pudge looked at him for a few seconds, ignored the rhetorical question, then continued with another question.

"I find your suggestion that revolutions never achieve their aims curious. Should I take it that you consider the Chinese Revolutions to have failed? I refer, of course, to the revolutions of 1911 and 1949. Have they failed to achieve their aims?"

"I'm not qualified to give an opinion, but I would have to say that, overall, those have succeeded and thus are the exception."

Pudge looked at Holroyd but said nothing. Then he rifled through the file until he came to a document that he appeared to study. He looked up at Holroyd again. "I notice that the records of your departure from China at that time are incomplete. How did you leave?"

"We made our way to Hong Kong. I don't remember many details, but it was an extraordinary journey. We met with hostility from Red Guards, most of whom I doubt could read or write, but other people risked a lot to help us."

"And your conclusion?"

"Sir, we were foreigners and guests in your country. I had no role to play in judging those events."

"I see." Pudge consulted the file again. "You have no contacts from, say, your previous visit? Old school friends?"

"No. Most of my school friends were young like me, and any friends we had were friends of my parents. Several friends went off somewhere during the Cultural Revolution, but I don't know what happened to them after that. With others, I have lost contact. They discouraged contact with foreigners for a while."

"How did you get your information to do this new research?"

"There are researchers of Chinese origin who now work in universities outside of China."

"There are. Have any of them suggested people in China with whom you might try to make contact?"

"No."

"Yet you intend to go. You intend to conduct research with no contacts or introductions?" Holroyd noticed a tone of disbelief.

"There is a letter of invitation attached to my application. I think such a letter means some people will meet and help me once I arrive. I accepted the letter as an introduction."

"I see that Fujinhaizhou University has invited you to do this work. How do you know Fujinhaizhou University?"

"I don't. However, an acquaintance of mine offered to make introductions to some people he thought would be of help. I assume those people work at Fujinhaizhou University."

"That all seems perfectly ordinary, except that while Fujinhaizhou University has a history department, I see no department and no expert in your field."

"Yes, I had noted that. But because the recommendation came from my acquaintance, I thought no more of it."

"Have you known this acquaintance for long?"

"No. I met him only recently."

"And yet you are prepared to go to China based on this casual acquaintance?"

"A friend in the British government introduced me."

"May I know the names of these people?"

Holroyd was becoming irritated by this circuitous and pointless line of questioning. "May I know why?" he asked, sensing a rising asperity in his voice.

"Professor, I'm charged with satisfying my government that the purpose of your visit is legitimate." Holroyd was amused at this display of pomposity.

"Legitimate? What could be illegitimate about researching such an arcane topic?"

"That, Professor, is precisely what we seek to find out."

"Might I ask who precisely this 'we' is?"

"The Chinese government, like any government, has many interests to protect. Such protection may be managed by politicians, state security departments, or a host of other official departments. It is not my role to inform you which department may be concerned; it is my role to respond to any concerns that are brought to my attention."

A silence settled over the room. Holroyd recognized he was facing a blank wall and pondered what the consequences might be if he admitted the identities of his dinner companions. He remembered that he should not divulge the purpose of his research, but he could see no reason to hide the names of his employers.

Holroyd explained he'd been introduced to Mr. Xiang Jin Leng and his son Deng Tan Liu by Viscount Huntington. "They asked about my line of work and offered to help me. Frankly, I found it curious that they offered to finance part of my work, but I questioned none of their motives as I have found the wealthy often have their agendas."

"They do. And did this Mr. Xiang Jin Leng offer any explanations?"

"No."

"And did you ask for any explanations?"

"No."

"Why not? Were you not or are you not curious?"

"Yes, I was. But I was being offered the help I needed to continue my work, and I'm not one to look a gift horse in the mouth."

"Gift horse? I see no mention of horses in the file or your application, nor do I see the relevance." Holroyd bit his tongue to keep from speaking.

"This Xiang Jin Leng, do you know anything about him?"

Holroyd shook his head.

"I find it strange that a person of your reported integrity should be prepared to travel to China at the suggestion of someone you do not know but has money to engage you on some academic quest in which I fail to see their interests. Is there anything else you would like to add?"

"Not that I can think of. But I will say, I'm surprised there is such concern about my application." Pudge looked at him, causing him to squirm in his seat. He hoped Pudge did not take his clear unease as a sign he had something to hide.

He felt a trickle of sweat running down his back even though the room was not warm. He hoped no sweat was shining on his face. Finally, he broke the silence. "Are you denying my application?"

"We will let you know."

"May I be so bold as to ask when you might let me know?"

"When we are ready, Professor and I hope that will be soon."

"May I go?"

"Yes, my assistant will show you the way."

He got up and extended his hand to Pudge. "May I have my passport back now?"

"Are you travelling somewhere else soon?"

"No."

"Then I'm sure you will not object if we keep it for a little while longer?"

"I don't see how objecting would help me."

"Thank you for your cooperation, Professor."

Finally, he received a call from the embassy telling him to come and collect his passport. Once again, they took him to Pudge's office. This time, however, they did not offer a seat or tea.

"Professor Holroyd, how good of you to come. It will please you to learn that we have approved your visa." His voice slipped half an octave lower as he added, "Upon instruction from Beijing." With that, he handed Holroyd his passport.

"Please be sure, Professor, that you break no laws nor associate with any criminal elements while in China. I wish you an enjoyable trip and every success with your research. We appreciate your cooperation."

Pudge nodded to the guide, who escorted Holroyd out.

Once outside, exited the embassy and looked for a taxi. He realized he would have a better chance of getting a cab on the opposite side of the road and crossed while musing over his treatment. *What was all that fuss about my visa? What does approval "on the instructions of Beijing" mean? Why would Beijing get involved with visa applications that are normally the prerogative of local embassies? Merry couldn't have had enough time to organize a diplomatic request, absent which I can't imagine why the central government would have gotten involved. Or did Xiang use his influence? Or has someone flagged me? But if that's the case, who and why?*

He was so deeply immersed in his thoughts that he stepped onto the crosswalk without noticing a van that suddenly pulled out of the curb. As it reached the crossing, the van screeched to a halt, the side door slid open, and someone tried to grab Holroyd to pull him in.

Holroyd failed to realize what was happening, and if not for a passing young man who grabbed him from behind, Holroyd would have been pulled inside. Finally, Holroyd reacted, and the balance of power shifted so that whoever was inside the van was almost pulled out. The assailant released Holroyd, shouted at the driver, and the van accelerated, disappearing around the corner into St. James Street before Holroyd could note the license plate number or any other identifying marks.

Shaken, he turned to his rescuer. "Did you see that? Someone just tried to grab me off the street!" He felt disoriented and dizzy, and he noticed his voice was unsteady.

"Yes. But we stopped the buggers, whoever they are." The young man looked at Holroyd. "Are you alright?"

"I think so. But what was that all about? Did you see who they were?"

"Looked Asian to me. But I didn't get the licence plate or anything. Bloody foreigners! Come here driving like madmen."

"Why would anyone want to get at me?"

"Can't help there, I'm afraid. Are you sure you're okay? Anything I can help with? Look, here's my card in case you need me for a follow-up, though I don't think there's much I can do."

"Think, I'll manage, thanks."

"Perhaps we should call the police. Not sure what we could tell them, though."

"No, no. I think I'd rather just get home." Still shocked but also beginning to feel outraged, Holroyd wondered what lay behind the incident. *This is the real world of London in the twenty-first century, not some fictional thriller novel.* He racked his brains, but nothing came to mind. *Better just to go home and enjoy a relaxing hot bath and a good stiff drink.*

Once home and feeling somewhat refreshed, he continued to mull over the incident without concluding.

11

Holroyd took out the paper Anderson had given him. Looking more closely at it, he thought it was a map, and the lines represented the contours of a hill or mountain and possibly the shoreline of an island. But where? He picked up the phone.

"Alfred, Peter Holroyd here." Rostwick expressed surprise and pleasure at the call. Holroyd continued. "I'm calling to see if you could help me." He gave a summary of the matter and concluded with an invitation. "Care to have lunch at the club? I can show you what I'm talking about."

"Oh, thanks. I'd be delighted. But not for lunch. Let's make it dinner."

They met at the Naval and Military Club and entered the Long Bar, where Holroyd asked for a Talisker. As he sipped it, he looked up at the walls where the paintings of long-dead generals and admirals had been hung.

There was a picture of an inane-looking George III in a military uniform over a samurai sword captured from the Japanese after their surrender. General Charles "Chinese" Gordon assiduously studied a book that Holroyd assumed to be the Bible because of Gordon's reported Christian beliefs.

Given that George had lost the American colonies and Gordon was butchered at Khartoum, Holroyd concluded morosely the memorabilia honoured losers more than winners.

Holroyd and Rostwick chatted about old times and caught up with each other's activities. They went upstairs to the Coffee Room overlooking St. James Square for dinner, after which Holroyd reached into his pocket and pulled out the envelope Anderson had given him. He extracted the piece of paper and showed it to Rostwick, who put on his reading glasses and scrutinized it.

"Alfred, do you have any idea what this is?"

Rostwick looked at it closely "By Jove! I think I do. If I'm right, this is a very interesting piece of paper. Would I be able to keep it and verify what it is?"

"Well, it's not mine to lend, and I was—"

"Peter, if this is what I think it is, it has great significance in certain circles in Whitehall. I'm pretty sure it's not something up your alley. And never fear, I'll make sure you get it back quickly."

"I have a better idea. Why not take a picture on your phone, and you can study that at your leisure?"

"I'd rather not, but let's see if we can get a copy downstairs."

They went to the reception to make a copy, only to be told the machine was out of order. After getting Alfred's solemn promise to safeguard and return it on completion of the verification, Holroyd agreed to let Rostwick take it and went home.

Upon arrival, he noticed his door was open, and the light was on in the living room. *What's this? Could I have been so careless or distracted as to forget to ensure the door was locked and turn the light off?*

Still shaken from the attack in the street, he nervously entered his flat, only to see a black leather shoe sticking out from behind the living room door.

"Hello, what are you doing in my home, and who are you?" he called out.

When he got no answer, he peeked inside and found a body lying face down on the floor with a pool of blood seeping out from a smashed upper torso. A wave of horror washed over him.

He felt weak and reached for something to hold on to. Luckily, the door jamb was at hand. Holroyd stood by the door as he steadied himself and took in what he saw. *What the hell is this?*

Somewhat steadier, he thought the body was Chinese or Japanese, dressed expensively but with little taste. He saw a gold necklace beneath a mauve shirt that stuck out from blue satin trousers, and a gold watch studded with diamonds was on one wrist. The other lay under the body.

Who is this man? Why is he lying in my flat? And then his mind switched irrelevantly to asking *Strange. If this were a robbery, why leave the necklace and the watch?*

He noted his papers scattered on his desk and the floor, as were several books. Someone had searched the place. But as far as he could see, they had taken nothing of value.

He entered the room but was hit by a heavy blow to the head from someone hidden behind the door and remembered nothing after that.

12

Holroyd woke up on in his bedroom with a splitting headache and a throbbing pain in the side of his skull. Disoriented, he looked around and realized he was not alone.

Standing at his bedside was a beautiful young Asian woman dressed in a white blouse and a dark business suit. She was about five feet five inches tall, slim, and had an oval face framing her almond eyes and high cheekbones.

She had cut her black hair in a fringe at the front but sported a full, modern ponytail that hung to her shoulders. Despite the ponytail, she reminded him of the pictures of the beautiful young court ladies during imperial China or perhaps of some heroine out of a Chinese film set in the times of the resistance against the Japanese or during the Civil War.

"What happened? Who are you?" He croaked.

"Oh, good! You're awake! I was worried that your injury was more severe," she said with a concerned look.

"But who are you, and why are you here?"

"My name is Wendy Liu, and I'm here at the request of Xiang Jin Leng. I have a letter here for you." She fumbled in her purse before handing him an envelope.

"But why are you in my flat?"

"Your door was wide open, and I came in to see why."

Holroyd struggled to get up. "But . . " He groaned as a wave of dizziness washed over him, and he sank back into his bed. He touched his head and felt a bandage he knew had not been there earlier in the evening.

"You hit your head. It was bleeding, so I dressed the wound for you. Now please lie back and rest."

"No, no. I have to call the police."

"The police? What for?"

"The body in my library."

"What body? I did not see a body."

"But someone came here, went through my stuff, and left a body on my floor." Holroyd struggled to get up and finally tottered to the living room despite Wendy's attempts to hold him back.

Once there, he looked to where he had seen the body. It was not there, and there was no sign it had ever been there. As he looked around, he realized his papers and books were no longer in disarray either, but an empty bottle lay by the desk next to the shards of a broken glass.

"Doctor Holroyd, what are you talking about?" Wendy came to his side. "There is no body on the floor. Your things appear to be in order, except for the empty bottle and broken glass by the desk."

"No, no! There was a body covered in blood, and my room had been ransacked. Someone coshed me as I came into the room. I mean, how else could I have this wound? I have to call the police."

"Doctor Holroyd, there is no body and no blood on the floor, other than perhaps your own from the injury to your head." Wendy looked at him with a puzzled expression on her face.

"I think you fell and hit your head on the edge of the desk. Do you really think you should call the police because you injured yourself?"

"I didn't injure myself. I was attacked." Despite his weakness, Holroyd became indignant.

"But if you decide to call the police, a policeman will come and look around, see nothing extraordinary, and smell your breath. To what conclusion do you think he will come? Perhaps he will think you're just another lonely old man who has been drinking too much. Is that what you want?"

"But that's not what happened!" He stopped. "How did you get into my flat? You said my door was open, but how did you get past the front door?"

"Just as I was about to ring your flat, someone came out and let me in when I explained I was about to visit you."

"But why was my door open?"

"Perhaps you did not close it properly when you came in."

"No, no. That's not possible. I'm calling the police."

"If you feel you must, but as I said, there is nothing to see, and if asked, I would have to explain how I found you with your door open, lying near the desk with a bleeding head, an empty bottle, and broken glass, which, I'm sure, will contain evidence of drinking."

"As I don't know you, you might have difficulty explaining why you came here in the first place."

"I doubt that. As I told you, I have a good reason for being here."

"Yes, you did, and that is very generous of Mr. Xiang. But you came unannounced, and I don't believe that's normal."

"I tried to call you, but you did not answer." Holroyd thought for a moment, but he still felt dizzy and confused.

"Well, you picked a good time to visit," Holroyd muttered sarcastically. Wendy did not seem to register his attitude.

"Oh, thank you! I'm pleased I could assist you and may have saved you from embarrassment."

"Saved me?"

"Yes. Consider if one of your neighbours had found you in this condition. I doubt this would create a good impression."

Holroyd closed his eyes and groaned softly. He sat on the couch, pondering what she had just said. She could be correct in thinking his story might not convince the police.

If she would not corroborate his story about a body and without any immediate evidence of a crime, the police might conclude he had been in a drunken delirium. And he doubted that bringing himself to the attention of the police with a story as far-fetched as his would be a good thing.

He wanted nothing more at that moment than to recover from the attack and try to understand what was happening. *I'm grateful for her presence, but surely, I can't be so wrong to have imagined what I saw. If I am, I'm losing my marbles, and I don't think that's quite the case yet.*

"Look, thank you for your help, but I don't know what's behind all this. I need to recover, and I think it's best I rest now. Let me get in touch with you later." He knew he was overly brusque, but he felt an overwhelming desire to get his thoughts together, for which Miss Liu was not very useful.

"If you're sure you can manage, I can go." She stood up, looked down at him, and then left, closing the door behind her. He thought he should have offered to help her and call a taxi, but the effort was too much.

He lay back, thinking. *What really happened? Did I imagine what I saw? Who is Wendy Liu? Perhaps her arrival was by chance and is part of Xiang's offer to help, but surely someone, be it Mr. Xiang himself would have called me in advance and at least asked if I would be happy to have her as an assistant. Let me see what's in the letter.*

He opened the letter she had given him and read that Mr. Xiang had every confidence and highly recommended Wendy to help Holroyd in his pending academic research. She had recently graduated from King's College with a first-class degree in Chinese history and literature and had done excellent work for Mr. Xiang.

Seems in order, but I wonder what work she did. He put the letter aside and then realized there were no contact details. *How do I get in touch with her? That's a strange oversight! I suppose I'll have to call Xiang if only to thank him for the suggestion.* He thought a bit more, trying to fight off another wave of dizziness. *Not much I can do now, and I really need to recover.*

Lying on the couch, he tried to relax but instead tried to make sense of recent events. "That can't be coincidental," he muttered. *Someone is out to get me or, more likely, get something I have or know. What does someone think I have or know that seems to fit? Unless it's linked to Xiang and the project.*

"If that's the case, sod it. Xiang can take his money and stuff it. Nothing is worth an attack on me and dropping a dead body on my floor."

But then, what was the real nature of this project? What could be so important that someone would go to such lengths? No doubt the sovereignty of Dejection Island was a matter of consequence, but there were other perhaps less satisfactory means to sort that out.

So, what really lay behind the events of the day? *I'm owed an explanation, if not an apology, for all this. But from whom? Merry? Xiang? Roggenback? Someone else? Or am I on my own here?* He got up, still feeling unsteady, and poured himself another drink and then another but with two painkillers to help him sleep.

Outrage and anger swept over him as he took his last swallow of the day. *Dammit, how dare people attack me? Who do they think they are? There's no way I'm going to crawl away and hide. I'm going to see this through. I'll do something for Queen and country, earn a good salary, save my career, and do the research I want. No! No one will scare me away. I'm an Englishman and proud to be so!*

It sounded a bit hollow but filled with a new resolve, or Dutch courage; he went to bed. That he might have placed Rostwick in danger did not occur to him.

*****

Once outside Holroyd's apartment building, Wendy reached into her handbag, extracted her cell phone, and speed-dialled a number.

"I have introduced myself successfully to Holroyd." The person at the other end grunted in acknowledgement and then hung up.

13

Feeling slightly better next morning, Holroyd called the number Xiang had given him. "Star Dragon Company Headquarters. Xiang Leng Gong si Zhong Xin. For English, please press one," followed by a string of Chinese. After a protracted search he was told they had no Wendy Liu in the company.

He asked for Mr. Xiang's office and was told Mr. Xiang was abroad, but they could pass a message to him. Exasperated, Holroyd hung up, his mood not improving for several hours, and set about making travel arrangements.

Rather than directly flying to China, he booked a detour through Singapore. There he would catch an 'island hopper' that would take him to Dejection Island.

If anyone challenged him, he would explain how it would advance his research, which, when done properly, was as much an art as a science. Many of the best discoveries in history—and in just about every other discipline—happened by accident, and Holroyd had long ago accepted the importance of opening himself up to such fortuitous accidents.

In his view, narrowing one's focus too early on a project could be a serious mistake. One had to wander around to find things one didn't know to look for. At the very least, going to Dejection Island would give him a firsthand sense of what was at stake.

The phone rang, and he picked up the receiver.

"Doctor Holroyd? Wendy Liu here. I'm calling because I was worried about you and just wanted to ensure you recovered."

"That's very thoughtful of you. I'm feeling better, thank you."

"I'm so glad. Please rest some more and recover quickly."

"I will." Holroyd paused. "I was trying to call you to thank you and because I didn't get to introduce myself properly, so I wonder if you would be free to meet today."

"Oh, thank you, but I have an engagement already. I thought you would need a few days to get better and arranged to meet with a relative in Glasgow later today. I hope you don't mind."

Holroyd reluctantly agreed and, wishing her a safe journey, hung up. *Unusual to start a working relationship that way, but I can see her logic. I suppose it'll work out fine, but I'd have preferred to get to know her sooner if she's going to be my assistant. Seeing as she is going to Glasgow, I won't suggest she come to the island with me, but she can meet me in China.*

With that thought, he continued with his travel plans. Fortuitously seats were available immediately, so he was able to board his flight for the following day.

14

Once on board in his first-class seat, Holroyd looked around the cabin and noted a Chinese man who, judging by his style of dress, was a government employee trying to look unobtrusively underpaid. But if he was a government employee, what, Holroyd wondered, was he doing in first class unless he was a highly placed official?

The man was sitting in a window seat and was already settling down with his laptop and a file folder. But Holroyd thought the man was covertly watching him, and Holroyd wondered why.

During the flight, Holroyd spent some time thinking over what he would do once on the island. He would look for records and talk to people who might have heard stories about the early settlers or even have family heirlooms dating from the start of the colony. He hoped that, if a clue were to present itself, he could recognize it.

The trouble with clues was that they often blended into the scenery and didn't come with clear labels. *Wouldn't it be wonderful if they came with a placard declaring in friendly red letters, "I'm a clue!"?* He must have giggled aloud at the thought because several other passengers looked at him in surprise.

In Singapore, he was politely directed to an information board on which he would find the information needed to catch his connection. He found no such information, and there was a long queue at the information desk.

Finally, after what seemed an interminable waiting time, he discovered his flight had already left. However, the agent reported there was an available seat in two days. After thinking about whether to cancel the visit to the island, Holroyd decided he would accept the delay. He was told he might want to stay at the airport hotel, the entrance to which was just after passing through Immigration and Customs.

Arriving at Immigration, his passport was scrutinized, but instead of stamping it and returning it, the officer asked him to wait and then spoke into an intercom. Another officer arrived, and the two discussed something Holroyd could not hear. Finally, the second officer nodded, and Holroyd was cleared for entry. He entered the hotel and approached the registration desk.

"Good day. Do you have a room available for two nights?"

"Let me check." The clerk consulted her computer and smiled, "Yes we do. Is a single with a double bed suitable?" Holroyd nodded. "Excellent. What name, sir?"

"Holroyd, Peter Holroyd." He pulled out his passport. The clerk started typing but then stopped suddenly. "Oh! You have a reservation, Doctor Holroyd. A prepaid suite for two nights."

"What? Are you sure? There must be a mistake."

"Oh no, sir. It's here, and the details conform to your passport."

"Who made the reservation?"

"Hariseng Imports. It's a large company here in Singapore." *Never heard of them, but perhaps this is Xiang's doing. But I didn't let him know my plans, and he could hardly have foreseen my missing my connecting flight, so how could he have made the reservation?*

With that question swirling through his mind, he went up to his room. On entering he found three Western people sitting in armchairs. Before he could say anything, one of the men got up and offered a handshake.

"Doctor Holroyd. Glad you could make it. Do come in. I'm Harry Stinnes, and these are my colleagues, Donald Porter, and Stan Harrison." He spoke with a distinct American drawl that Holroyd associated with the southern part of the USA.

"Now, who are you, and what are you doing in my room? Come to that, how did you know this was my room?" Holroyd asked.

"We were advised of your coming, and knowing you would need a place, we took the liberty of making the arrangements for you. I trust they are satisfactory?"

"The room is very satisfactory, but how you came to know I would need it is more to the point."

"You got it! Why don't we just get to the point?" Porter said from his chair. *They didn't answer my question about knowing I'd need a room!* "We want to talk to you about your project and the people who employed you." He, too, spoke with an American accent.

"Who are you? I take it you're all Americans, so why are you wanting to question me?" Holroyd demanded.

"Who we are is immaterial, but our questions are not. So, put your bag in the bedroom, and let's get started."

"Now, just stop there. I don't know you and have no intention of discussing anything with you. Kindly leave." Harrison sat impassively, but Porter opened his mouth as if to say something, but Stinnes cut in.

"Donald, leave this to me. Doctor Holroyd, hang on for a moment. We've got off base here, so would you be so kind as to put your bag in your room and freshen up while we order some room service? Okay, Doc?" After a moment's thought, Holroyd allowed curiosity to gain the upper hand and agreed.

When he returned, he sat down and looked at the men. Stinnes and Porter wore business suits, but Harrison wore an open-necked button-down shirt, slacks, and loafers. Holroyd had the impression of a young blond-haired college football quarterback, but something more sinister about him did not quite fit the business-like image the other two conveyed.

"Well?"

Stinnes opened the conversation. "Our apologies, Doc, for coming at you like this, but we're here now. We've been asked to talk to you about your project."

"Asked by whom? And why?"

"You don't need to know by whom or why. We ask the questions here," Porter broke in, but before Holroyd could react, Stinnes intervened.

"We're here on orders of the American government. We know you have been asked to do some research on Dejection Island, and we want to know what you're proposing to do."

"The American government? What on earth has caught the attention of the American government?" Holroyd was surprised.

"That's why we want to talk to you. As you probably know, the situation around the island is tense right now, and we want assurances that you are not about to piss in the pool."

"That's a quaint expression if I might say so. As far as I'm aware, I have no obligations to the American government, so I don't see the point of this meeting."

"An American has employed you, and we want to ensure the employment is above board," Porter growled.

"There was a verbal suggestion of some employment by an American, but that's all. Nothing further came of it. Now, if there is nothing else, perhaps you would be so good as to leave."

"I see. Well, Doc, let's just say we would take it as a gesture of goodwill if you decided not to complete your task yet."

"Should I take that as a warning?"

"Take it in any way you want," Porter said

"Then good day to you." Holroyd got up and opened the door to show the men out. They left without a further word.

After the Americans were gone, Holroyd thought over the meeting. *What was that all about? I've been warned off by the American government, no less.*

He felt a trickle of sweat running down his back, and it wasn't because of the heat in the room. *They obviously know about Roggenback's offer, but not that there's been no follow-up. Yet somehow, someone in America knew I was going to the island and arranged for me to miss my connecting flight. If the American government runs interference, I could be in for a lot of trouble.*

He felt a mounting dismay intermingled with fury before a further thought struck him. *I've lost two days of research. Or have I?* He got up and phoned the concierge.

"Would you see if any seats are available on the next flight to Dejection Island?"

"Let me inquire and call you back, sir."

Ten minutes later Holroyd was informed there were nine seats available for the following day's flight. *So, the information I got at the flight counter was false, probably at the instigation of the Americans. Fine, let me see if I can also play the game. I won't change my flight now, but I'll gamble that at least one seat will be available to book just before departure. Hopefully, inaction now will lull any watchers into a sense of security, and an unexpected departure might catch them off guard.* After checking his email, he spent the rest of the day relaxing.

The next morning, abandoning some belongings and taking only immediate necessities and his laptop, he left as late as he could to book and catch the flight. Dashing down the corridor toward the gate, he perversely noted that they had closed the travelling footpath for maintenance, and crowds of slowly moving passengers, often with trailing baggage and fractious children, impeded his progress.

As he hurried along, he seethed (and not for the first time) that there was no pleasure in modern travel and that his athletic days were long past.

By the time he arrived at the gate, he was sweating and out of breath. Giving him no time to rest, a reproachful passenger agent waved him down the stairs to where a small twin-prop twelve-seater amphibious plane was waiting.

Three passengers were already in the plane, strapped in and waiting for him to arrive. One passenger was a middle-aged white woman, another was an Asian man (Holroyd could not decide from where), and the other was a Chinese man who might have been his cabin-mate on the flight from London. Holroyd nodded in recognition but received a stony stare in return.

Oh, well, he had difficulty distinguishing between individual Asian races, and his eyes weren't as good as they once were. Anyway, if it was his cabin-mate from London, how had he got on that flight, where was his laptop on which he had been working, and what was he doing there? How many people, let alone Chinese people who had just flown in from London, flew to Dejection Island? He pondered that question as he strapped himself into his narrow seat.

Before takeoff, the co-pilot addressed the passengers. "Welcome aboard. Please remain in your seats for the entire flight. Please keep your life vest handy, keep your seat belts fastened, and refrain from using any electrical devices during the flight. The flight takes approximately two hours. Upon arrival, you will get onshore using a tender. Any heavy luggage you may have brought will follow by sea and should be available at customs in two days. Relax, and have a good flight." With that, he started the departure countdown.

The ride was a little bumpy, and he snoozed until the plane descended and landed in a lagoon where a tender came alongside to ferry the passengers ashore. He had arrived safely but had forgotten how hot it could be in the tropics. Despite a desultory breeze, he was soon sweating heavily.

After clearing immigration and customs, he was surprised to be greeted by a man who introduced himself as the governor's driver.

"Welcome to the island, Doctor Holroyd, " the man said, "I'm here to take you to Government House where his excellency has arranged for you to stay."

15

As Holroyd was being driven to Government House, he thought the rest of the world most likely would ignore this island with less than fifty thousand inhabitants who seemed happy but were probably as poor as church mice. He was reminded of some of the villages in the Caribbean he had visited as a student.

Government House was a modest two-story whitewashed building between palm trees and surrounded by a carefully tended garden. A sprinkler kept the grass green, and the occasional wind-driven spray supplied a cool respite from the heat.

On arrival, a butler greeted and escorted him to a room furnished in a typically colonial style, complete with a ceiling fan, mosquito-netted four-poster bed, night table lights, a chaise lounge, and a large dressing-room mirror. The adjacent bathroom was spacious and modern.

"If you care to refresh yourself, sir, his excellency will meet with you later this afternoon. I will find some fresh laundry for you until your things arrive. Meanwhile, I can have your own washed." Holroyd gratefully accepted the offer, asked that someone contact the Singapore hotel to have his things forwarded, and after a refreshing shower, lay down to sleep until a knock on the door awakened him a few hours later.

"Here you are, sir. Some fresh clothing. When you're ready, his excellency will meet you on the terrace."

His Excellency Jonathan Sotherby-Wynne, Her Majesty's Governor of Dejection Island, proved to be affable and invited Holroyd to enjoy a sundowner on the terrace.

"Nice to welcome you, Doctor Holroyd. We don't get too many visitors here."

"I can imagine, but how did you know I was coming?"

"Oh, I saw your name on the passenger lists due to arrive over the next few days. Checked with London to learn a bit about you and got the green light. Today's update told me you would arrive today rather than as planned. I confess a bit of curiosity at all the changes, but here you are."

"Well, I encountered a bit of an unexpected bother on my way." There was silence while the governor scrutinized Holroyd.

"I'm not aware of what London may have passed on, but let's just say the real reason for my trip must remain hidden." Holroyd felt the need to explain himself. "May I suggest doing research for a book on remote colonial islands?"

Then he recognized how foolish he had been. If the governor's driver met him at the airport, the governor would have already had a sense of the purpose of Holroyd's visit. "I'm sorry. Of course, you are aware of the real reason for my visit. It's just that matters seem to be going haywire." He went on to relate the events of the last few days.

"Well, I was aware of your task, but I did not know about the rest. That's quite a tale. Wouldn't have believed it if you hadn't told me. Did you tell anyone else?"

"Actually, no. I wasn't sure what I could report."

"Hmm… yes. Do you know anything about this woman who turned up at your flat?"

"She told me she had been directed by my employer, or rather one of my employers, to help me. I think she will turn out to be helpful, and she seems pleasant enough."

"And this employer is a Chinaman? Curious, that!"

"May I ask why?"

"It may just be coincidental, but we have a Chinese naval squadron nearby. Until just before you landed, we had no contact with them at all.

Didn't need one. But while you were napping, we got a call asking for help.

"Seems one of the ships had an engine room accident, and three men were badly injured. Asked if they could land the injured men into our hospital.

"I had to reply that our facilities are limited, but we could try to help arrange a medical evacuation to Singapore or somewhere where better treatment is available. Could we send our doctor out to see what's needed? Haven't heard back.

"Given the politics, I don't feel comfortable allowing a bunch of military men to come ashore even if it's an emergency, but at the same time, we can't refuse to help if it's needed."

"What did London say?"

"Nothing so far. Probably all asleep."

"But you think the presence of the ships and this request is related to my task?"

"Maybe and maybe not. Just a gut feel that things aren't quite as they seem. Reminds me a bit of my childhood in Malaya during the troubles." He took a swallow from his drink.

"My father managed a rubber plantation there. All was quiet, but we still felt uneasy, and then suddenly all hell would break loose as the rebels started firing out of the trees. I doubt, though, we'll be under attack by naval bombardment because I don't think those ships have the capability. But if a bunch of marines came ashore under some pretext, we wouldn't be able to resist."

"Nice thought, but let's hope it won't come to that. If they did land, my task will be concluded very quickly indeed. I'm not sure London is prepared for that; in fact, I think I've been engaged to make sure it won't happen."

The governor looked into his drink. "Good luck, then." Both men sat in silence until the governor suggested supper. A few minutes after the meal ended, Holroyd made his excuses and retired to his room.

16

The next day, sitting over a breakfast of tropical fruits, English eggs, and bacon, the governor suggested Holroyd might take the time to go down to the church and look at parish records. "The archives there might be in line with your *literary interests*," he added in a tone that Holroyd could have mistaken for ironic.

He was gratified that the governor was supporting the public reason for his visit in case any servants nearby were eavesdropping. "Government archives may not be of much use to you. They relate primarily to regulations, customs, immigration, and public works. However, the parish records cover births, marriages, and deaths going back to a missionary in the mid-eighteen hundreds." At first, the suggestion puzzled Holroyd until he realized that such records might confirm who was on the island and where they came from.

Breakfast over, he walked to the church, which proved to be conveniently close. He was soon sweating in the heat and could feel the sun burning his head. Once he arrived at the church, he entered the shaded but not much cooler wooden building. The vicar welcomed him and after exchanging pleasantries, led him into a study where he kept the parish records.

Holroyd received an old-fashioned leather-bound volume detailing in carefully entered longhand the parish records going back over one hundred years.

The first entries, dated 1851, were of marriages. As he looked over the names, he noted with disappointment they were all English surnames. Even births registered in the following months recorded the parents' names as English. He was disappointed because, based on the names, the original settlers were all English, meaning that the British claim was valid.

However, it suddenly dawned on him that all these people would have been second or third-generation islanders. Of the first generation, there were no records.

These entered names would be of islanders whose mothers would have taken their husband's names on marriage. Therefore, if any women came ashore from the wreck they would have been the offspring of English mothers. But if there had been people already on the island when the sailors came ashore these people could have been the offspring of women of some other nationality.

There was no point in examining later records. He closed the book, thanked the vicar, and took his leave. Frustrated, he recognized he was no further ahead in his search. Perhaps going to the island has been a foolish detour.

As he walked back into the heat, he passed under a shady tree, only to be surprised when splinters suddenly shot off the trunk. Shocked, he stared at the scarred trunk before realising that something moving at great velocity had hit the wood. *What in god's name was that?*

He looked at the scar. *That could have been a stone or a bullet.* He scanned the area and thought he saw a figure duck behind the low wall marking the limit of the church property. He was not sure, but he thought the figure was dressed in dark clothing, perhaps a business suit, which struck him as odd.

Who would wear a dark business suit outside in the tropics? And why duck behind the wall? Something nagged the back of his mind, and he remembered the Asians on his flights. *Could one have them be the figure I saw?*

Turning, he ran toward the wall, but when he reached it, he was gasping for breath, and there was no sign of anyone. He sat down to regain his composure. *Did I just see someone spying and shooting at me? If so, who and why?*

He returned to the government house, but the governor was away. However, the butler informed him that the governor offered his driver to take him on a tour around the island. With no other plan in mind, Holroyd accepted and, supplied with a Fortnum and Mason hamper for snacks, set off.

17

The governor's car turned out to be a jeep that might have survived the war but possibly came from a later time. The engine was noisy, but the shocks managed to absorb most of the jolts of the uneven road. The roof was down, so Holroyd could enjoy the wind, and he didn't mind at all that the wind made conversation impossible. Unfortunately, he forgot to take a hat and resigned himself to getting a sunburn.

Progress was slow, but eventually, the jeep left the town for the countryside until the paved road became a dirt track. Swirls of dust blown by sporadic puffs of wind settled on Holroyd. The jeep's passage contributed to the mini dust storms, and he could only trust that the contents of the snack hamper were safe. He had no desire to crunch on gritty sandwiches or drink tepid sludge.

In the fields, scrawny cattle rooted for whatever meagre fodder they could find. He saw a water buffalo wallowing in one of the mud pools by the side of the road as a child herder tried in vain to urge it back into the field.

He passed roadside stalls, usually tended by women, displaying meagre selections of vegetables or fruits. Sometimes, a sleeping child or dog accompanied the attendant, and once or twice, a tethered dog or cow. What he saw seemed remote from the world of politics and big business that lay only two hours away by plane.

On coming to a plantation, the driver, a tall, slim man with dark skin and a dazzling smile who had introduced himself as James, turned off the road and drove more slowly.

"The governor thought you might like to see one of the better farms. Mrs. Hardcastle runs this one. An old family, the Hardcastles is. Go back to the original settlers, they do. Her husband was the doctor here for many years, but he passed away only last year. The governor called to let her know you might come by."

As Holroyd digested this information, he experienced a sudden surge of hope. Would Mrs. Hardcastle be able to confirm if her ancestors both came from the Steadfast? If so, he might succeed sooner than he had expected.

But then he realized that even if Mrs. Hardcastle confirmed her ancestry as wholly British, that did not preclude the possibility of prior settlers. He decided to ask her anyway.

Holroyd looked around as they went up what could have been a side road or the entrance lane to a large estate. Sturdy palm trees grew thickly on either side of a paved lane, beyond which he saw banana orchards alternating with open spaces.

Workers were busy among the palms and in the open spaces.

"Looks like we may have company. Another car just turned off here. Strange, though, that's Mr. Aitoko's car. I wonder what he's doing here."

"Mr. Aitoko?"

"Local Japanese businessman, sir."

"What does he do?"

"Can't rightly say, sir. Seems successful, though. Has a staff but keeps mostly to himself. Has visitors from time to time, usually from Asian countries."

Without warning, the windscreen developed several cracks radiating out from what appeared to be a small hole. James jerked in surprise, and the car veered off the road and lurched over the ditch before hitting a tree with a screech of tearing metal, bringing it to a jarring stop.

Instinctively, Holroyd threw out his hand to brace himself, but he fell forward, feeling a sharp pain in his arm, and hit his head on something solid. Though groggy, he knew he was alive, but James was resting his head on the steering wheel and seemed unresponsive.

Aitoko's car stopped, and two men dressed in dark suits rushed over to the wreck. Holroyd was confused and in pain, but dimly thought they could be Chinese or Japanese. Shoving James aside, they reached for Holroyd. He felt his arm being pulled by one hand while another grabbed a fistful of his shirt, as he was dragged rather than helped out of his seat. He thought he saw a gun pointing at him, and suddenly he felt very afraid.

"What... what are you doing?" he mumbled, struggling in their grip. He received a stinging slap across his face in reply.

Holroyd was taken completely by surprise. Outrage temporarily overcame fear

"What the hell do you think you're doing?" In reply, he received another stinging slap. The man holding the gun said something that might have been Japanese, and Holroyd felt the hold on him relax for a moment. Both men were looking over to where the workers were. Holroyd felt himself manhandled again, but the men seemed more hurried.

"Is anyone hurt?" a woman's voice asked. One of the men grunted something Holroyd could not understand. "Now you stop that right now!" the woman yelled.

There was a pause, and Holroyd dimly realized some workers had come over to inspect the crash. Grunting something again, the men released Holroyd, ran back to their car, and sped off.

"You alright, dear?" the woman asked as she helped him out of the wreck and to his feet.

"I think so, thanks." He stood up, still feeling a bit groggy. "Yes, I think I'm a bit shaken but okay. Thank you, and thank you for coming to help me." The other workers either looked at Holroyd or watched the disappearing car.

"What happened? Who were those men? Are you alright? Can you walk?"

Holroyd suddenly felt dizzy and grabbed the side of the car for support. He quickly withdrew his hand as he touched the metal, which was hot from the sun, and began to sway dizzily.

One of the workers steadied him. "Now, you just sit down," the woman said. "Jacob, run to the house and tell Mrs. Hardcastle what happened."

"No, no! Thank you all very much, but I'll be alright. Just give me a minute." He sagged to the ground and looked around. That's when he saw James still slumped over with blood trickling down his forehead, around which insects were already buzzing eagerly, anticipating a feast.

"The driver?"

One of the men gently lifted James's head, at which he groaned. Reaching into a satchel, the helper pulled out a bottle and gave James a drink.

Judging from James's reaction, Holroyd assumed that whatever was in the bottle was stronger than water, but it seemed to revive the injured man.

"Are you alright?" Holroyd asked James, who was now showing renewed signs of life.

"I will be, sir. Shook up, though."

"Is anything broken? Pain?"

"Nothing as far as I can tell. Probably got a few bruises though. How about you, sir?"

"Seems I may have dislocated a finger." Holroyd looked at one of his fingers bent at an unnatural angle. With trepidation, he grit his teeth and pulled sharply. There was a short and painful snap, and the finger returned to normal.

A wave of dizziness washed over him, and he paused until it passed. He felt the back of his head but detected no blood. He had no headache or blurred vision, so he concluded he might have made it out of the crash without a concussion.

He felt a mounting fury at the attackers, and their brazen assault before an icy fear stopped him from letting his feelings show. *This attack and the shot at the church have to be connected.* He put on a brave face.

"Well, looks like we made it out safely." He surveyed the mangled hood and the enormous spider web of cracks stretching across the windshield. "The car, less so. What the hell happened?"

"Everything seemed alright until the windshield cracked. I must have lost control for an instant and swerved into the trees," James replied weakly.

"Any idea what caused the window to crack like that?"

"Not sure, sir. I've seen windshields crack like that when hit by a small stone, but that's not the case here. I remember when some children were playing with a catapult, and the shot went through the governor's window, but I see no young rascals around here." He looked at the windshield, scrutinizing the crack. "I'd have said it looks like a bullet hole."

Holroyd had never seen a bullet hole in real life, but he had to agree that the damage looked very much like what he had seen in films and on television.

"Did you hear a shot?"

"No, sir. But the noise of the wind might have drowned it out." After a moment, James continued. "Looks as if a shot from Mr. Aitoko's car could've caused that there hole. What was Mr. Aitoko's car doing here?" At the mention of Aitoko, the workers started whispering among themselves and drifted away.

"Well, I wonder why Mr. Aitoko's car stopped in the first place and why no one came over to help us or make sure we were safe."

"Not quite what happened," Holroyd replied. "They stopped but not to help. They seemed to want me."

This was not what he expected while on a tour in the governor's car. He almost allowed himself to yell in anger and frustration but then had an image of himself as a middle-aged, pale white professor yelling from a tropical ditch with his wrecked car. Maybe it would have been the logical thing to do, but it seemed embarrassing to him. What would the workers think?

"Wouldn't be like Mr. Aitoko not to offer help, sir."

"What did you say?"

"Isn't like Mr. Aitoko to create an accident."

"It would be if Mr. Aitoko was not in the car, and whoever was in the car wasn't out to help us. They sped off when the workers came over to see what happened. Lucky for us that they did." As these words sunk in, neither of them said anything.

"Best we wait until the boy tells the house what happened, and they sends help, sir."

Holroyd's hand hurt, his head was burning, and now he felt pain in other parts of his body, though as far as he could tell, nothing was broken. He suspected that bruises would soon bloom all over his body. Above all, he felt anger, frustration, and curiosity.

Holroyd tried to stand up but winced with pain as his foot touched the ground, though as far as he could tell, he had broken nothing. Holroyd looked at James. "I don't feel too fit, and you don't look too good. I heard one of the workers tell someone to go up to the house. We'd better just sit and wait here."

"If we really needs help, I can holler at them blacks over there."

Holroyd sat down. As far as he knew, the road only led to the plantation house, so, because the car had not turned around, it should be there. If that was the case, he could get answers about what happened. But did the road also lead elsewhere? The shooter might be up ahead at some track and take another shot, or the men might try for another grab at him, neither of which were comforting thoughts.

He felt his shirt clinging to his back and the sweat running down his neck, into his eyes, and his groin.

His balding head was hurting from the effects of the sun. He felt dizzy again and hoped it would wear off soon. He lowered his head to touch his knees and closed his eyes.

Absent-mindedly, he waved away the myriad of insects flying about his head and suddenly wondered what disease he might contract if bitten or stung. Should he have had inoculations before leaving London? If so, for what? Malaria? Yellow Fever? Dengue Fever? Could he get treated on the island, or was it too late?

In a sudden wave of panic, he envisioned himself expiring on a hospital bed, raving deliriously as he breathed his last. He took a deep breath and shook to steady himself.

Finally, he saw two cars heading his way. The first one he recognized as Mr. Aitoko's car, but it sped back toward the open road without stopping. He did not recognize the second car and assumed it was the help from the plantation.

By then his injuries were hurting a lot, and he could sense that he was getting severely sunburned. Mrs. Hardcastle greeted him with open-mouthed surprise but graciously said nothing about his appearance and welcomed him into the car. After looking over James, she told her driver to stay and watch over him until she sent help.

Once back at the house, she took Holroyd to the veranda and offered the choice of iced tea or something stronger. He chose the latter.

While surveying the garden and the plantation, he thought about what had just happened. *What in hell's name is going on? Who were those people, and what did they want from me? Was one of them on the plane with me? Was one of them the person I thought I saw at the church?*

He had experienced indifference to violent attacks and accidents in China, where people were reluctant to get involved in anything that might draw police attention, but never in any other country.

But was it so surprising? *Put into the context of the other happenings, I'm sure now that someone is out to interfere with my task. But who and why? These were Asians, so could they be tied back to Xiang as the most likely villain? But why would he interfere with a task he commissioned? And how does this Japanese businessman fit into what's happening? And how many people know where I'm to be found? I wonder if Merry knows anything about this.*

Before he could think any more, Mrs. Hardcastle came out to make sure he was not seriously hurt and to tell him she had informed the governor and that the police were on their way. The governor was sending another car to collect him. But if he was in pain Mrs. Hardcastle would call for a doctor immediately, though it might be quicker for him to go directly to the hospital than to wait.

"Thank you so very much for your assistance, Mrs. Hardcastle. I think I can wait till I get back to town. I'm sorry to have caused all this trouble."

"Oh! Don't apologize. Haven't had this much excitement for ages. Very quiet usually, just trying to survive managing the plantation." She smiled. "I think I'll have lots to talk about at my next bridge evening."

"The driver said your family has been here since the original sailors landed."

"Oh, yes! I can trace my ancestry back to one of the officers. Not many of us around, though." Holroyd detected pride in her voice. He debated whether to ask about her other ancestor but decided that his task overrode any delicacy.

"I say, that's rather special. And may I ask about your other ancestor?"

"Are you referring to the officer's wife?" Mrs. Hardcastle let a frown escape before she laughed. "We're not too sure about her. That's always been a taboo subject in the family. Could be she wasn't considered suitable to be an officer's wife. Might have been an illicit frolic with someone else's sister or daughter or even a wife or one of the servants."

She paused before going on "Living on the plantation meant secrets could be kept quite easily. Not so unusual in those days, especially out here in the middle of nowhere."

"So, there would not have been any records or gossip?"

"Oh, my goodness, no records and if there was gossip, no one on the island would have been immune. I doubt there were too many women around at the beginning, so I imagine morals were a lot looser then than now."

"But there were women."

"But of course! How else could the population have survived? Naturally, the urgency slowed down once other people began to arrive, and morals became stricter."

"What is known about those early women? Were they already here, or were they off the ship?"

"Curiously, no one seems to know for certain. I've heard stories that either or both could be true. Some seem to think there were settlers or visitors from Malaya, Indo-China, or even the Philippines. Others maintain the ship had some women on board, but no proofs have been found to support any of the theories."

"But eventually, there were children. How would that have been explained?"

"I'm sure there was an explanation if one was needed. But this wasn't the salons of Regency London. I doubt too many people here got uptight about such things back then. Remember, survival would have been uppermost in people's minds, and a newborn might have been very welcome, preferably if one or both parents were White Anglo-Saxon Protestants."

"Both?"

"Perhaps. We've never really gone into that, and anyway, no records exist as far as I know. Unfortunately, the plantation house burned to the ground in the 1860s, and I've always assumed any private records or letters that might have offered some insight went up in flames."

At that point, a servant announced that Holroyd's driver had been brought in, and Mrs. Hardcastle excused herself.

Holroyd sighed. *A dead end! How damned frustrating, but other avenues of research are still open.*

While he was on his second drink, a policeman arrived to take down notes of the event. He did not comment when Holroyd described the damage to the windshield and talked about Mr. Aitoko's car.

Nor did he react visibly to Holroyd's suggestion of an attempted kidnapping though he did ask for greater detail. In due course, he left Holroyd to nurse his by then increasingly painful bruises and disappeared to talk to James.

"You're sure, sir, the other car passed you on your way here?" the policeman asked when he returned.

"Yes, why?" Holroyd sensed a note of incredulity creeping into the policeman's voice.

"Well, sir, why was the stay so short if it came here and then left? And why not stop and offer help or ask if everyone was alright?"

"I agree. Odd. Did you ask Mrs. Hardcastle?" Just then Mrs. Hardcastle came in.

"Oh, yes. That was some Asian man. Wanted to buy the plantation, and when I refused, he demanded to know why Doctor Holroyd was coming to visit. Damned cheek! Told him the place was not for sale and Doctor Holroyd's visit was none of his business. Sent him away with a flea in his ear. How silly of me. Now that I think of it, I wonder why he was so interested. Maybe he has an ulterior motive. Can't think what it could be, though."

Curious indeed, Holroyd thought. *How does the attack on me tie in with an apparent demand for the plantation? If the events are linked, what could it be unless both were designed to stop my research?*

If that's the case, the attackers might think there are records here that could shed light on the earlier settlements, and the attackers might not have known such records would have been lost in the fire.

But why would Xiang hire me and then try to stop me? But perhaps Xiang is not behind this, but then, who is? And how can I find out? Just then, the governor's official car arrived and took Holroyd home.

Once back, they informed him that the governor was unavailable, but a doctor would stop by shortly. In the meantime, he took a bath and relaxed until the evening. Before dinner, the governor called him in to ask about the incident at the plantation. Holroyd mentioned the Asian man's visit, and together they wondered about the purpose of asking to buy the plantation. After further questioning, the governor sat for a moment.

"You know, I can't help but feel you've taken on more than you expected. This could get nasty, and you might want to take some precautions as you go along."

"Such as?"

"Don't think I have an answer to that, but you'd best be prepared."

Neither reassuring nor helpful, Holroyd thought.

The evening started with a small semi-formal dinner with some prominent members of the island's society in attendance. Despite the formality, it turned out to be a pleasant affair.

Holroyd scrutinized his fellow guests to see if he could discern any Eurasian features that could suggest Asian ancestors but came to no conclusion.

An excellent chilled New Zealand white wine accompanied a local seafood dish, a spicy chicken curry, and tropical fruits. In the relaxed atmosphere, the conversation flowed easily. As a guest with assumed good connections in Whitehall, Holroyd ended up being the focus of attention.

What everyone wanted to know was why he was there. What was the government's position regarding the South China Sea dispute? Would the government seriously consider handing the island over to the Chinese? What about the citizens?

He tried to navigate these rather sensitive questions, but it was difficult. Again, he trotted out his book excuse, but despite some offers of help, he feared he was unconvincing at best.

The governor finally came to his rescue. "Would you care to join us tomorrow at council? Might let you give an unofficial report and give you a taste of colonial island concerns. Not as dramatic or exciting as a book, but it might be useful to see what makes us tick." Grateful for the interruption, Holroyd accepted with alacrity.

Before going to sleep. Holroyd checked his emails and found one from Wendy. He was surprised given his earlier failed attempts to reach her. Mr. Xiang, she wrote, asked where he was, as he was expected in Beijing. Still unsure of what role he wanted her to play, he wrote back to tell her he would let her know.

He was awakened by what sounded like thunder, and he saw flashes of light through the curtains. There was no sound of rain, and he thought it was probably an offshore storm. He remembered a similar storm at sea in the Caribbean and turned over to go back to sleep.

18

The next day, Holroyd followed the governor into the council chamber, which proved to be a small, ordinary, and unimpressive room. Once seated, the governor introduced him formally and then opened the meeting. "Doctor Holroyd, would you care to say a few words?"

"Thank you, governor." Inwardly, he hated being put in the hot seat, but he managed a weak grin. "It is a great honour to join you this morning, but I'm not sure what to say. I dropped by to look at the island. Perhaps the best way to proceed is to invite questions that I will try to answer to the best of my abilities."

"We're happy to welcome you here, Doctor Holroyd, but just what decided you to visit our little island?"

"I'm doing research for a book on how the location of small islands, such as this one, influenced maritime voyages during the fifteenth and sixteenth Centuries. A friend of mine in London suggested Dejection Island would be worth a visit."

"Didn't know we were so important." Remarked one council member drily.

"Do you have an official task that could affect the future of this island?" another council member asked.

"No, I have no official standing, so Whitehall could and probably will disavow anything I might say. I do have a request to conduct, or at least assist, in some government research."

"Does that research bear on the future of this island as a colony and its citizens?"

"I'm sorry, but I really can't answer that. I can only guess what my employers could do with the results of my research, and any guess could be wide of the mark. It would be irresponsible of me even to suggest an opinion."

"May we know who your employer or employers are?"

"I'm sorry, but I'm not at liberty to divulge that information."

"Are you aware that China is claiming all the South China Sea as its territorial waters?"

"Yes, I had heard that."

"And did you also hear this puts the island in a very precarious position should China pursue its claims?"

"No, I had heard nothing like that, but it's easy to come to that conclusion." Holroyd could only hope the evasiveness of his answers would not damn him when the Day of Judgement arrived.

"My name is Elsie Watson, and I wonder if you know we voted overwhelmingly to remain a British colony."

Another council member cut in. "Can you give us any assurances that we will remain British subjects? I have no desire to become a citizen of any foreign power, especially none from around here."

"I can't comment on the future of the island, but to me, it sounds rather like a prototype of the Pitcairn Islands or perhaps a repeat of the Falklands."

"Prototype, eh? I'm not sure I like the sound of that. Makes me feel like a specimen in a petri dish."

Holroyd felt himself getting warm under the collar and not because the temperature outside was rising as midday approached. *I'm not ready for these questions, but I grant I'd be asking the same ones if I were in their shoes.*

"I think we'd better let our guest catch his breath," the governor said, taking charge of the meeting. "Thank you, Doctor Holroyd. We appreciate your attendance here, and I'm sure you will be available while you're on the island if council members wish to chat more with you. Let's move on, shall we?"

For about an hour, the meeting droned on. As the morning progressed, and the temperature increased, Holroyd felt the effects of jet lag and almost fell asleep. He jolted awake when he heard a council member say, "Those warships are still out there."

"Yes, I know that. But they're outside the twelve-mile limit. So, what's the problem?"

"What are they doing there?"

"No idea, and not much we can do about it."

"Well, I heard gunfire last night, so it looks like they're trying to provoke something, and I don't like it." A few others agreed with a hearty "Hear, hear!"

"They could send in a landing party, rape us while we sleep," Elsie Watson said.

"Oh, come off it, Elsie!" the governor retorted, losing his composure for the first time in the meeting. "I don't think you're in any danger, but we can cross that bridge if and when we get there."

Elsie glared at him.

"Should we ask the Americans for help?"

"Oh, yes! That's a splendid idea," David Pullman noted wryly "Don't forget the Americans just sent in a fleet to cow the North Koreans, only it was sailing somewhere off Indonesia. Fat lot of good that did."

"Careful, now," the governor said. "We may need them."

Recognizing the futility of further discussion, David chipped in. "Have any of you been following international events at all?"

"I have," Paul said, "and it looks like Pakistan will beat England in the Test match. Bloody awful state of affairs if you ask me."

"That's not what I meant," David said, thoroughly irritated at the irreverence of this comment.

"Well, is London going to do anything? Do they even know or care that there are warships out there?" Elsie sounded ready to go on the warpath again.

"I'm sure they do," the governor interjected, recovering control of the meeting before Elsie could derail it with another outburst. "I sent them a note in the last dispatch, but, as usual, no one has come back with anything yet. Probably think it's not urgent, and I must agree with them. I doubt the Chinese will start a war. Anyway, until London advises us to the contrary, we let it lie.."

"I think you and your masters are ignoring the issue." Elsie gave every sign that pressure was building up inside, and she would soon blow. "This is serious, but no one is doing anything about it."

"Elsie, as I have told you, there's not much anyone can do."

"Well, I can, and I will! I have friends in London who can raise the matter in the House and in the press. I intend to write to them and get their help. I hope to raise enough of a stink that people will take action."

"You mean an action like holding their noses?" someone commented.

The governor rapped the table and addressed Elsie. "You will do what you think is best, but the situation is volatile, and I ask you to be careful." He looked at Elsie as if to invite a reply. When none came, the governor continued.

"One other matter. I've received a notice from the Americans asking for permission to conduct research on the island. They didn't specify the purpose of the research, but they want to land some dozen people." He stopped to wait for comments.

"Other than supplying them with victuals, I can't see a problem. I propose to give permission but with a proviso that they supply themselves." There were nods around the table. The governor paused and gathered up his papers. "Anything else?"

"Yes, just a question," Paul said. "Did you get a reply about sea levels rising due to climate change?"

"Not yet, but I'm sure someone is beavering away at it."

"They know a rise of even a few feet could flood the livable area and severely jeopardize our farming here, don't they?"

"I'm not sure it's that urgent, so I wouldn't worry. We aren't the only nation that's threatened. I believe the Maldives have expressed a similar concern. Apparently, they could lose over seventy percent of their land if seas rise five feet or more. There's some work being done to see how to solve the problem."

"So, we could be in the same situation?"

"Yes, but it's not expected for another few years, so there's still time to do something about it."

"You'll keep us up to date?"

"If I hear anything, I will inform you. And, yes, I will keep reminding London that there is a potential problem. Meanwhile, I suggest we get on with our lives as normal. So, if there's no other business." He looked around the table but got no response. "Well then, I declare the meeting adjourned."

Everyone stood up. As the council members trickled out, the governor pulled Holroyd aside. "As you can see, council members are uneasy, and frankly, I share their concerns. I hope you'll bear that in mind because the sooner you complete your task, the sooner we can move on with our lives."

Holroyd nodded. *As if I needed more pressure to get on with the task. I think it's time for me to move on.*

As he mentally went over the arrangements for his departure, he heard the governor ask, "Coming over to the club for a drink, David?"

"Not this time, John. Promised the wife and children I would join them on the beach. I say, would you care to join us, Doctor Holroyd?" Now that the council meeting was over, Holroyd could see David was of average height, slim, and, in Holroyd's opinion, sported distinctly Eurasian features. *Perhaps there might be proof of early Asian settlers after all, but maybe not enough to suggest when such settlers could have arrived.*

But David was taller than the average Asian and sported a small moustache that Holroyd associated with British military men. *I wonder if he's got a regimental background and has seen combat somewhere.*

"Well, that is most kind, but I have to make the arrangements for my departure."

"Nonsense. The plane doesn't leave until tomorrow afternoon, and there will be plenty of space, so you might as well relax with us today."

"In that case, yes, I'd love to."

"Right. Well, while we're there, you can help me watch out for the children's safety. Wouldn't want any of the ankle biters to get into trouble." David grinned as they walked out of the room together.

An aide came up to the governor and whispered something. John turned to David. "Seems our Chinese friends have left us. Moved out early this morning before dawn and were seen heading possibly back toward China, according to the last report. That should please Paul."

The governor went into his office as Holroyd and David headed out to David's car. As they passed into the parking area, David looked toward the entrance gates. "Oh! That's Aitoko's car parked there. I wonder why? I thought he was away somewhere. Unusual for anyone to park their car here."

19

Lookout Point was the place where, so folklore had it, the original shipwrecked survivors kept watch for possible rescue but now served as the main recreation area for swimming. To get there one had to drive along a road that branched off the island's main highway near the church.

Other than a stone monument to mark its historical significance, the place was undeveloped. Palm trees provided shade and flanked a half-crescent of golden sands and clear blue waters.

At the east end of the beach, an occasional spray from a breaking wave marked a jumble of rocks over which seabirds circled and dived after small sea creatures that scuttled among rock crevices. To the west end, the beach ended among mangroves that harboured the occasional snake.

After parking the car in a spot shaded by one of the palm trees along the shore, David led Holroyd to join his family under some palm trees. Introductions were quickly made and, leaving Holroyd in the shade, David accompanied his boys, Harry, and Martin, to inspect the rocks.

Harry was the elder of the two. His hair was fair, and he had startlingly blue eyes strangely set in slightly Eurasian features that promised a certain handsomeness later in life. At age twelve, his physique was showing signs that his as-yet undeveloped frame might one day take on a shape that many American women like to call "hunky."

Martin, age ten, looked to be more serious and lacked his brother's physical presence. His hair was darker than his brother's, but he had the same startlingly blue eyes.

As he watched the progress of David and his sons climbing carefully over the rocks, Holroyd noted a nearby flock of seabirds that appeared to be squabbling over what could be a fish. As Holroyd studied the birds, he realized it would have to be something large to get so many birds so excited.

Curiosity overcame his fear of aggravating his sunburn, and he made his way over to the place. On arrival, he looked down at the water gurgling and surging sluggishly between the rocks and noted an object that he knew should not be there.

At first, he didn't quite recognize what he was looking at, but then he made out dark dress trousers and an arm sticking out from a white shirt. Black hair topped a partially submerged head. He was looking at human remains.

The boys had also spotted the seagulls' activity and came over to look. "Daddy, come look!" Harry shouted and gesticulated.

Martin, who was by then as white as a sheet, stammered, "Is that… Is that…"

David came over and took one look. "Both of you, go to your mother, now! And tell her to get hold of the police." Harry trudged off sullenly, but Martin didn't budge. David had to grab him by the arm and send him on his way.

With the boys gone, David and Holroyd squatted over the body and gave it a closer look. David descended over the rocks until he could grasp the corpse by the shirt and haul it out of the water. Despite its small size, it was heavy, and he had to use both hands to get it onto the rocks.

Looking down, Holroyd noted one arm dangled at an odd angle, broken above the elbow, and one foot was missing below the ankle. He hoped nothing would come apart as David dragged it up. A few small crabs that had been feeding on the remains scuttled away. After the body was out of the water, the two men examined it more closely.

The man wore a short-sleeved shirt, a pair of dress trousers, and a black leather loafer on the remaining foot. With the body fully extracted from the water, Holroyd could discern the man as Asian.

David looked over at Holroyd. "I wonder how long the body's been in the water and where it came from. Can't have been long because there is little bloating."

Feeling nauseous, Holroyd sat on a rock to steady himself. It was not a comfortable seat, and he looked around for something better. He saw nothing suitable nearby and resigned himself to suffer longer. His discomfort increased as he felt the hot sun on his back signalling the onset of a massive sunburn.

"Perhaps he fell overboard from a ship and grabbed onto some flotsam before finally succumbing to exhaustion. If so, it must have been from a vessel close to the island because the body would not be in such shape otherwise." He sat silently for a moment.

"You know, I can't help but feel there's something familiar about him. I may have seen the man somewhere. Maybe on the plane with me or even more recently, he could have been one of the men who tried to get at me at the Hardcastle plantation."

They sat there pondering the body's origins until they heard voices. Turning toward the sound, they saw a small crowd approaching. Harry led George Wilson, the island's head of police, with David's wife and the children trailing not far behind.

David got up as Wilson reached the rocks, greeting him with a perversely cordial, "Morning, George."

"Morning, sir. What do we have here?"

"Looks like a body. Could be someone who fell overboard." Wilson knelt and looked at the remains. Then he pulled out his radio and called for help to take the body away. He turned to David. "Perhaps the children should go back to the beach?"

David looked at his wife, who ushered the kids away. Martin went along at once, but Harry seemed reluctant to go. "Go on, young man," David said, shooing him away.

Wilson examined the remains and after searching the pockets stood up. "Well, a pretty kettle of fish, if you'll pardon the pun. Wonder where he came from. There don't seem to be any ID on him. Can't find a wallet."

"We think he could not have been in the water more than a few hours," David said, "so with wind and currents, I would say he must have entered the water perhaps five miles out." David's arm swept an arc between west and northwest.

"That's about where them warships was yesterday evening," Wilson said as he stared out over the water.

"Yes, could be, but I doubt this man had anything to do with that. He's not wearing a uniform." He paused, "But if not from one of the warships, then what? Have you heard of any missing people?"

"No, sir. Not yet, that is. A boat might still be out there, and it could be someone hasn't reported a loss." He looked at the body. "Curious though. I can't recollect any of the local crewmen being Asians, least-a-ways not as Asian as this man.

"I doubt any of them would dress this way," David replied

"You have a point. But surely you don't just lose someone and not report it."

Wilson nodded. "Unless you don't want to report it or hope you won't have to. Or perhaps you were unaware of the loss."

"Have any ships big enough not to notice a loss passed close enough to the island?" Holroyd asked. Wilson looked at him as if seeing him for the first time.

"A Japanese freighter is due, but she hasn't arrived yet. But that's a cargo ship delivering agricultural produce, so I doubt she'd be big enough to lose someone without notice. Otherwise, I dunno, sir. But I'll be making inquiries. Meantime, we had better get the body back to town. Looks like he drowned, but we'd better do an autopsy."

"Better be quick about it, or it'll decompose pretty quickly."

"Yes, sir. Ah, here comes the ambulance boys."

The ambulance crew removed the body for examination before burial. Wilson remained writing up notes but David and Holroyd rejoined David's family. After the experience, the joy had gone out of the outing, so everyone went home earlier than planned. Gloomily, Holroyd noted his departure plan had likely gone awry.

David invited Holroyd to share supper with them. Although the evening started on a sombre note, Harry's spirits recovered halfway through. "I say, Daddy, who do you think the man was? I mean, he was dressed rather funny for someone going to the beach." So, Harry had noticed the anomalies.

"I mean, why keep those trousers on? Why wasn't he wearing shorts? And the shoe doesn't fit. And how come he had only one leg? He can't have been here long 'cause he wasn't brown enough." Holroyd studied the young boy, taken aback by his sharp eye for details.

"Yes, Harry, all great questions," David said. "But let's leave that to the police, shall we?"

"That's enough of that discussion for the dinner table," David's wife said. "Who wants dessert?" She looked around. There were no eager claims until she added, "There's ice cream and pudding." There were expressions of delight this time, and the atmosphere lightened perceptibly as they all tackled the dessert and tried to put the afternoon's events out of their minds.

A phone call came after supper. David got up to answer it and then returned to the table. "Sorry about that, but the governor wants me and Doctor Holroyd down at the hospital." He turned to Holroyd. "I mentioned to the governor that you thought you might have seen the man somewhere, and the governor thought it might help if you had another look. Don't come if you'd rather not."

"No, I'd like to tag along and see if I remember him."

As Holroyd stood up, David turned to his wife. "Darling, put the boys to bed, would you? And don't wait up for me. I don't know how long I shall be." With that, he and Holroyd made their departure.

Once at the hospital, David, the governor, and Holroyd went to the operating room where the body lay. Doctor Haskin pulled back the sheet.

"Doesn't look to me like he drowned," Holroyd said, looking at the body. "I've seen drowned bodies in the service, and he looks to me as if he was killed on land."

"Well? Do you recognize him?" The governor looked at Holroyd.

"I'm not sure. It could be one of the men that attacked me, but the crash rather dazed me."

The governor nodded.

"Someone knifed this man before he went into the water," Haskin said, pointing to a small, discoloured hole above the heart.

Holroyd felt an urgent need to vomit but managed, with some difficulty, not to.

"Murder?" the governor asked.

"That's most likely."

No one spoke until Haskins recovered the body. "I won't know whether he was dead before he went into the water until I've done an autopsy," he said. "The other thing is, I don't know his nationality. I will send a blood sample for analysis. Until then, I won't know what to put on the death certificate."

The governor nodded. "I don't think we should be too hasty. I can't help feeling we need to know more. Can we keep the body for a few days?"

"We don't have a morgue here, governor. We rarely need one since we bury the bodies the same day. If we can't ship him off quickly, the only place I can think of where we could store him would be the butcher's freezer."

"What about loading him onto the air ambulance and sending him to Singapore or Indonesia?"

"There would be no problem if this were a medical emergency, but I doubt a corpse meets that criterion."

"Even though this might be a murder investigation?"

"I'm not sure how such a request would be received. I don't know much about murders, but I suspect any hospital or morgue receiving a stuck corpse might want to ask questions that we can't answer yet, if ever."

"I agree. I'll ask Robert if we can use part of his freezer."

"Better make sure it's nowhere near the frozen meat counter," David said, smirking. The governor gave him a stony glare.

Once back outside the hospital, the governor looked at Holroyd. "You may have wondered why I dragged you into this. My instructions were to ensure you have every help in the matter concerning Whitehall. I have a gut instinct that this corpse may somehow bear on the matter. Therefore, I thought you'd better stay fully informed.

"And another thing. We made inquiries about yesterday's accident. The car belongs to a local businessman, so we asked a few questions. It seems, however, that Mr. Aitoko has been away for almost two weeks.

"Finally, as you noticed this morning, the car was parked outside Government House. No one came to move it, and so in the evening, we had a look inside. Found what could be some bloodstains in the boot."

"I can't help but feel there's a plan behind all this," Holroyd said, before continuing. "Did Aitoko's people say anything about who was staying there?""

"They told us he left instructions with his staff to expect a couple of visitors and to give said visitors every help. No one knew anything about who they were or the relationship between them and Mr. Aitoko. The visitors may have been Japanese, though they weren't sure.

"The staff reported that the men used the car yesterday morning and returned it in the afternoon. It was dusty, and the gas tank they usually keep full needed petrol. One of the staff took the car to fill it up, and the total pumped supports that it was driven farther than just out to the Hardcastle place and back.

"The visitors, or at least one of them, used the car again to go somewhere and then left it parked outside my office. I'm thinking there are Japanese actors in your play, and I think you should ponder that."

Holroyd thought the advice was not welcome at all, but he couldn't figure out why, and he couldn't think of a reason for any such interest.

"Are they still here?"

"One Asian was on the flight out the day after your incident. The other has not been seen since."

"So the corpse could be the missing man."

"Could be," the governor agreed, "but that raises the question why he was murdered."

"Have you done anything to attract an interest from Japan?" asked David.

"Not as far as I know." Holroyd replied.

Holroyd and David returned to David's home in silence, each immersed in his own thoughts. Upon opening the door, they learned that David's sons had waited to ambush them with questions. The two men reported the absolute minimum they thought would satisfy the boys' curiosity, but Harry turned out to know far more than either of them realized.

"But, Dad, Mr. Aitoko's car went to the beach before we did."

"Well," David began, looking quizzically at Holroyd. "Quite a few people drive out there…"

"Yes, but why would Mr. Aitoko go to the beach?" Harry asked, insistent.

"He probably wanted to go for a swim, or perhaps someone from his house. Nothing unusual in that." Before David could say any more, Holroyd broke in.

"How do you know that, Harry?"

"Martin and I were playing by the church when we saw the car drive up to the beach."

"What were you two rascals doing at the church?" David asked. "Did you tell your mum?"

"No, we didn't. Sorry, Dad."

Holroyd didn't think he really meant it, but David remained stern. "Thank you, Harry. That could be useful."

"Yes, Dad." Harry beamed at his father's approval, and Martin, who had been silent throughout the exchange, basked in the glow of his brother's achievement. With grins, the boys scampered back to their room upstairs.

"Drink before you go home, Doctor Holroyd?"

"Oh, please call me Peter, and yes, I think the occasion merits a drink."

"What are you thinking?"

"I think this incident is interesting. One answer could be that someone drove out to the beach in Aitoko's car and dumped the body into the water."

David nodded his assent as Holroyd continued. "But something has been bothering me. As I said, I may have seen that man before. There were Asians on the plane when I flew here, and this one looks like he may have been one of the two who tried to grab me at the Hardcastle plantation." He stopped.

"There may be no connection, but I can't help feeling it's all too coincidental. Perhaps our corpse had some link to this Aitoko and got knifed after an argument. That raises a question: what's the link?"

"Perhaps you're onto something," David observed after a short pause.

"What do you mean?"

"Well, here we have the body of a man who may have travelled with you from London and may have attacked you but is now freezing in the local butcher's, and if Harry is right, we have our local Japanese businessman's car seen going to where the body was found. That suggests you and the businessman are linked somehow. Do you know of any possible connection?"

"No. But if there is such a link, why was our corpse knifed? Who did the knifing? Where is the knifer now?"

"That's the irritating part. I don't know." With more questions than answers swirling in his mind, Holroyd left David and returned to the governor's residence.

Once there, he reflected further on the recent developments that had happened after the meeting with Xiang. But Xiang was Chinese, so where did this Japanese businessman fit in? And why would the Japanese want to attack him? Was it possible that Xiang's real intent related to a Japanese involvement?

If the Japanese were trying to harm him, a logical conclusion would be that these Japanese interests did not want the island's sovereignty to change. But why?

He felt as if he had become a pawn in a game, the purpose and rules were unknown to him. He felt uneasy, and the thought briefly crossed his mind that he should quit, but he had given his word to undertake the task. A perverse sense of outrage overcame his fears and strengthened his resolve. That, at least, is what he told himself.

He could do little more on the island without arousing suspicions, so he arranged his departure and then sent a message to Xiang's office to let Wendy know of his intended arrival in Beijing.

20

Upon arrival in Beijing, despite almost choking on the air, Holroyd felt relief at stretching his legs after so many hours on the plane. He exited the international arrival concourse, as did several hundred passengers from other flights.

It was noisy as people screamed with delight at recognizing waiting relatives and friends. Some people held up placards with names, but Holroyd noted his name conspicuously absent.

"Doctor Holroyd!" someone called above the din. He turned and, with a sense of relief, saw Wendy approaching.

"Welcome to Beijing. Mr. Xiang apologizes that he is not here to welcome you in person, but he sends his best wishes. Now that you are in China, I will be honoured to assist you." She turned to a large muscular man beside her "Guo Li, *Xingli!*" The man moved forward and grasped Holroyd's luggage.

"Is this your first visit to Beijing?" Wendy asked.

"Yes, although I visited China during the Cultural Revolution, I never got to Beijing."

"I think you may find that much has changed since then. It is my task to make your stay in our capital memorably pleasurable."

She led him outside to a large black car with tinted windows. A chauffeur jumped out and ran around the car to open the door for him while Guo Li put the bags in the boot. As Guo Li sat next to the driver, Wendy and Holroyd settled into the backseats.

"Doctor Holroyd, how was your flight? I hope it was not too tiring." Holroyd acknowledged it had not been too bad.

"I'm so glad! Mr. Xiang suggested I arrange a short program for you before we go to FujinHaiZhou. Tonight, we will dine with a group of people including some academic professors. It will be a very important meeting for you." He breathed an inaudible (he hoped) sigh of relief. He would not have to arrange his stay on his own.

Once at their destination, the hotel was a modern high-rise building, like those in any major city in the world. The lobby, the receptionist desk, and the lifts gave no hint that he was in China.

He unpacked the necessities for his stay and then checked his emails. One was from David, reporting that the man found in the water had been staying with Mr. Aitoko and might have been an employee of the Japanese government.

David also mentioned the blood found in Aitoko's car was probably human, but definitive test results had not yet arrived. *Just what I bloody well need, the Japanese and American governments teaming up against me. Fine, the gloves are off. Let's see who first cries, "Hold, enough."* He lay down for a short rest and was woken when the phone rang

"Doctor Holroyd, are you ready to leave for dinner?"

Wendy took him to what appeared to be a very exclusive restaurant. Eight people were waiting in a private room where Wendy helped him remove his jacket before taking him around the table to meet the guests.

Hospitality was warm but challenging, given his lack of fluency in Chinese. As the meal progressed, without an end to the variety of dishes appearing at the table, discretion suggested that a slower eating rate would be wise. This prompted a concern, "Is this dish not your liking?"

Assurance that the dish was delicious resulted in the delivery of yet another morsel to his plate. Faster eating suggested that Holroyd was still hungry because more food appeared before him, and the vicious circle continued.

The Chinese usually served tea or beer at Chinese dinners, and Holroyd remembered that they limited spirits (other than imported spirits) to what they euphemistically called "White wine" (*Bai Jiu*).

He learned to beware of the colourless contents of small green glass bottles because, while delicious after a few swallows, the viscous liquid was sneakily vicious. The Lonely Planet travel guide accurately referred to the concoction as "Liquid Lobotomy."

One guest succumbed to the effects of Bai Jiu and quietly disappeared under the table, which caused much ribaldry among the other guests.

"I see you have learned the dangers of Bai Jiu," the man next to Holroyd said with a smile.

"Yes." Holroyd laughed. "I'm sorry, but I did not quite catch your name during the introductions."

"I'm Li Wen Yao. Again, I'm pleased to meet you."

"Likewise." They toasted each other with Bai Jiu.

"And what do you do here? If I may ask."

"Oh! I'm here as a translator in case that should prove necessary. Otherwise, I work in an office."

"How nice. Thank you. I will call on you if I need to."

"It will be my pleasure. I hear you are a distinguished professor specializing in early Chinese travels."

"I wouldn't call myself distinguished, but that is my interest."

"Then may I ask your opinion on reports that a Chinese admiral named Zheng He discovered America before Columbus did?"

"I think it's probably true the Chinese came to America before Columbus. There are many reasons for me to question the truth of Columbus being the first. The evidence is that the Vikings, probably the Irish, and maybe the ancient Egyptians all arrived before Columbus. And let us not forget there were several civilizations there before Columbus arrived, so he discovered nothing, but he did establish contact. It's like saying Marco Polo discovered China when the Chinese were there long before Polo was born." Holroyd grinned.

"And are you here to find support for your belief?"

"Yes."

"Then I hope you will find what you are looking for. Should you need any help, please call me."

"Thank you. That is most kind."

Holroyd turned to chat with the guest sitting on his other side. Only later did he wonder how an office worker who doubled as a translator could help in his search.

By the time dinner ended, Holroyd felt the effects of too many toasts that, together with travel fatigue, made him feel groggy and the worse for wear. He stumbled a few times as he left the restaurant and would have fallen but for Wendy's help.

He almost tripped getting out of the lift, but she managed to steady him as he fumbled for his access card, opened the door, and, surrendering to jet lag, collapsed into bed, only to awake several hours later to the sound of his alarm.

He took a shower, the water alternating unpredictably between scalding hot and freezing cold. He felt groggy, and his tongue reminded him of a long-dead sea cucumber. It was not an auspicious start to the day. He wished only to go back to sleep but knew it was impossible. Wearily, he checked his emails.

One from Merry asked about his whereabouts and whether he knew anything that might have caused excitement on the island. He had had a long conversation with the governor, and there had been unusual communication traffic from the island to Japan. What, Merry asked, had Holroyd done to invite Japanese interests?

Given his recent experience on the island, Holroyd called Merry and, given the time differences between Beijing and London, was lucky to reach him and gave him an update on what had transpired but omitted the attack or the discovery of the corpse. Merry made a few non-committal noises before switching subjects.

"I have a question for you on a completely different matter. Some time ago, I got a call from a mutual friend, Alfred Rostwick. Said you gave him a document. Wouldn't tell me too much over the phone but said it was urgent and wanted to meet with me soon. Care to tell me more about this?"

"It was a document my bookseller asked me to look at. I borrowed it to look further, but then I thought Alfred would be more qualified than I." Holroyd was surprised that Alfred had contacted Merry about it.

"Why was that?"

"The document looked like it had Japanese writing, and that's Alfred's specialty."

"I see. Took it with him, did he? Nothing further? No idea what it might have been? No? The funny thing is, he never turned up, and now he's gone missing. I suppose he'll turn up eventually. Meanwhile, enjoy your stay." Holroyd hoped he would be able to do so.

How come Rostwick is missing? Missing usually means wandering off without anyone knowing where or that some accident had happened of which no one was aware. It would be very unusual for Rostwick to wander off, so did that mean he had had an accident? Holroyd hoped that would not prove to be the case.

What about the document? Was that missing too? In retrospect, Rostwick's reaction suggests it might have been very valuable. Could Rostwick's disappearance be linked to that? I was stupid to loan it before determining what it was. Damn! What is so important about that document?

Suddenly, the question hit him. *Was the document in any way linked to my task? If that were so, the document has to do with Dejection Island. The lines on the document might have been contours or the outlines of an island, so it may have been a map of the island. If that were so, there was some linkage between the island and Japan and possibly something to do with the Japanese occupation.*

Might the document have had to do with military matters though I didn't see any signs of gun emplacements or fortifications. But perhaps that was the point. The document refers to hidden construction. What purpose would a document of hidden construction serve unless the builders wanted to return to the site? And why would they want to return unless there was something buried that had value… something like treasure? I think a call to the island might help. He looked at his watch and decided it would have to wait. After all, if the treasure had been there for several decades, an extra day wouldn't make much difference.

After a breakfast that barely assuaged his hunger pangs, he went out to the lobby where Wendy was already waiting for him and greeted him enthusiastically.

"Good morning, Doctor Holroyd. I trust you slept well? I know your flight tired you," she said, which was an understatement, "but we leave for FujinHaiZhou shortly. The flight will need a change of planes in Xi Tung Piao, a small provincial town, but the stopover is short. Do not take too much hand luggage as the second flight is in a small plane. Please be ready."

The flight to Xi Tung Piao proved uneventful, and there was only a thirty-minute wait before boarding the next flight. On entering the small plane, the cabin staff politely welcomed him with smiles that did not reach their eyes and showed him to his window seat in the business class section.

Wendy sat next to him. As the flight settled at its cruising altitude, Holroyd turned to Wendy. "Thank you for the arrangements so far but tell me something about you and your background."

"I was born in Liaoning Province, the second child of the local hospital's chief doctor. My parents managed to get me to Japan to evade the One Child Policy, and from there, I was sent to relatives in England. I attended the City of London School for Girls before studying at King's College. After graduating, I worked for Mr. Xiang."

"What did you study?"

"Political science and economics. I managed to achieve a first in both." She let her pride show.

"Well done! And how did you come to meet him?"

"My relatives had guanxi[2] or good relations with him and introduced me to him. He offered me a job."

"Ah, yes! Guanxi helps every time." Holroyd grinned.

"Oh, but it's not that simple. You always have to return the favour in some way. Failure to do so would cause a big loss of face with bad social consequences."

---

2 Guanxi (in China) the system of social networks and influential relationships that facilitate business and other dealings

Holroyd nodded. "And what work did you do for Mr. Xiang?"

"Economic research to help his machinery business."

"And do you have a boyfriend?" Wendy blushed and started to laugh.

"I did, but he went to America."

"And you didn't want to go with him?"

"He wasn't interested! Told me his parents wouldn't allow him to marry a banana."

"A banana?"

"Someone who is yellow outside but white inside. Or, to put it simply, a Chinese person who has lived and been educated for too long in the West and has adopted Western ideas."

"Oh, bad luck! And do you have hobbies or interests?"

"Not really. I want to earn money to help my parents in their old age."

"Ah! You kept in touch with them?"

"Yes! Contacts between relatives in and outside China became much easier once China opened up. I visited them two years ago."

Holroyd sat back *All reassuring and satisfactory. I think she'll work out quite well. Nice girl and seems competent. Xiang is keeping his promise to help.*

The rest of the flight proved uneventful, but he could see nothing of the terrain they passed because of cloud cover. They landed at a modern air terminal, retrieved their luggage, and went out. Again, a chauffeur awaited them and drove them to the Auspicious Friendship Hotel.

The hotel pleasantly surprised Holroyd. His experiences of hotels ranged from staying (at someone else's expense) in cozy two- or three-story hotels like the Ritz London or the Storchen in Zurich or multi-story impersonal structures like the New Otani in Tokyo with its battery of elevators, each with a polite hostess welcoming the potential rider with a smile and a bow.

The Auspicious Friendly Hotel was somewhere in between the two extremes. Surrounded by trees and fountains suggesting a rural setting, the hotel was of a modern design.

Once inside, Holroyd could not identify a focal point in the immense lobby, but he noted a staggering amount of marble. To one side, closed glass doors led to a dining room open only for mealtimes. Opposite the dining room, an open door led to the bar, where he could see only a few customers.

The reception desk was against one wall, almost hidden behind marble columns and potted plants. Several receptionists stood behind the desk, engaged in deep discussion.

A concierge desk was between the glass doors leading to the dining room and the outside doors. On a table nearby lay travel brochures and rental car announcements. A small sitting area that doubled as a café was outside the bar, but a red rope stretched across the entrance to show it was closed.

Aside from Wendy and Holroyd, the lobby was empty of anyone but the staff, and no wonder. There was no seating in the lobby, so they expected guests to go directly to their rooms, go to the bar, or go out.

Once they had registered, a bellboy appeared, grabbed their luggage, and led them to the lifts. Arriving at the door to their suite, the bellboy swiped their card, held the door open, and invited them to enter before him. Leading the way, Wendy surveyed the sitting room and proceeded to the bedroom and adjoining bathroom.

"Doctor Holroyd, this looks very suitable. I will be in the room next door."

"That's very convenient, thank you." The hotel would be his *pied-à-terre*, which satisfied him for now.

"May I suggest we go to the university once unpacked?"

"Oh no! Mr. Xiang suggested we go to the FujinHaiZhou library because the university owns no information that could be of use. I apologize for not informing you earlier, but I hope that will not be inconvenient."

Holroyd was surprised, but Wendy looked contrite, hoping Holroyd would not refuse or cause a scene. He had no counterargument or alternative suggestion and agreed to meet in the lobby.

21

Outside the hotel doors, their car took them through the town to the library. On arrival, they looked at the building's architectural style which was Soviet ugliness topped by a classical Chinese-style roof. The entrance daunted potential readers more than it welcomed them.

Holroyd thought it a disagreeable combination testifying to some unfathomable political concept of beauty. He doubted many citizens of FujinHaiZhou would disagree.

On entering the vast lobby, Holroyd noted how quiet it was: no one was moving about, and no computers or air conditioners could be heard humming. As they stood there wondering where to go, a man and a woman approached with smiles.

The man was about five feet four inches tall, thin almost to the point of emaciation, and had a sallow, even unhealthy, tint to his skin. Holroyd would have guessed his age to be about forty-five, but his luxuriant hair was still jet black. Likely due to many years of poring over a desk, he stooped somewhat. Dressed in a white shirt, grey trousers, and black Chinese slippers, he came forward diffidently.

"Welcome, Dr. Holroyd! I'm Ding Qu Wan, the chief librarian. I have been advised of your intended visit. It is my honour to welcome you to our poor library. We are very proud that you have selected us where you wish to conduct your research. We will cooperate with you in every way possible." His tone left Holroyd feeling that his version of cooperation and Holroyd's might be very different.

"Dr. Holroyd, welcome." A diminutive woman stepped forward. "I'm Shao Yao, or Chrysanthemum Pearl. I'm the deputy director. She smiled and immediately dispelled Holroyd's previously negative impressions about the library and its staff.

She must have been in her late twenties or early thirties but had retained a slim, almost girlish figure. Her face reminded him of Audrey Hepburn, with almond-shaped eyes and a perfectly shaped mouth. Her smile had a warmth that no officialdom could dispel entirely. *She is lovely. No, more than lovely; she is exquisitely beautiful and must be very competent to become the deputy director quickly. My search might not produce the evidence I'm looking for, but Chrysanthemum Pearl's presence might make the task enjoyable.*

"Please call me Pearl. I will be most pleased to assist you however I can."

"That will be most kind of you," Holroyd said, though his voice sounded strangled to his ears. He heard a sound and turned to see Wendy looking at him puzzledly.

"We do not understand how we might be of help," Ding interrupted. "Perhaps I might inquire of your particular interests here?"

"Thank you. Yes, well, my interests are in Ming and Qing Dynasty explorations and cartography. I understand you have one of the great collections of maps and reports from that period. Until now, I could not find much information for use in my research. I suppose Western search engines do not have full access to Chinese libraries. However, there was enough for me to wish to look at what you may have and do some further research."

"That is delightful, and we will be most pleased to help in any way we can. However, I fear they have misinformed you. Our collection is small and not, I believe, of great interest. Nonetheless, please examine what we have. Is there anything in particular you might look for?"

Holroyd thought he detected a slight suggestion of concern, and he wondered why. "My interest is to find any records of who travelled to or in the area we now call the South China Sea. As you probably know, Zhang Xie wrote a study of the eastern and western seas, though you may know it as the Dong Xi Yang Kao. I'm looking for a copy of that and any other reports of such activities."

At the mention of the South China Sea, Ding looked surprised and became very attentive. "Ah, the Dong Xi Yang Kao? I have heard of it but am not familiar with that book. I don't believe we have it in our collection."

Holroyd was surprised. *How come the librarian is unfamiliar with the Dong Xi Yang Kao? That would be like an English librarian who never heard of the Venerable Bede!*

"*Women you ma*? Oh! Sorry, I spoke Chinese!" Ding turned to Pearl "Do we have that?" She looked at him with a hint of reproach.

"Yes, we have it, Director. As I remember, Dr. Nicholson asked for that when he was here."

Holroyd was taken aback. *Who is this Nicholson person, and when did he visit? And why would he want the same book I'm looking for? The Dong Xi Yang Kao is hardly the sort of book in popular demand, but if it were, surely the person would be someone in my field of interest. I don't think I've ever heard of this Doctor Nicholson.*

"Ah, so it will be in our historical section," Ding said, turning to Holroyd with a grimace that he probably intended as a smile.

"Director Ding, you will remember that you allowed Dr. Nicholson to take the book out of the library." There was a moment's silence, and Ding's smile disappeared. Holroyd thought Ding turned pale.

Why? Holroyd stifled a groan. *Now, I'm going to need the cooperation of some academic of whom I've never heard. Or is this yet another attempt at frustrating my search? Is this an American or possibly a Japanese interference? That could mean whoever is out to stop me may have succeeded, and I'm not sure what I can do about that right now.* He got no further before Ding replied to Pearl's announcement.

"Ah, yes. I remember. That was a special situation." He looked at his watch. "However, perhaps you might excuse me, as I have another meeting to attend, but Shao Yao will help you find whatever you need." He grimaced again, turned, and hurried toward a bank of lifts at the far end of the reception area.

"Dr. Nicholson?" Holroyd asked, turning to Pearl. "I have not heard of this gentleman. May I know who he is?"

"Oh, have you not heard of him? Dr. Nicholson is a very distinguished American researcher at the University of Mississippi who also studies early Chinese explorations and activities in the South China Sea. I understand he has written several papers and books, and is highly respected."

"Really?" Holroyd became certain he had never heard of Dr. Nicholson at the mention of papers. His ignorance irked him because he thought himself knowledgeable and possibly even an expert. However, he thought it best not to reveal his surprise at this stage.

"Is he still here? I want to catch up with him."

"I believe he is staying at the Auspicious Friendship Hotel. What will you catch with him? Do you both like fishing? I'm not aware of many fish here."

"'Catch up' means exchanging information about activities since our last meeting."

"Oh, like when I get together with my classmates, and we tell each other about our lives. Yes, that will be nice. It is always nice to… how you say it? Catch up?"

"Yes, it is. But perhaps I could see the collection?" He changed the subject quickly.

"Yes, please excuse my irrelevant chattering. Please follow me." Pearl led him to the same bank of lifts and, on entering, pressed the button for the second floor. "I will bring you an entry card for future use, but I will always be ready to help if you have questions."

They reached the second floor and entered a large, air-conditioned room with rows of computer monitors similar to an internet café. Several people whom Holroyd assumed to be researchers were bent over their respective screens and so engrossed in their work that they did not look up as Holroyd, Wendy, and Pearl entered.

"This is our research room," Pearl said. "Here, you can look for any document you may wish for and call it up for you to read on the screen. It is a modern system, like the one we have at our best universities." She smiled proudly as she led him to a console.

His heart plummeted as he saw everything was in Chinese, as it would be. Although he could read some Chinese, undertaking a search would be a slow process. His disappointment must have shown.

"Do you have access to Western search engines?"

"Search engines?" Pearl looked confused.

"Yes, a means of finding information on a particular subject. Like Google or some university libraries."

"Oh! Google is not available. We have a Chinese search engine, Baidu, and access to most Chinese university libraries. And we hope to have much wider interlibrary exchange agreements soon." This was not what he had hoped for, even if, at the back of his mind, he had half expected it.

Perhaps recognizing Holroyd's concerns, Pearl gestured to the computer. "Please, just to let me know which document you would like to view, and I will be happy to put it on the screen." Pearl sat down and let her fingers dance over the keyboard until what appeared to be a search site appeared.

Holroyd looked at it with dismay because it looked like nothing he had ever seen. He was used to a screen that asked for keywords, title, author, or publication information. However, this showed almost two dozen preliminary choices before reaching his desired search criteria.

"I'm unclear how you set up your retrieval system, but let's try a few keywords."

"Yes, that is how we arrange this."

"Good, then let's try 'maritime exploration in the Ming Dynasty, and then the same for the Qing Dynasty.'"

"I'm sorry, but what is maritime?"

"Oh. Well, let's try 'explorations by sea in the Ming and Qing Dynasties.'"

Pearl nodded, and again, her fingers danced over the keyboard. "We have several articles on file. Is there anyone in particular that you would like to review now?" She pushed back to let him look at the screen. Over a dozen references appeared, of which he recognized maybe three, but Nicholson's name was not among them,

"Perhaps you could print this list for me?"

Pearl nodded, pressed a few keys, and went to a printer near the door.

"Who is Doctor Nicholson?" Wendy asked.

"No idea. I never heard of him. Strange, I thought I knew of anyone notable in the field. But I've never come across the name in my area before."

"We can check it out at our hotel. I think Miss Pearl said Doctor Nicholson was also staying there."

"So she did. Good point."

"Perhaps you could help me review the list to see which might be useful. I recognize a few authors, but if those are the papers that I think they might be, they won't be of much use." Wendy nodded.

Holroyd explained "The problem with published research by Chinese academicians is that seventy percent repeats or validates already published stuff. Many of these people publish only for publication without trying to advance knowledge in the field, and plagiarism is rife. But perhaps there is something we can use."

Pearl returned with a few sheets of paper. "Here is the list, Doctor Holroyd." Scanning the publication dates showed nothing in the collection was over twenty years old and thus not much use.

"Is the Zhang Xie book included in this list?"

"Oh no. We list the Zhang Xie book in our special collection. We only allow specially approved researchers access to that."

"Am I a specially approved researcher?"

Pearl looked confused. "That is not a problem." She paused as if to collect her thoughts. "Would you like to see the special collection now?" He nodded. "Please follow me then."

Turning away, she led them back to the lifts and the basement. Once on the basement level, they followed Pearl along a corridor and into a brightly lit, warm, and disordered room.

"What's this?" Holroyd asked as he surveyed the room.

"This is our room for storing any document or book we have not yet catalogued, repaired, stored, or otherwise arranged."

"Repaired?" He could not hide his concern.

"Yes. We repair old coverings, clean away any dirt or bacteriological contamination, and repair any pictures or lettering that may have become damaged." Pearl smiled proudly, but he was aghast.

"Won't that destroy whatever you are repairing?" he croaked.

"Perhaps, but what use is a book that no one can read?"

"Yes, but... how do you know what they wrote before you repair it?"

"Oh, there are usually other copies from which we repair things correctly."

"So, these are not rare books or documents?"

"No! We would touch nothing on a rare book." Pearl looked at him scornfully. "We record, catalogue, and place rare books directly in the rare book section of the library. Only Director Ding and I touch those books because we have the proper training."

He felt relieved. "The rare books storage is through here." She led them through yet another door.

The rare books storage was large and, from what he could see by a control panel, temperature and moisture-controlled. The library stored several books and documents in glass cases, and he could see what he thought were huge metal storage containers against one wall. Not up to the standards of the British Museum or the Bodleian, but respectable.

"How is everything arranged here?"

"We have sectioned the room so that documents from one reign are all in the same area. For instance, there," Pearl waved to her left, "are the documents from the time of the Kangxi Emperor. Over there," she pointed to another section of the room, "are the documents from the Yongle Emperor's reign."

Holroyd thought for a moment. "I think anything after 1840 would not be useful unless a more modern publication reports on early travels. Did anyone do any research?"

"We can ask one of our staff to inquire. Please let us know what you are looking for."

"I will let you know the keywords. But perhaps you could show us the Ming Dynasty and the early Qing Dynasty sections of the room?"

"Yes, that is not a problem. Here is the Yongle Emperor, and over there is the Wanli Emperor."

"Ah, the Wanli Emperor," Holroyd said. "He was on the throne when Zhang Xie completed his book."

Wendy nodded politely while Pearl gave a puzzled look.

"Yes, but he was a lazy, useless man."

"He was, but his Grand Secretary, Zhang Juzheng, was anything but. Unfortunately, Zhang died less than ten years into the reign, and everything went to pot from then on."

"Went to pot?" Pearl looked lost. "Does that mean cooked?" Holroyd smiled, and even Wendy looked amused.

"Became disorganized, got destroyed."

"Ah. Like our Cultural Revolution?"

"Er, yes, possibly." Despite the government's recent acknowledgement that the Revolution had been a disaster that would never happen again, he thought it best to hedge his bets on whether to agree.

He had heard in China that they could interpret historical events in various ways, but none of them were within a visitor's remit. He decided a quick change of topic was proper.

"Pearl, how does the library gain its collection?"

"Oh, the government gives us many books. We also inherit books and other objects when noble citizens donate them. Sometimes, someone comes in with something special, and we can get permission to buy it."

Given China's history, Holroyd thought few citizens would be noble enough to donate without active persuasion. However, again, he decided discretion would be the better part of valour and kept quiet.

"For example, not so long ago, one of our student researchers delivered a document she had found, or someone gave to her," Pearl continued. "She told me it was old, but I don't know what it was. Our staff was examining it but had placed it in the rare books collection before I completed the examination. I expect to examine it soon."

"Has the library ever lost anything?"

"I don't know. It is possible because the Cultural Revolution interfered with our work. During that time, the library was closed, and the staff could not continue cataloguing and repairing. When the Red Guards were in control, they destroyed many records of great historical value. After the Revolution, we recovered a few things but lost others. They burned many things. My parents told me there was a great fire in the town, and all citizens had to go watch."

"Did you go?"

"I was too young."

"Is it possible they destroyed or stole documents during that time?"

"I think it is possible."

He looked around the room and noted an empty case.

Pearl followed his gaze. "Yes, that is where we keep our copy of Zhang Xie's book, but as I told you, Director Ding allowed Dr. Nicholson to take it out of the library."

"And in this case?" He pointed to another empty one.

"Oh!" Pearl looked confused and anxious. "Please excuse me, but I have not been in this room for quite some time, so I do not recall what was in that case." He sensed her embarrassment and even agitation, as did Wendy.

"But the case is in the section where you keep the documents from the time of the Wanli Emperor, so perhaps whatever should be in this case would be from that time?"

"Yes, I think that is right."

"Do you think there is a record somewhere of what was in the case? Or perhaps where the item may be now?"

"I will look for you."

"Thank you. Is it possible that Doctor Nicholson borrowed this item also?"

"Doctor Holroyd," Wendy cut in, "perhaps we can go back to the hotel now and prepare a list of keywords for Miss Pearl? Then we will be better prepared for tomorrow. We can also try to meet Doctor Nicholson."

This calmed Pearl down. "If that is acceptable, let me call for a taxi to take you back to your hotel."

Once in the taxi, Holroyd looked at Wendy. "Why did you interrupt me when I asked about that second document?"

"Pearl does not know or does not want to reveal what happened to the document, and I thought it would be embarrassing if she had to admit that to you. She would have lost face in front of a *laowai* foreigner. I will ask her again when you are not nearby." Holroyd nodded and let his mind wander.

How strange, he thought, that Zhang Xie had written his book during the reign of the Wanli Emperor when maritime activities stopped. And, come to that, just why had the Wanli Emperor curtailed maritime activities? He doubted the conventional wisdom that held it was the eunuchs who had done so, but that still left the question of who had decided and why.

He thought it would be a research project worth undertaking once he finished this task. *What am I thinking? A project worth undertaking! I might not have a job when I return to London, and even if I do, I probably won't have the necessary resources.*

"I'm curious about that second empty glass case," Wendy said, interrupting his reverie. "I wonder what was in it. It seemed the empty case worried Pearl. I don't believe she knows nothing about it. I think Pearl knows more than she was admitting."

"I agree. I'm also curious about how the library gained its artifacts. What was that story about a student handing in some document? It's strange that Pearl could not or would not say what it was, where the student found it, or how she got it."

"We didn't ask."

"True, but we should ask tomorrow."

"Do you think the story has anything to do with our quest?"

"I have a funny feeling that perhaps we should look further. I mean, it's purely a gut feeling, and there's no way I can explain it, but we might as well follow up. You never know, and stranger things have happened. And it's not as if we have unlimited leads to chase."

"Yes, Dr. Holroyd. I will make inquiries to see what I can find out."

Once back at the hotel, Wendy went over to the reception desk before coming back and reporting that no Doctor Nicholson was or had been a registered guest. That, Holroyd thought, was disconcerting.

Without Nicholson, consulting the Dong Xi Yang Kao could prove problematic, and now Nicholson was not where he was reported to be. Unbidden, Hamlet's "There is something rotten in the state of Denmark" sprang to mind.

Holroyd had no idea but had several suspicions about what might be rotten, but this was not Denmark or any other Western country for that matter. That meant resources such as the police might not be available, or if they were, might not be helpful.

The only resource he had at hand was Wendy, and though she had been helpful so far, he wondered how much further she could help. At that moment, he felt unsure of his next step. Not the best position in which to find himself.

What about Pearl? She seems nice and helpful. Would she be willing to help further than her official obligations? But maybe what I'm trying for is something more personal. Perhaps if I ask if she would be prepared to show me the sights of the town. Would she then be amenable for me to take her out for coffee or dinner? Dammit, why not give it a try?

As he reflected on his problem, he decided to take a break.

"Wendy, unless you suggest our next move, I need a short break. Let's get some fresh air after dinner."

"I think that's an excellent idea, Doctor Holroyd; why not go down to the lake?"

22

Inspector Fang Wei closed the file he had been reading and rubbed his eyes. He leaned forward and poured hot water into his cup for a second infusion of tea. With a warm cup in his hand, he sat back in his chair and considered yesterday's events.

The office had received reports of three cases of theft, four fender benders, three domestic unrests, a lost child, and fourteen drunks. None of these issues required a police inspector, but then only a few of his subordinates seemed willing to accept responsibility, preferring instead to defer to a senior authority.

He remembered the old Chinese saying, "Do a little work, make few mistakes. Do nothing, make no mistakes." He wryly recognized too many of the city's police officers were fervent advocates of that philosophy.

Tomorrow, he thought, he was to meet with some Party functionary from Beijing and discuss a matter that someone else considered of utmost importance. Could be anything from discussing the city's crime records, providing security for some visiting dignitary, or just exhortations to do more. More what?

There had not been a serious capital crime in over four months, and there were no rumours about spies or anti-government protests. To tell the truth, he had no interest in what said dignitary might want or who he might be. Besides, he didn't think it was his place to have that meeting; it should have been his superior.

However, FujinHaiZhou's commissioner, Fu Li, had left a message saying it would be inconvenient for him to attend, and he would appreciate it if Inspector Fang Wei would replace him. Fang Wei was sure Fu Li had already informed the functionary.

"The bastard left me no way out," Fang Wei muttered, "but then why am I surprised? It's not as if Fu Li does not shine in his role as police commissioner, at least as far as appearances go and for sucking up to the higher-ups in the Party." He did not need to go on.

Fang Wei reached into his pocket to grab a cigarette before remembering the directive that forbade smoking in public buildings. Sourly, he concluded that today was not going to be among the best days of his twenty-two-year career.

The door opened, revealing Police Lieutenant Wu Shi Ming. He was about to enter but, on considering the inspector's face, decided he should pause for a moment. He stood by the door and contemplated his superior.

In appearance, Fang Wei was thin and wiry. His hair had not yet turned grey, but there were signs of aging or stress. His face retained the lean look that was a hallmark of younger Chinese, but Wu could see worry lines around the eyes and mouth. He was stooping a little, probably the result of sitting too long in an office chair and too little time exercising. His fingers were nicotine-stained, evidence of a lifetime habit of smoking at least a pack a day.

Fang Wei was wearing his uniform with a crisply ironed shirt under the open jacket. Unlike so many police officers, his shoes were solidly utilitarian and polished to a high gleam. Looking at him, even a casual observer would feel confident in but perhaps not impressed by this representative of the law. By comparison, Wu Shi Ming could have passed for a model on a police force recruiting advertisement.

Wu was tall for a Chinese, over six feet. He had an athletic frame and carried himself with a mixture of grace and authority. He rarely wore his uniform but instead dressed sombrely but fastidiously in grey or blue suits. He walked with an air of authority that belied his youth. People almost instinctively deferred to him when meeting him.

Wu shifted as Fang Wei looked up at him.

"If you have a moment, we got a call from the Auspicious Friendship Hotel. It seems a guest was attacked. Could you come and have a look?"

Fang Wei looked up, surprised.

"An attack? Is that not something you can handle?"

"Well, normally, I would not trouble you. But my wife and I are to host her company's boss all day. In the evening we are to go down to the lake to watch the light and music display. Her boss is in from Wuhan and," he paused, "I don't think she will want me to be absent."

Wu Shi Ming's wife was a second cousin to Fang Wei's aunt's brother-in-law, which meant family obligations hovered over the discussion, even though no one would ever openly suggest that or that such obligations featured in Wu's assignment to Fang Wei's division.

Still, the family issues might surface later if Fang insisted now that Wu take charge. If they could solve the matter quickly, sending Wu would bring no repercussions because Wu could still meet his family. And Fang Wei could go home.

If, however, the matter turned out to be something more complicated or something he could not lose in an unsolved case drawer, Fang Wei would have to explain why he, as a senior officer, did not take charge.

The Auspicious Friendly Hotel was among FujinHaiZhou's premier accommodations for visitors, so the victim might be important. Fang Wei realized it would be safer if he went down there himself.

A sudden thought popped into his mind, and Fang Wei winced at the thought of domestic recriminations if it looked as if he had put business, even the murder of a possibly important visitor, ahead of family obligations.

Wu's wife would be swift to incriminate if she thought she was being slighted in any way—not that anyone would justify the recriminations. Still, relatives rarely included justification when women folk perceived a possible slight. Fang Wei could envision his aunt accompanied by Wu's wife in full battle mode, reproaching him in front of a smug commissioner. The vision was an unpleasant one.

"What about Lu Ping Wan or Zhang Hu Wing?"

"Lu is sick, and Zhang is already out on a case."

"Why not send your sergeant?" Both men recognized this to be a last-ditch effort.

Wu shook his head. "My sergeant will accompany you." Fang Wei surrendered to what had been inevitable from the beginning.

"Is there anything else I should know?"

"The incident took place in one of the upscale hotel suites, suggesting this might involve someone important or at least rich. It might just be a robbery or some misbehaved chicken with an aggressive handler."

"Is he dead?"

"Don't know yet."

"Okay. I'll go along but join me there as soon as you can get away."

Fang Wei went down to the garage, where he found Wu's sergeant and a driver, and then set out.

Although acquainted with both the sergeant and the driver, Fang Wei was in no mood to chat. He would gain nothing by speculating on what they might find on arrival at the hotel, and neither subordinate would be comfortable chatting with such an august officer.

On arrival in the hotel's driveway, an agitated but obsequious member of the hotel staff came out to greet them. He was wearing a dark suit with the concierge's crossed keys on the lapels.

"Good evening, Inspector; thank you for coming so quickly. I'm the day manager, and I will provide you with any help you may need. Please come this way." He led the police through to the lobby and toward the elevator banks. "This is a terrible experience."

Fang Wei nodded without listening but instead looked over the lobby. The passage of the police did not distract the receptionists, who seemed bored because no one was demanding their attention.

Fang Wei noted that the hotel staff and a rather shabby-looking westerner accompanied by a beautiful Chinese woman exiting toward the street were the only people in the lobby. *Probably, a tourist and a local guide, although she might have other talents than showing a visitor the sights of the town.*

As the lift rose, the manager handed over his business card. "A chambermaid reported a commotion inside a suite on the twelfth floor and called me. It's registered to an American, Mr. Norris Brugge. He registered just last week, and his passport was in order with a visa and port of entry stamps. I will, of course, produce a scanned copy for you."

He stopped to see if there was a comment, but Fang Wei only nodded, so the manager continued. "I went to the suite and viewed the scene. A foreign male, about thirty years of age and dressed in a blue shirt and light-coloured trousers, was lying on the floor covered with lots of blood. I could see he was dead, so I left and locked the door before calling the police. No one has entered the room since that time.”

“Did you feel for a pulse to make sure he was dead?”

“Inspector, I was in the army and have seen dead men before. I don’t need to check for pulses.”

“Did anyone else report this disturbance?”

“None. The floor is unoccupied except for an English professor and his assistant and a Mexican businessman. The Englishman and his assistant just went out but have not yet returned. The businessman checked out this morning.”

Arriving at the suite, the manager swiped his card, held the door open, and invited the police to enter before him. Leading the way, Fang Wei surveyed what was the sitting room and motioned to the sergeant to go into the bedroom and adjoining bathroom.

Fang Wei sensed the odourless neutrality of an air-conditioning system and concluded that nothing was out of the ordinary. He scrutinized the furniture and the carpet. There was no sign that anyone had occupied the room, at least since its last cleaning.

“Well, where’s this body?” Fang Wei asked the manager as the sergeant came back shaking his head.

The manager shook his head as he stared at the spot on the floor. "I don't know. It was here, and there was blood on the carpet. There was even a burnt smell in the room."

"Yes, so you said, but as you can see, the body is missing, and there is no blood, no burnt smell, and no sign of disorder." The manager continued to look blank.

"Sergeant Li, are there any signs of occupancy? Any clothing, toiletries, or luggage? Any signs of usage in the wastebaskets?"

"Nothing, sir."

"I don't understand… The body and the blood were here." The manager seemed close to tears.

"I see. Perhaps it might be useful to interview the member of your staff who reported this incident."

"I think she is off duty now, but I will see if I can find her address for you."

"That would be helpful—" Before he could continue, a staff member appeared at the door looking somewhat flustered. Going over to the night manager, he whispered something. The night manager frowned and then turned to Fang Wei.

"Inspector, there seems to be a problem in finding the copy of Mr. Brugge's passport and registration."

The statement was met with silence. Fang Wei looked at the room and then turned to the manager.

"Without a body, blood, and evidence that someone has been staying here, we don't have a crime that would allow us to investigate. We will be back to talk with your staff and see what else we may find. In the meantime, I need not remind you that misleading the police is a serious crime. We need not trouble you any further now."

Fang Wei left the room, followed by the sergeant. "Well, at least Wu Shi Ming had his day with his family and did not come here for some fool's errand. Anyway, I want you to follow up and check the closed-circuit television to see if what's his name is registered and if there are any records of him in the corridors and entering his room." He stopped as if mentally going over a list.

"Talk to the staff to see what they know and if he had any luggage or used room service. Find out if anybody entered the room to clean it after they called us. I'm not sure if you will find anything, but we had better check. If there is anything to the story, we can expect calls from the consulates and the ministry, so we better be prepared." He paused and then continued.

"Oh, and run a quick check on those other foreigners staying on the floor. I doubt they will be of help, but one never knows. Then return and brief Wu Shi Ming when he gets in tomorrow."

The sergeant nodded. He knew the drill, and he knew the inspector knew this, but he also acknowledged the inspector was covering all bases.

"It's not easy to clean up a room after a murder, especially if there's blood on the carpet." Fang Wei mused. "I wonder if they showed us the correct room."

"If it's not the correct room, how would we find the correct one? We would have to search the entire hotel."

"Perhaps. But that raises a question: why the deception? Why call the police instead of keeping everything quiet? See if you can find out who called the police."

As they crossed the lobby, leaving by the front door, they sensed the stares from the page boys and the concierge. By chance, the sergeant looked straight into the concierge's eyes and stopped.

"You go ahead, sir. I want to check on something," he said as he went over to the desk.

Fang Wei had a long-awaited smoke while he waited outside. He had smoked about half the stick when the sergeant came out.

"The concierge knows something but isn't talking yet. One of the page boys said he overheard a lady asking for a foreigner's room last night. He did not hear the name of the person she was asking for. They must have given her some information because then she went over to the lifts. But nobody else remembers the incident."

"Perhaps, perhaps not. Check CCTV to see where she went."

Fang Wei regarded the traffic passing the hotel. "I wonder why there is no proof of Brugge's visit." He was sure that the night manager was not lying, if only because he would know the consequences of police obstruction. Yet, nothing he had seen suggested that anything untoward had happened. Fang Wei was intrigued.

An avid watcher of Western television crime series like The *Midsummer Murders*, *Miss Marple*, *Hercule Poirot*, and *CSI*, he relished the thought of investigating a case that contained a mystery and a crime. He needed to think, and he concluded a walk would help clear his head. Normally, he would never think of strolling downtown in uniform. Attacks on policemen were rare but did happen.

The case of Yang Jia, who had attacked and killed six police officers in Shanghai over some trifling crime, was still fresh in every police officer's mind.

However, Fang Wei believed there was no ill will toward the police in FujinHaiZhou, and he felt safe.

"Sergeant, please take the car and return to the office. Write the report before you go home and put it on my desk tomorrow morning. It's late now and I don't need to return to the office. I will walk awhile and then take a taxi."

"Yes, sir." The sergeant saluted and then went off to find the car. Fang watched him go before walking down the steps and turning toward Serenity Lake.

Serenity Lake stretched about three kilometres across to the far shore. The shoreline nearest the town was busy. Families and couples ambled along, with many consuming different fast foods.

Under a cloudless sky, the evening was warm. Fang Wei sat on a bench, relaxed, looked up at the stars and then watched the Son et Lumiere, and cleared his mind of all thoughts.

As he watched, he thought he heard a commotion somewhere further up the park from where he sat but decided it was probably a noisy celebration of some sort. *Nothing for me to get involved in.* He lit another cigarette.

The waterworks display ended, and Fang Wei, along with several other members of the crowd, moved back toward the road and transportation home. A passing taxi observed his wave and, defying all other drivers and traffic rules, swerved across two lanes to pull up in front of him. Fang Wei got in, gave his address, and then sank back into the upholstery.

"There's no hurry, and I'm not on duty." He noted how the driver relaxed at his words. "And you may smoke if we both do."

The driver smiled, reached into the glove compartment, and pulled out a pack of Zhong Nan Hai. "Beijing cigarette, Captain? A previous passenger left them behind."

"I don't mind if I do, thank you." A respectful silence ensued while both men savoured the cigarettes, which were milder than most Chinese brands.

Fang Wei's cell phone buzzed. Wu Shi Ming was calling. "Yes?"

"I wanted to thank you for your cooperation this evening. The entertainment has ended, and I just wanted to know if there was anything you would like me to do now."

"No, there's nothing that can't wait till morning. I trust you had a more productive evening."

"Yes, we did, thank you."

Fang Wei understood the message and, while satisfied that he had made the right decision over Wu's duties. "Good! Please check with your sergeant tomorrow morning to make sure he has completed the paperwork. Have a good rest of the evening." He hung up as the driver stopped the car.

Fang Wei paid the fare and exited the cab but then turned back. "You know the government forbids you to smoke in taxi cabs?"

"Oh yes, Captain, I know it as you do."

Fang Wei, paused, looked at the driver for a moment, and then turned to the entrance to his apartment. *Tomorrow*, he thought, *is another day.*

23

Shuang Yang Ma, the English teacher at Number 4 Middle School, sat on a bench contentedly watching the lakeside activity. There was a joyful atmosphere as kids ran screaming under the watchful eyes of parents or grandparents, and some small children played football close by.

She saw a foreigner accompanied by a beautiful Chinese woman walk slowly along the shore before finding a bench and sitting, probably to watch the light and water display.

A toddler chased a ball, squealing with delight, the ball rolling over to stop at the foreigner's foot. Amused, Shuang observed the kid wanting the ball back but afraid to come too close to the *laowai*.

The foreigner bent forward to grab and return the ball when a man standing behind the *laowai's* bench fell forward and almost pushed the foreigner to the ground. *Curious! What happened? Is the man drunk? Has he collapsed, perhaps, from a heart attack?* Shuang got up and went over to see what had happened. Other park visitors also gathered around, curious.

The foreigner stood up, and Shuang heard him say something to the fallen man, who did not respond. The woman with him bent over the recumbent figure and shook him but got no response. Shining her cell phone light on him, she looked more closely, finally focusing on his back where there was a widening dark stain. She said something that Shuang could not hear. She moved closer, so she could listen.

"What?" the man asked, horrified. "What did you say? Shot? Who is he? Shot by whom? What the fuck is happening?"

"Doctor Holroyd! Distressing as this is, there is no need for profanity!" The woman protested in a pleading tone. "Please!" Her tone suggested she was requesting cooperation.

"Have you lost your mind? A man next to me gets shot, and you want me to stop swearing?"

"Yes, that would be most appropriate. But I do not think this is the time or place for further discussion. We should not stay and get involved with the police, who will only become suspicious that a foreigner was this close to a shooting."

"But shouldn't we go for help?"

"No, I'm sure others here have already made calls. Please, let us leave now."

The man, addressed as Doctor Holroyd, stared at her. "I could have been hit," he said in a mollified tone.

"Luckily, you bent forward, or else they could have hit you. But they did not."

"Why would anyone shoot this man?" Holroyd persisted.

"Perhaps they were not aiming at him."

"If that's so, who was the target? Me? You? Someone standing near us?"

Shuang became very attentive. *What are they talking about? Why would they think they were the target of a shooting? Who are these two people?* She heard and felt something whiz by.

A woman in the crowd cried out and sank to the ground clutching her leg, from which a dark stain was seeping toward her foot. Other bystanders moved back nervously, although one or two attended to the stricken woman.

Shuang turned to watch the foreigner and his companion and noted that the man had peed his pants. *Not surprising, but at least it's dark, and not too many people will notice the widening stain in his trousers.*

"Wendy," she heard him say in an urgent tone, "I think they are shooting at us. We should leave immediately."

"I agree." She reached for his arm but then looked at his head. "You're bleeding."

"What? Where?"

"At the back of your head. It doesn't look serious, so we can deal with that later, but now we have to run."

He reached up and touched the back of his head. "Oh, my! I've been hit!"

"Doctor Holroyd, we need to get to a safer place immediately."

The woman grabbed Holroyd by his jacket. "Come on, we have to go." As they left, Shuang heard people commenting on his presence and his appearance. She also saw the flashing lights of an approaching police car and left without waiting to report what she had seen and heard. *Best not to get involved with the police.*

*****

Once away from the scene, Holroyd stopped. "Wait, Wendy. We must wait and give an account to the police."

"Yes, Doctor Holroyd, that is what you would do in your country. But not here. Come!" Dragging Holroyd along, she pushed toward the park exit. They reached a small, shuttered stall away from the crowd, where Holroyd stopped to regain his breath and his composure.

"Let me look at your head." She opened her handbag, took out her cell phone, and switched on the light. "Yes, you have a cut there, and it's still bleeding. We should go to a hospital and have a doctor look at it, but meanwhile, let me try to staunch it with this." She pulled out a handkerchief and held it to the back of his head. "Hold still and hold this handkerchief in place!"

He obeyed but felt a rising sense of outrage. *This is getting past a joke. Given everything that has happened to me, someone now wants to shoot me. Why? Or is Wendy the target? If so, who in God's name is she?*

Holroyd's thoughts began to clear. "Who was that man who got shot? Or were we the target? For all I know, you could have been the target. I mean, there could be an overly jealous husband or a boyfriend after you. Or you could be a spy whom someone finds irritating."

As his emotions took hold, he thought *this was the woman who had entered my London flat, probably cleaned up a body, and coolly recommended against calling the police. Does she have an aversion to the police? Is there some secret that causes her to want to remain out of officialdom's sight?*

"For Christ's sake, woman! Every time you turn up, so does a body. You know, you're beginning to make me very nervous. Who are you?"

"Doctor Holroyd, if I displease you, I'm very sorry! But I think you are being fanciful and are giving me far too much credit. I assure you there is no jealous husband or boyfriend, and I'm not a spy. However, please let us return to the hotel, so I can look closely at your wound and dress it properly. We do not want to risk infection. But we may stop on the way and try to clean the rest of you. Even if no one sees you, the smell alone could draw attention."

With that, she took him by the arm toward the road, where they hailed a taxi. Once underway, Holroyd continued to feel pain, discomfort, embarrassment, and fear. To add to his discomfort, he thought the driver was unimpressed by the smell emanating from the back seat.

"Why are we not calling the police?" he asked. Wendy sat silently for a minute.

"This is China. A report to the police takes time, a lot of time, and we do not have time to waste. You are a foreigner, and that makes the police nervous. Why, they would ask, were you so near someone who got shot? Did you know the man or the woman? If they were not the targets, were you? If you were the target, why would someone want to shoot at you? What will you tell them?" She stopped to let Holroyd consider her question.

"You do not have an answer that might satisfy them. Even if you have a story, the police may not believe your version of events. I think if someone meant the bullets for you, and this was an attempt on your life, they could try again. If we were merely in the wrong place at the wrong time, then our hurried departure is of no consequence."

"If someone is taking potshots at me, I want to know why."

"I agree, but remaining there would not have provided an answer and may have gotten you harmed."

As they got out of the taxi outside the hotel, Holroyd thought he heard the squeal of brakes behind him, followed by a shout.

"What was that?" Temporarily forgetting his appearance and discomfort, he turned to look. Wendy grabbed his arm.

"Probably a traffic accident, but you're in no condition to go and look. Now, please come, and let's go to your room."

24

As Holroyd and Wendy approached the lift, a policeman stopped them and asked where they wanted to go. Wendy answered and then began raising her voice. The policeman shrugged and with an exasperated "*heng*" Wendy grasped Holroyd's arm and led him to the bar.

"There has been a reported incident on your floor, and no one can go up until the police have finished their investigation."

"What kind of incident?"

"Wait." Wendy listened to a conversation the bartender was having. "Oh! It seems someone was killed in one of the rooms near yours."

"What? Killed?" Holroyd suddenly began to panic. *Another body turns up near me?*

"It doesn't seem to have anything to do with you. It may have been a sex meeting that went wrong." Holroyd looked at her, at a loss for words.

He started to say something but then stopped, thinking how what he wanted to say might sound. *I've almost been kidnapped twice, I've come across two corpses, and two people have been shot standing near me, and you think this incident has nothing to do with me? I don't believe that.* He paused *I don't think even the author of the worst trashy thriller would dare to write this up.*

Just then Holroyd noticed policemen exiting the lift and, after a few comments to a staff member hovering nearby, allowing people to enter. Holroyd stood up and headed toward the lift.

"Let's go upstairs," he said. "I've had enough of all this."

Once out of the lift, Holroyd could see no evidence of a police visit to his floor. He entered his room where he discarded his soiled clothing and put it in a plastic laundry bag for cleaning. Wendy washed the wound and, from somewhere, produced an antiseptic lotion that stung like hell when she applied it.

"Well, the bleeding has stopped, it's not a deep wound, and now I have cleaned it, we need to protect it." She produced a dressing that she carefully applied to his scalp. He knew when the time came to remove it, he would also remove several hairs.

"You know, this is getting very, very worrisome," Holroyd said.

"What do you mean?"

"If someone at the park meant those shots for me, then that's the third time someone has taken a shot at me. I don't relish being the target for a bunch of trigger-happy snipers. And now a report of another murder close by. I'm getting worried."

"What do you mean, the third time?"

Holroyd told her about the attempts on the island.

"Oh, my goodness. I can see how you must be terribly upset. I did not know. But I think you may be overreacting. You have no proof anyone is trying to kill you."

Holroyd looked at her in amazement. *Three attempts aren't enough to prove someone is out to kill me?* "I am most certainly not overreacting. How do we know that this murder next door wasn't aimed at me?"

"I really can't see how it could have anything to do with you. We don't know who the victim was or if you even knew him. But I will ask the staff to see if they will tell me anything. Now, please lie down, and get some rest. Do you need any sleeping medicine?"

"No, thank you."

"Goodnight then." With that Wendy turned off the light and exited.

After she left the room, he lay in bed going over the events of the past few days. He felt very unsure of himself. What is happening to me? *My predictable life has suddenly become unforeseeable in ways with which I'm not sure I can cope. I'm in the middle of a provincial Chinese city, tripping over bodies, the subject of repeated attacks on my life, and there is no end in sight. Am I the target, or do I attract murderers like jam attracts wasps?*

To whom can I turn for advice or help? The police back on the island? I can see the faces of the island police and hear their sympathy. "Did you say you are in danger, sir? From whom? Now, why would anyone be interested in harming you, sir? Oh! In London also, sir, yes, I see. And then again in China, sir? Little out of our jurisdiction, London and China are. We can let them know, sir, but otherwise, there's little we can do, barring more information."

The Metropolitan Police? I can hear the inspector saying, "A body, you said, sir? In your flat, was it? Murdered, sir? And you didn't report it? And then you flew off to Asia, did you? Now, why would that be, sir? And you say there were attacks on you on this island and in China? Now, why would so many people try to harm you? Perhaps there's something that you're not telling us, and I can't help wondering why."

The Chinese police? I can imagine meeting a friendly or perhaps not-so-friendly officer looking at me and saying something like, "Protection from assassins? What makes you think you are of interest to any assassin? Oh? Someone took shots at you last night, did they? Reported it, did you? Oh? You didn't? Now, why was that?" But then I would need Wendy to communicate with the police, and she is against it.

But why was she so reluctant to go to the police? Nothing I know of her suggests any previous contact with the police that could cause her to be so disinclined.

Perhaps it's just a general desire to avoid any police involvement regardless of the need, a trait many Chinese display. I suppose I can't really hold that against her. But it's strange because she grew up in England where there's little antipathy toward the police.

What about Merry? I can almost hear his reaction. "I say, that sounds very dangerous. Are you sure you feel comfortable?" *Comfortable? Oh! Although expressing concern, Merry would expect me to carry on but unlikely be able to do much to stop another and possibly successful attempt on my life. I wonder how much help Merry could or would be.*

How about Mr. Xiang? Where could I find him, and what could he do? He had warned me that the project could be dangerous, although he had not been specific. Would it be reasonable for me to ask for help? If I were in his shoes, he would want to distance himself from any unpleasantness.

Going mentally over his list of friends and family, he realized he had become a lonely if not isolated individual, and there was no one he felt he could confide in or look to for comfort. In the dark and silence of the room, he shivered under the bedclothes like an abandoned child afraid of the night.

Clearly, he had been wrong not to be more assertive. *I should have followed my instincts about the body in my flat. I should have linked the events under the rubric of some game of which I am not aware, and I should have made further inquiries about Xiang and Wendy before carrying on as if this was a normal academic research project.*

Then he felt a surge of resolve and defiance. *I won't meekly allow events to dictate my every move any longer. I will see this matter through, come what may. I have allowed myself to be lulled into a false sense of security, confident that events were influencing but not controlling me.*

Two Aspirins later, he reflected that nothing in his life had quite prepared him for this, and he fell asleep hoping the next few days would be less interesting.

25

The next day Fang Wei read a report of a shooting at the lake. Looking over the report, he wondered if the commotion he had heard was tied to the event. *A foreigner accompanied by a Chinese woman was seen at the site and may have been wounded but left before either could be interviewed. Tian ba! One more headache to deal with.*

*****

Holroyd woke and found his wound was no longer throbbing painfully.

Pearl called to say the library researchers were still compiling the documents he had asked for, and they should be ready in a day or two. However, Director Ding had invited them to dinner the day after tomorrow. That meant there was little point in going to the library now.

Holroyd wondered about this strange Doctor Nicholson. How could he go about tracing an individual foreign visitor? What reason could he give for trying to contact this man? If he were a relative or friend, people would have expected that he could have made contact by cell phone or email. *As far as I know, there is no law forbidding anyone from presenting themselves as someone else unless by doing so, they received benefits that they otherwise didn't deserve. That Doctor Nicholson has obtained a book is not necessarily a crime unless he does not return it. And it's too soon to see whether he will return it.*

Frustrated, Holroyd decided to follow up on the missing document. Beyond a faint hope and a gut instinct, there was no reason to think the document would help further his search, but he could think of no alternative.

He was saved from further thoughts when his phone rang. To his surprise, Pearl called to tell him the student who had brought the document that was missing, had come from a small village called Wang Tang Cun situated some 150 kilometres from FujinHaiZhou.

Holroyd became excited because there was a chance the clue was linked to an email he had received from his Taiwanese colleague so long ago. He decided he should talk to the person or persons who had come into possession of what he hoped could prove to be a vital piece of evidence.

He phoned Wendy to make the arrangements. "I want to follow up on the researcher or the student who delivered the document to the library."

"But Doctor Holroyd, how did you discover where we should go?"

"Pearl called."

"Why would she do that? I thought she didn't know how much information she could give us. Do you trust her?"

"Yes, I think I do. And I suspect she needed time to find the records of that document, which would explain her initial reply."

"What did she tell you?" Holroyd gave the information, and Wendy agreed to make the necessary arrangements.

His thoughts were interrupted when Wendy called to say arrangements had been made and she would meet him in the lobby.

As they exited the lobby, Holroyd noticed police and a group of people arguing by the side of the road opposite the hotel entrance. "What's that all about?" he asked.

"I'm sure it's nothing to concern us."

"Isn't that where the traffic accident occurred last night?"

"Possibly, but please, let's not involve ourselves in matters that do not concern us."

"No, no. Please go over and find out what that's about."

Grimacing in frustration, Wendy crossed the road, chatted with a few bystanders, and then came back. "The son of a prominent local businessman ran down a foreigner. It seems the man was seriously injured."

"That's awful. But why are so many people upset? I mean, such things happen."

"Yes, but this particular businessman, called Xun Fan Ting, is very prominent and has friends in high places."

"It happens. Even in England, where the Queen's husband was involved in a traffic accident."

"Yes, but here the local police are known to protect such prominent individuals, and people are getting fed up."

"I see. Thanks for finding that out. As you say, looks as if it's nothing to concern us. Okay, off we go then."

When they arrived at the station, near Wang Tang Cun, he looked down from the train, searching for the non-existent platform. Instead, descent required a risky three-foot leap onto the rocky rail bed.

He hesitated, envisioning a sprained ankle and the following pain and inconvenience. When Wendy leapt nimbly to the ground, he followed as best he could. Once on the ground, he looked around.

The scene reminded him of *Doctor Zhivago* wherein the hero flees the city and arrives at a desolate country station. Unlike in the film, there was no old family retainer with a horse and coach to welcome them.

When the train had cleared the station, he saw a taxi on the other side of the tracks, and he wondered whether the driver met every train in the hope of passengers or if Wendy had arranged the meeting. At that point, he did not care. He was happy to see any kind of transportation even though, upon closer inspection, it turned out to be an *xiali* long past its best-before date.

The *xiali* (Chinese for "charade") was a tiny car, underpowered and shoddily built, that served Beijing as the standard taxi for several years. On being retired, the cars were handed down from municipality to municipality until they found a last working place in the Chinese equivalent of the boondocks.

It could fit either three passengers or one passenger and two suitcases. When the cars were built, the average Chinese was tiny by Western standards, and seeing as no one changed the design of the cars, they were always a tight squeeze for foreigners.

Once inside the car, Holroyd found the seat had surrendered any pretense of comfort, and he could hear the snap of electricity across the car battery. The windshield was in decent shape, but one side mirror was missing, and the other had only one-half of the glass remaining. Dangling Red Chinese knots obscured the rear-view mirror unless a sudden lurch caused the ornaments to gyrate wildly.

The road initially was of a standard macadamized sort. Still, it soon changed into little more than a dirt track that led through mountains along the side of overhanging clay cliffs with mournful vegetation clinging precariously to the soil for survival. Precipitous and seemingly bottomless drops bordered the other side.

Along the way, the road often narrowed to the width of a single car at points that always seemed to coincide with blind corners. Less than a foot separated the wheels from the edge of the precipice.

Holroyd suffered from vertigo and did not dare to look anywhere but straight ahead or up at the sky.

The driver seemed unconcerned and continued chatting volubly, never slowing down, while Wendy smiled and preserved her dignified silence. Later, Holroyd wondered whether the smile was one of enjoyment or a death's head rictus.

There was little traffic, but trucks or cars came in the opposite direction, and always, it seemed, when the road was wide enough for only one vehicle.

When this happened, one vehicle would stop and allow the other to inch past. On one such occasion, Holroyd noticed a motorcycle had stopped behind them.

The rider was riding a brightly coloured Kawasaki and wearing a leather suit with a helmet that obscured his face. A girl was riding pillion behind him, probably oblivious to the surroundings because she was texting or playing a computer game on her cell phone. Holroyd briefly wondered about cell phone coverage there.

The motorcyclist continued to follow them and never attempted to pass until they had almost reached Wang Tang Cun, where he put on a burst of speed and disappeared ahead.

Once they arrived, their driver obligingly opened the door for them. Holroyd only then noticed he wore a jacket emblazoned with a Pirelli Racing Team badge.

Their arrival caused excitement. Villagers came out of their homes to look at the *laowai*, and he realized that for many of them, this was the first time they had seen a Westerner.

His appearance fascinated the children, who didn't seem to know whether they wanted to come closer to greet the strangers or run away and hide.

Wendy consulted one local who, after a lengthy conversation, turned and walked toward a house, motioning for Wendy and Holroyd to follow.

The house they approached did not differ in appearance from its neighbours, and there was no one at the door to welcome them. They knocked and then entered.

It was a one-room house. The beaten earthen floor was bare. A platform, called a *kang,* was covered with folded quilts and served as a bed and a couch. The family slept together on this platform, sharing quilts and bodily warmth. It also served as an oven, which heated the bed and the room and a part of the top surface was used for cooking.

A small table stood against a faded green wall that was bare except for a picture of Chairman Mao and an advertising calendar. Two rickety chairs, one on each side of the table, completed the furniture.

Battered cooking and eating utensils cluttered shelving built against the third wall. Corn cobs, garlic, and what looked like onions hung from hooks in the ceiling. A bowl containing four brown eggs, some slightly wilted green Chinese cabbages, and half a bag of rice stood near one corner of the *kang.*

A kettle was heating on the *kang.* Spread across the table was a jar containing tea, two tin cups, a chipped porcelain mug with red-and-gold lettering, and biscuits arranged on a cracked plate. The house smelled of cooking mixed with the odour of old age. Holroyd wrinkled his nose in distaste while noting poverty yet without misery.

An old man and an old woman were sitting on the chairs. The woman, who Holroyd presumed was the old man's wife, wore a red head scarf patterned with flowers, a ragged brown padded jacket, and padded light-green pants. On her feet, she wore tattered slippers and what looked like mismatched cotton socks. Her face, seamed with wrinkles, showed she was used to worries, but she smiled a toothless welcome.

The man was wearing an old fur-lined Mongolian-style army hat with earflaps. He wore a grey-blue Mao-style 'five-pockets jacket' over army fatigue pants and woven straw peasant sandals that had already served many years. His face also bore witness to many years of toil and suffering. He had cataracts, and his teeth were rotten and tobacco-stained.

The old woman said something Holroyd did not understand, smiled, and offered them tea and biscuits. The old man appeared oblivious to his surroundings but responded when the old woman spoke loudly and sharply to him.

Wendy explained who they were and why they had come. The old man listened uncomprehendingly. The old woman, however, rocked back and forth in her chair.

Wendy asked a question that neither of the couple answered, at which point the old woman began crying. Suddenly, she screamed at the old man. Wendy said something sternly, and for a moment, there was silence. Then the old woman started to speak again, though not so loud.

"It seems we have come to the right place," Wendy whispered to Holroyd. "The old woman is yelling at her husband for not following her advice and so committing a crime. It seems the old man engaged in tomb robbing."

They waited for the tirade to subside. The old man grumbled something that set the old woman off again.

"She warned him that selling the artifacts instead of reporting them would lead to trouble," Wendy translated. "Now we have come here, and your presence as a foreigner means the authorities will also come, and she thinks they will go to prison." The old woman stopped her verbal assault and moaned, wiping her eyes on the sleeve of her jacket.

"Now she is asking what will happen to their children if they end up in prison."

Holroyd looked around for some evidence of children but saw none. "What children?"

Wendy gave him a stony look.

"Ah, wait a moment." He reached into his pocket, pulled out his wallet, and extricated five one hundred-yuan notes. When the old woman saw the red notes, she stopped, wiped her eyes again, stared at the money, and then looked at them expectantly.

"Tell her," Holroyd said, "that we understand the temptations that can come when one is living poorly, and we have no desire to worsen conditions. Instead, we would like to pay for information."

"Put that money away, Dr. Holroyd." Wendy looked at him aghast. "Offering money is illegal, and to do so openly is disrespectful. Give it to me."

Wendy turned her back to the old woman and reached into her purse, withdrawing another red envelope. Taking the money from him, she slid the notes into the envelope and returned to face the room again.

She spoke to the old woman, who replied almost uninterruptedly and occasionally looked to the old man for support. After she stopped, Wendy addressed her sternly, whereupon the old woman yelled at the old man. She only stopped when Wendy spoke again more conciliatory and offered the red envelope. The old woman nodded and accepted the proffered gift with a smile.

"Let's go." Wendy turned to Holroyd and led the way out, but a buxom woman wearing a Mongolian-style fur hat with a red star and an army green jacket with a broad red armband with yellow lettering blocked their exit. She looked angry and spoke to them in a tone that Holroyd would have classed as hectoring.

Wendy engaged her in conversation, producing various documents, including his passport, which the woman scrutinized.

"Who is this woman?" Holroyd asked.

"Please, Doctor Holroyd, don't interrupt. She is the village leader and local party secretary. She wants to know who we are and why we are here."

Wendy walked outside with the woman, and he heard the conversation getting loud. A man's voice interrupted, and matters became quiet.

By craning his neck, Holroyd could see out the door to where Wendy was talking to the officious woman, but a man dressed as a motorcyclist had joined them. Holroyd wasn't certain but thought the same man had passed them on the way up. Their conversation lasted a few minutes before Wendy returned.

"Let's go, Doctor Holroyd," she said.

"What was that all about?"

"Oh, nothing serious. I needed to explain who you are and the purpose of our mission."

"You told her *everything*?"

"Not quite everything. Some things are better left unsaid, and she need not know everything."

"And who was the man?"

"A village member who wanted to know what the fuss was about."

"He was dressed for a motorcycle ride."

"Yes, he was. Shall we go?" Wendy smiled and led the way back to the waiting car. As they moved to the car, several villagers gathered to watch them go. Holroyd heard comments and, from their tone, deduced they were not friendly.

"What's got into them?" he asked Wendy.

"Never mind," Wendy answered, "We should leave." She held the door open for him. "Please get in. We have a long way to go."

On the way, Wendy summarized what the old woman had told her. The old woman admitted that the old man was part of a group of villagers who had discovered an ancient tomb nearby.

The tomb belonged to an official from a place called Haicheng, but she did not know where that place might be. They determined the place from the inscriptions on some bronze bowls.

The villagers had sold the contents to dealers rather than reporting the artifacts to authorities. Among the findings had been documents that were of no interest to them. They had used a few documents as fuel for household ovens until a young villager noticed that they may have value.

The old woman only remembered one, a *jiandu* tied with a ribbon that might have been red. She remembered it because she had never seen one before. Inside the *jiandu,* she had seen what looked like a paper slip or note.

A young man or woman (the old woman could not remember who) had taken some of the documents, which, when last heard of, she had handed over to a library or museum in a nearby town. The town may have been FujinHaiZhou, or perhaps it was another town.

Wendy asked for a description of the documents given to a library. There, the old woman had paused, and Wendy had the impression she wanted another red envelope, which was not forthcoming.

"Strange, because *jiandus* were expensive and labour intensive. Printing on paper was much more usual, so preparing the bamboo sticks, writing on them, and binding them together would mean the author had a special reason for doing so. Perhaps it was his hobby, or maybe the contents were of special significance. I wonder what happened to it, and I'm curious about this paper inside the *jiandu*. That seems out of place." She stopped and looked at Holroyd.

"Do you think," Wendy asked, "this paper or the book has anything to do with our search?"

"Well, she said they gave it to one of the village children who worked in a library. I suppose FujinHaiZhou is the nearest and, therefore, most likely." He paused. "We don't know the date of the tomb or what the book or the paper was about, nor anything about the author. I think we have little to go on at this stage."

"There's a Haicheng in Liaoning Province where I remember correct predictions and timely evacuations saved many lives during an earthquake. But what is the connection with this part of China? That's very far from here."

"You said Haicheng?" Holroyd could hardly hide his excitement.

"Yes."

"There is another Haicheng that was near here but later became part of Longhai in the Ming times.

This Haicheng was the port for Zhangzhou, where Zhang Xie came from. So, there's a possibility that the tomb belonged to some official attached to the port. If that's the case, then maybe, just maybe, this book or the paper will have records of activity in the port. If such records exist, they might help our search. We need to see what's in there." He sat back and let his mind wander.

A connection with my quest seems possible, but only if the documents have a report of people that might have set out and gone to Dejection Island, or whatever they called it then.

"But if this official was from the Haicheng you mentioned, why is his tomb here? Surely, he would have been buried there. This village is quite far from the coast," he asked.

"Not necessarily if he came from here. People from all walks of life could rise high through the imperial examination system. So, it's possible he got his position by academic achievement. Once he died, his body would have been returned here, so he would be with his ancestors." Wendy explained.

Another thought struck him. "Did the old woman say anything about the other artifacts the tomb robbers found?"

"No."

"Tomb robbing has become sophisticated," Holroyd said. "There are even classes advertised on the Internet on how to go about it. But it's not that simple. Think about it: a farmer is digging in his fields and stumbles on a tomb. Alone or with others, he opens it and discovers a coffin and some artifacts.

"Now, he knows from reports that the tomb's contents could have value, but he also knows not reporting the find and keeping the contents are criminal offences. China only recently removed the death penalty for tomb-robbing and selling cultural artifacts.

"What will he do? He can't just go onto eBay and offer his trove for sale. The authorities would notice. So, somehow, he must find someone who will buy his treasures and keep the whole thing secret. How to find such a person? Particularly how to make contact if this is the first time our farmer has found and robbed a tomb.

"Does he have a friend in the business? That may be so; tomb robbing has been a pastime for so long that informal networks are common. But if our man is not part of a network or has no friend to whom he can turn, how does he make contact? I saw no computers or cell phones during our visit, so how do our tomb robbers get their wares to the market?"

"Maybe it went the other way."

"What do you mean?"

"Our man," Wendy said, "comes home and shows one or more objects—a bronze bowl or a weapon. Everyone gathers around to admire the find and discuss its value. Then they raise the question of how to enjoy their discovery. Someone says he is going to town and can take the find to a friend or acquaintance who can help. Not everyone will think it's a good idea, but there may be no alternative, so that's what they do. But he takes only one object.

"In town, he goes to his friend. Now, if the friend is honest, he will advise going to the authorities. In that case, the search for a suitable contact will continue. Once the finder stumbles upon a contact who will buy the artifact and keep the secret, the search ends, and they have set up the pipeline from the finder to the buyer. They will use this pipeline for the remaining artifacts.

"If the authorities get wind of the matter, they will either push criminal charges—which the locals will meet with denials and feigned innocence—or they will join in on the activity and offer to act as middlemen. It's not unusual in China to find corruption." She stopped and looked at Holroyd to see what he thought of this.

"Sounds reasonable. In our case, we have one possible link. We know that the documents, or maybe just one document, went from the village to a library, probably in a nearby town. We also know the library in FujinHaiZhou got a document from a student researcher from Wang Tang Cun.:" He stopped to think and then continued.

"We can reasonably assume we are talking about the same document. That being so, maybe the library or someone in the library is the conduit for the stolen artifacts."

He sat back and thought. Suddenly, he realized they were not alone and, looking out the car's rear window, he saw the same motorcyclist they had met on the way into the village. This time, as before, the motorcyclist did not pass but was tailgating. Holroyd nudged Wendy.

"What do you think that rider is up to? Why not overtake us?"

"What makes you curious?" She looked back, "Motorbikes are common, and he may just be hanging back until it is safe to pass."

"He had several opportunities to pass. So, why hasn't he done so?"

"Perhaps he's not in a hurry or is being cautious on this road."

"Yes, but the same guy followed us on the way up. Maybe the same man you met in the village."

"I'm not sure it's the same man. Even if it is, I still don't see the problem. He is without a passenger now, so perhaps he dropped her off, and now, like us, he is returning. It's not that unusual."

Holroyd nodded and settled back, looking out the side window.

They had reached one of those narrow sections with a precipitous cliff on both sides, one a solid rock wall, the other a long drop to the river below.

As Holroyd looked at the scenery, his attention shifted when he noticed the motorcyclist speed up and squeeze past, only to brake suddenly in front of them. Their driver jammed on the brakes, and the car lurched and began to slide.

Holroyd had a kaleidoscopic view of the adjacent cliffs, the long drop into the void, the back of the driver's head, the Chinese knot wildly gyrating in the windscreen, and a vision of a mangled wreck with dismembered and bloodied bodies at the bottom of the valley. His heartbeat took off and, grabbing the nearest solid object, which happened to be Wendy, he felt a rush of adrenaline.

The driver swore loudly and, turning the wheel away from the abyss, accelerated to regain control. The car slowed its slide and regained traction before reaching the road's edge. The motorcyclist sped off around the next corner.

Holroyd's heart began to slow, and he relaxed his grip on Wendy. For a few seconds, there was silence before they resumed their journey with the driver and Wendy talking animatedly. Holroyd understood little of the exchange, but he gathered that they agreed on several uncomplimentary descriptions of the motorcyclist's behaviour and probably his parentage.

"That does not fit someone being cautious! Wendy, that fellow meant to do us harm or at least scare us."

"I admit his action was dangerous. But to say he intended to harm us is unreasonable. He may be uncomfortable that a foreigner came to the village asking about the sale of ancient artifacts and wants to warn us to stay away."

"It's possible," Holroyd conceded. "But I think we had better be on our guard if he tries again." Wendy nodded and spoke to the driver, who laughed but nodded.

A mile or so later, as they came around another corner, the motorcyclist suddenly appeared behind a rock and sped directly toward them. A collision seemed inevitable, and Wendy screamed.

Unlike the previous encounter, the motorcyclist intended for them to slide over the cliff. Their driver swore viciously and jammed on the brakes, sliding the car dangerously toward the abyss below.

Holroyd felt a renewed rush of adrenaline and paralyzing fear. He was thrown against the car door in the direction of the abyss with enough force that he bruised his arm, and the thought flashed through his mind that the force of the impact would send the car hurtling into the void. He may have screamed. For what seemed like an eternity, the car approached the edge.

Luckily for them but not for himself, the motorcyclist misjudged his trajectory and plunged over the cliff, glancing off the car's front fender. If the motorcyclist screamed, nobody heard it.

The car slid before mercifully halting with one front wheel half over the edge. The driver tried to reverse back to safety, but the car spun its back wheels and lurched nearer the void. He stopped trying. No one moved.

Holroyd watched as the driver gingerly opened his window and, on looking down, shook his head before carefully moving over to get out of the car. The car shifted slightly, and Holroyd took a deep breath to steady himself.

"Wendy! Get out but move very gently."

Shaken, Wendy slowly opened her door and stepped out. As she exited, the car shifted as the weight distribution inside changed. Holroyd realized his situation was getting worse, and he moved as quickly as possible, hoping to get out before the car plunged over the edge.

Finally, they were all standing on firm ground. Holroyd wiped his brow. "Thank goodness we're safe."

The cliff's edge under the front wheel slowly crumbled as they surveyed the situation. Holroyd moved back quickly to the other side of the road but was almost run over by a truck coming in the opposite direction. The truck stopped, and the driver came over to look. After some discussion, he towed the car back into the middle of the road. Holroyd thought that such events were common on that road.

While all this was going on, Wendy and Holroyd sat on the side of the road. Holroyd looked at Wendy, hugging her knees and staring into the distance.

"Wendy, how are you feeling? Are you alright?" Wendy showed no signs of having heard. "Wendy!" This time she started and looked at him.

"We could have been killed! No one told me that working for you could get me killed!" She started to cry. "What was that motorcyclist trying to do?" she wailed. "If he was just trying to warn us, he would not have acted as he did. But it seemed as if he was trying to push us off the road.”

Her voice trembled. Holroyd hugged her to comfort her and tried to assume a soothing tone, even though he, too, was frightened.

“But why would he want to do that?”

“Perhaps someone worries that we have discovered too much about the tomb-robbing activities.”

“But we don’t know anything more than it takes place at the village and that an item was taken away,” Holroyd protested. Wendy stopped crying and composed herself.

“Perhaps that item is of more significance than we know, or perhaps there is more than just tomb robbing here. In any case, someone seems to want to stop us.”

“Who?”

“Perhaps a seller or a buyer. I don’t know.”

“But the only person who might have known we were coming here was Pearl. Would she have told anyone else?”

“Perhaps she told her boss, Ding Qu Wan.”

"If you're correct, what can we do?"

"What can we do?" she repeated. "I don't know. I'm a research assistant engaged to help you, not a detective." Wendy shrugged and started to cry again. Holroyd let her weep until she finally settled down.

"We don't know the rider, and if we report this matter, the police will assume it was an accident. Happens all the time in China. If it's bigger than just the villagers trying to warn us off, we don't know enough to do anything yet."

"But he was trying to drive us off the road," Holroyd protested.

"Possibly, but even if he was, he failed, didn't he? I agree it is worrying that this may or may not have been an attempt on our lives, but I think it was probably an accident." Wendy was recovering her composure.

"Come off it, Wendy! What if next time whoever tries succeeds? What then?"

"I don't think we need to worry."

"What?" He was astounded.

"Doctor Holroyd, I doubt very much that anyone will make another attempt before we get back to FujinHaiZhou. Whoever might have arranged this will wait to hear of the outcome of this attempt before trying again.”

“I don’t like that I have become a sitting duck,” he said, his fury rising.

“Doctor Holroyd, you in no way look like a duck. You don’t have any feathers on your head, and I doubt you have webbed feet.” Wendy giggled, although she was beginning to sound a bit like an exasperated parent dealing with a fractious child.

Holroyd looked at her with concern, wondering if she was close to hysteria after their narrow escape. Wendy seemed to recover, though. “But perhaps we should take precautions to improve our safety in case assassins are after you around every corner,” she said.

It was hard to disagree with her, but her attitude surprised him, and Holroyd was frustrated at having to react rather than take control of events. Wendy was there to help, but again he wondered how far she could go.

The rest of the return journey was uneventful. They were even lucky because they had only an hour to wait for a train. Once it arrived in FujinHaiZhou, they hailed a taxi to take them to the hotel. As they got into the taxi, Holroyd had a thought.

"Why don't we stop by and see if the librarian is there? I'm sure he will welcome a visit."

"That is not a good idea, Dr. Holroyd. Please let me arrange it for you."

"No, no. This won't take long."

In the library, they found the location of the director's office on the notice board and went over to the bank of lifts. When they arrived outside his office, Holroyd knocked and entered without waiting for a reply.

Director Ding was at his desk, typing on his computer. He looked up from the monitor with a mixture of irritation and curiosity, quickly changing to a more noncommittal look as he recognized them.

"Doctor Holroyd. Please, come in." *A fatuous comment*, Holroyd thought, *given we're already halfway across the floor.*

"How may I help?"

"We wondered," Holroyd began, "about a document that the library received from a small village in the region."

"We receive many documents here, as you can well imagine." Ding pushed back from the computer and put his hands on the desk. "Can you be more precise?"

"I was told that the document in question belonged to a Ming Dynasty official who lived in Haicheng."

"Haicheng? I'm sorry, but what or where is Haicheng?"

"Haicheng is the city where Zhang Xie wrote his Dong Xi Yang Kao. The city is now part of Longhai."

"Ah, yes. Now I remember. And you say you discovered a Ming Dynasty document?"

"No. I said we discovered its existence."

"I see. And this document found its way here? To this library?"

"We believe so."

"Oh! So, you are uncertain?"

"Well, no. What we know is that its finders gave the document to a library. We also know this library received a document from the same source. Given the proximity of this library to the village where the document came from, we thought it likely that the document arrived here. But, as you have remarked, we are not certain."

"I see. Well, it is possible! So, let us accept that this Ming Dynasty document arrived in our collection, but unless you can tell me how access to it helps or even concerns you, I'm not sure I can authorise your access to it."

"The document was written by a Ming Dynasty official in Haicheng near Zhangzhou, which was an important port at that time. We don't know whether the official concerned himself with port activities, but if so, we believe the official's responsibilities might have demanded he keep records of his activities. If the document we are discussing recorded port activities, it might help me enormously in furthering my research. So, we need to examine the document."

Ding nodded.

"We need to know where it is now."

"Yes, I can see your interest." Ding nodded again and turned back to his computer. "Please wait a moment." His fingers danced over the console, after which he waited a moment.

"Oh! Yes, we received the document to which you refer. But someone destroyed it in the excesses of the Cultural Revolution. Those maniacs destroyed many of our documents."

"Is there a record of the document's contents?"

Ding typed on his keyboard again. "I can see they found the document near or in a village called Wang Tang Cun." Wendy and Holroyd looked at each other and smiled. "I see that one of our researchers gave an initial inspection and labelled it as a document which needed a record of the author and provenance. The entry notes that the contents appear to be records of some port revenues. That is all because I scheduled it for further inspection. There is no further mention of its contents."

"Oh," Holroyd said. "That is too bad. My principals will be very disappointed. They were ready to pay handsomely for the document. We cannot be sure that this document was the one we were looking for, but had it been so, and if it were still available, it would be worth a lot of money. Even a photograph or a scanned version of the document."

"How unfortunate," Ding said. "I regret that I have no further information."

"Is the researcher who inspected the document available?"

"Alas, no. He is among so many of his colleagues who disappeared during the Revolution."

"Disappeared?"

"Passed over."

"He's dead," Wendy whispered.

"Oh, that is unfortunate. I'm sure you must miss those people and their expertise."

"A very grave loss."

"Do you think there might be anyone who would know of him? Someone with whom he may have talked or discussed his work and mentioned this document?"

"I would very much doubt it. People are reluctant to talk about those terrible times or about family members or other people they may have known who disappeared. Perhaps one day people will discuss these events more fully."

"Yes, one can only hope. It seems, however, that I have come to a dead end."

"I'm sorry I could not help in this matter. However, I look forward to our dinner tomorrow." With that, he rose and extended his hand for Holroyd to shake, ending the meeting.

"Wendy, do we know when exactly the villagers got the document and when they delivered it to the library?" Holroyd asked after leaving Ding's office.

"Oh! I didn't ask."

"Pity. It would be useful to know."

"Yes, Doctor Holroyd, I will try to get an answer as quickly as I can."

Holroyd nodded, before continuing. "You know, I didn't like Ding's attitude. With all those disappearances, I wonder how he survived."

"I agree, Doctor Holroyd. We need to help him overcome his reluctance. But I need to think more about how to do that."

26

Holroyd and Wendy duly arrived at the restaurant for the dinner with Director Ding and were greeted by Pearl, who led them to a small room with just one table.

Ding was already there and clearly had not waited for them before he had started to drink, but he welcomed them warmly. "It is a great honour, Doctor Holroyd, for us to welcome you here. We rarely have the chance to welcome foreign researchers. I'm very pleased you could join me. Please take a seat."

They sat down and, after a few minutes, servers placed several delicacies before them. As the meal progressed, Director Ding spoke up. "The subject of your research is fascinating."

Holroyd waited to see where he was heading, but Ding had stopped to take another drink. He put down his glass and looked at Holroyd. "It rather surprised me that it would involve the British government. I asked myself, what could be of such importance that your embassy in Beijing would ask for cooperation?"

So that was the party that intervened in the process of getting my visa.

"I received a copy of that request, and that is also unusual," Ding continued. "Then, I thought the

British government is not interested in ancient Chinese documents but is instead interested in the person interested in ancient Chinese documents. So, Doctor Holroyd, who are you?"

"Oh no, no. I'm just a professor at a lesser university. I'm no one in particular."

"But if it is not you that concerns the embassy, then their concern must be about your mission, the reason for your visit."

That's getting near the bone Holroyd recognized, *but good luck in finding that out from me. But I'm curious that Ding received a copy of the embassy's request. Before Wendy told me of the visit to the library, the library had not been the first place I had intended to visit, and yet Ding is saying he was aware of my intended visit presumably before I had arrived in China. How did that happen?*

Holroyd felt he had been manipulated somehow, but why and by whom? He decided it would be better not to raise the question but to play along as if he had planned the visit from the start.

"Director Ding, I think you may have misread the intentions of our embassy. Knowing my plans included research here in your distinguished library, they sent their letter out of respect for yourself as an eminent scholar." *I can only hope that no one will count this flattery against me on the Day of Judgement.*

A peacock in full display would not have looked prouder than Director Ding at that instant. Out of the corner of his eye, Holroyd saw that his comment puzzled Pearl while Wendy looked at him in astonishment.

Holroyd wondered if Wendy had known about the library right from the beginning of the project. If so, was she or Xiang behind the embassy's request? What other surprises might there be? His train of thought was interrupted by Ding's call for another toast.

It was getting warm in the room, and both he and Ding had removed their jackets. Ding had also loosened his tie and rolled up his shirtsleeves. A sheen appeared on Ding's forehead, and Holroyd thought his eyes were losing their focus. His voice had become louder, and he was speaking with animation. If Ding was not yet drunk, he soon would be.

"You know, Doctor Holroyd, China has much to teach the West. And yet, so many Westerners come to China and try to teach us as if we are children. But the West now understands that China is more developed than they realize and has much to contribute. Take yourself and Doctor Nicholson, for example. Are you not proof of that recognition?"

"I suppose so. But now you mention Doctor Nicholson, we cannot find him or any sign he was ever here."

"Oh? Well, I'm sure he will turn up." Ding poured himself another glass and then launched into a lecture about China's cultural heritage.

"But here you both are, eager to examine or maybe even obtain ancient objects that have lain beneath the ground for hundreds of years, and I find that curious. What relevance, I ask myself, could such objects have today? Why leave them hidden underground? And perhaps more relevant, what value do these objects have to the original owners? The answer to both questions is surely none. So, why leave them where they were placed?"

Holroyd suddenly became very attentive. *Where is Ding going with this*? Ding paused to take another swallow and then to call for more refreshments.

"What need do these mouldering corpses have of jewellery, porcelain, and other valuables? Can they still read the books of poetry? Do they still need the silk gowns, the golden brooches, and the glass vessels to store long-lost wines? On the other hand, such objects have value today because people are eager to possess them. Why not help them fulfill such desires?"

"Ding Qu, what are you saying? Should we desecrate tombs and sell the contents to whoever might want to buy them?"

"Desecrate, Doctor Holroyd? That suggests they are sacred." He paused and took another healthy swig of liquor.

"Sacred? That is a superstition fit for illiterate peasants, but you and I, Doctor Holroyd, are above such obsolete ideas. Why would a rotting corpse be sacred? Oh! Yes, the ancient Chinese believed that, after death, individuals joined their ancestors and continued to play a role in the daily lives of their offspring. They also believed there was an afterlife, for which the living had to make provisions. Hence the custom of building tombs and burying the corpse together with many goods and chattels. At one time even concubines, household slaves, and horses went into the tombs. But does that mean tombs became sacred?" He stopped to wipe his face.

"Does it not make more sense for us to enjoy the heritage these ancestors left behind? Should we not benefit from our inheritance from the past?"

"I suppose so, but I have to ask what you mean by 'benefit.'"

"I mean enjoy the use of the items our ancestors left behind for us."

Holroyd balked at the implication that anyone should dig up ancient artifacts once entombed and continue to use them like so much Tupperware, but he was not aghast at the idea.

He remembered one of his aunts used a chamber pot that had come down through several generations and was supposed to have been used by Anne Boleyn during her stay in the Tower of London. The difference was they had not recovered it from Boleyn's tomb.

"I doubt anyone would want to wear the silk clothing that was fashionable thousands of years ago, let alone stored next to a corpse for any length of time."

"No! But jewellery and other ornaments have value in the modern world because collectors pay lots of money for them."

"Director Ding, you believe buried artifacts should be recovered and sold to collectors for their private benefit?"

"Why not?"

"So, you approve of robbing tombs?"

"Robbing? That has such an evil meaning. Why not recognize that 'recovering' is a better term?"

"But you approve of the practice?"

"Why not?"

"Do you engage in this practice?"

"Me? Never! That would mean committing a crime for which the punishment, until recently, was death."

"But you do not disapprove of the practice?"

Ding gave Holroyd a careful if unfocused look. "No. People took many of the items in the library from tombs. Our collection would be boring were it not for such, shall we say, donations? Sometimes I accept items of historical significance as part of the heritage of the people of China, but that does not mean I know someone has taken them from a tomb." He stopped to take another swallow.

"I suppose they could accuse me of not notifying the authorities of such items, but the trade in such items involves so many people that I think no one would notice my errors of omission, and it's not as if it's difficult to hide the practice. Things and records disappear, and people can always find reasons. Look at how much disappeared during the Cultural Revolution. That helped a lot." He looked at Holroyd as if daring him to challenge the assertion.

"But if you accept these 'donations,' and if you know or believe or even suspect that the items come from a tomb, are you not condoning the practice by accepting them?"

"How so? I let others do the robbing and yet others do the selling." Ding giggled. "I would be stupid to do anything that might implicate me directly."

"But indirectly?"

"Let me put it this way. Suppose I were to become aware of an item that a buyer is interested in acquiring. I might consider passing on such information to the relevant people."

"Of course, you would benefit too!"

"Of course. And why not?"

Holroyd had a sudden flash of insight. "Is that what happened when you approved the loan of the book to Doctor Nicholson?" Before Ding could answer, Pearl interjected.

"Oh no, Doctor Nicholson promised he would return the book shortly."

"But we can't seem to find Doctor Nicholson or the book," Holroyd observed.

"Oh, come now, Doctor Holroyd," Ding said. "Why do you look so horrified? Are you not yourself in the business of researching ancient documents? Where do you think many of those documents you examine come from? If I do not have such documents in my library, how would you go about finding the document you want to look at?"

"The documents I examine have come from people's libraries or auctioned collections of privately held documents. I do not go around opening tombs. And if for any reason someone opens a tomb in my country, they do so under very strict regulations by people who have the qualifications to make sure they do not disturb the remains. Can you say the same is true for China?"

"Never!" Ding blurted, then corrected himself. "Sometimes." By then he was so drunk he seemed in danger of falling off his chair. Regaining his balance, he squinted at Holroyd. "But why are you against the practice? Are you upset? That's what's paying for dinner tonight. I may even have the document you want, or I may know where it is."

"Did you just say you have the document I'm looking for?"

"No. I said I *may* have it, or at least I *may* know where it is."

"And where is it?"

Ding laughed, but no one else did. Perhaps aware that he had said too much, he stopped and shook his head as if to sober up.

"Come now, Professor. I'm not quite such a fool. You can hardly expect me to reveal everything to you, however distinguished you might be." He took another swallow from his glass and then.

"W-why would I confide in you? C-can you offer me money or perhaps a p-promotion? No? I thought not, so you won't g-g-get what you want from me." He giggled almost hysterically, but then started to cry. Holroyd regarded the snivelling man with contempt.

Pearl looked aghast at her colleague. Wendy remained stone-faced, but Holroyd realized that a new avenue for his research had just opened.

There was silence until Ding said something in Chinese, though he slurred his words. He looked at Holroyd with unfocused eyes. "I'm so… shorry, so sh-hilly of me." He hiccupped and then stood up, grabbing the table to maintain his balance but then collapsed back in his chair.

"Wendy," Holroyd said, "I think it's getting late. Perhaps we should get back to the hotel." He turned back to Ding. "Ding Qu Wan, thank you for an excellent dinner." Holroyd got up with Wendy and left the room. He felt elated that Ding's admissions had been so candid.

Once outside and on the way back, he turned to Wendy. "Well, what do you think of that? I think I have to get our distinguished librarian to be more forthright. He didn't lend anything to Nicholson or whoever it was; he probably sold it to him. Oh yes! Our Ding is up to his scrawny neck in the trade of ancient documents. Now all I have to figure out is how to squeeze what I want out of him."

"I agree that Director Ding is being less than prudent. If people heard what he told us, he would find himself in a very unpleasant position. He would go to jail because they removed the death penalty for tomb-robbing just last year."

"Do you think Pearl knew?"

"I don't know. Most Chinese people prefer to keep a low profile when it comes to unpleasantness unless there's a clear matter that they cannot ignore. I don't think Pearl knew what Ding was doing, and I think she will do her best to forget what she heard this evening."

"Do you think Pearl will report him?"

"Again, I don't know. I suppose she might if she wanted to get rid of Ding, perhaps to take his place. Somehow, I doubt she will do that because if she tries and fails, she might lose her position, and if she succeeds, there's no guarantee she will get his position."

"I wonder how far the rot has spread."

"A lot further than you may want to believe," Wendy replied.

"We know that Ding might know where the missing document can be found. Let's see what happens if we suggest we're interested in buying it."

"We already hinted at it but got no response."

"Yes, but that was before he opened up this evening in front of witnesses. I think we have enough to start putting some pressure on him."

"That is a possible plan, but it will need careful handling. We can hardly go to Ding directly. We have no guarantee he will cooperate or if he will report us to the authorities. Or he might report us to his contacts in the sale of recovered artifacts, and they may not welcome our interest. Let me think about it."

27

Holroyd suspected that Ding, given his admissions at dinner, knew exactly where the missing document could be found and even what was written on it. How Holroyd could persuade Ding to open up was another question, but Holroyd thought he could shake Ding into revealing the information by pursuing the topic forcefully. He decided that together with Wendy another visit would be the next step.

They went up to Ding's office but found it locked. Nor did they find Pearl, so they descended and went out to the street through the main door.

"Right," Holroyd said. "I think we should try the police and see if we can find out anything about this missing Doctor Nicholson."

They stepped out of the library's front door, only to see a crowd of thirty or forty people, mostly of student age, gathered outside. They were looking at Wendy and Holroyd shouting what Holroyd thought were insults or threats and making threatening gestures.

Sensing things were ugly, Holroyd looked around for help and saw a policeman standing by a lamppost not far off to the right. He was looking in their direction.

Wendy stepped closer to him and gripped his arm. "Be careful," she whispered, though Holroyd felt that being careful might not be enough.

His suspicions were realized when he saw an object flying toward them and stepped aside but not far enough to escape the splatter of a ripe tomato. Jeers came from the crowd as another vegetable, followed by an egg, hit him in the chest. He looked down in horror at the gooey mess slipping toward his fly. A memory of Fagin cowering from an angry mob in the film *Oliver Twist* popped into his mind.

"Hooligans!" he shouted, waving frantically at the policeman, who looked back indifferently.

"Please, Doctor Holroyd, do not antagonize them further," Wendy pleaded with a tremble in her voice.

"Me, antagonize them? What have I done? And why is that policeman just standing there?"

Someone in the group yelled something in Chinese that others repeated. More yells and chorused jeers followed.

"They are accusing you of stealing valuable cultural artifacts and a few other crimes."

"That's ridiculous. What caused this?"

"I do not know. Sometimes Chinese people just get upset about foreigners—something their home governments may have done that upset someone here. For example, there were many anti-Japanese demonstrations when the Japanese government issued a new textbook that denied any wrongdoing in Nanjing during the war. Also, when a French crowd was disrespectful to the Chinese girl carrying the Olympic flame through Paris, many people here attacked the French." She stopped and looked at the crowd.

"Perhaps we had better go back inside and wait a while."

Holroyd thought fleetingly about facing the crowd but, on second thought, decided discretion might be the better part of valour. They turned to go back in but discovered that some demonstrators had got between them and the door, blocking them from their intended escape route and almost hemming them in.

Looking to the left and right, the only reasonable escape route appeared to lead past the crowd and over to the policeman, still standing impassively on the same spot, as though his job were to ensure the lamppost did not fall over.

"See that policeman?" Holroyd said as another missile landed on his suit, and a rotten tomato splattered one of his lenses. "Head straight toward him. The mob will hit him with some of their rubbish if we're lucky. That might ginger him into action."

He held her hand and ran, though later he would characterize the sprint as a rattled dash.

More missiles landed on or near them, but the volume diminished as they drew near to the policeman. When they reached him, they stopped, and the mob threw no more objects.

Holroyd was sweating and needed to regain his breath. That was more exercise than he had had in a decade. He felt relieved and safer but could still hear hoots of derision and laughter. Wendy neither looked nor sounded in much better shape.

"What was that all about?" he asked.

"I do not know," Wendy said, then turned to address the policeman. He looked at her but remained stolidly impassive for a long time until he finally barked back at her. The exchange continued until the policeman moved forward threateningly, reaching for his baton.

With an exasperated, "*Heng!*" Wendy finally gave up her tirade, backed away, and took Holroyd by the hand, leading him away.

"What did the policeman say?"

"He said that people are entitled to show their displeasure at foreign visitors who abuse China's hospitality by engaging in criminal activities, such as stealing ancient artifacts."

Holroyd was outraged. "But we did no such thing! I—" He got no further as Wendy pulled his arm and led him away from the scene.

"Doctor Holroyd, please! We need to get out of here."

"Yes, but why were we attacked?"

"If you'd been listening, I already told you why!" Wendy snapped. "This is China, and people can get angry for many reasons we know nothing about. Perhaps this is one such occasion."

"No, Wendy, we are being told to back off from something they think we know."

"Such as?"

"My research. Someone or perhaps several persons do not want me to succeed in my task, and I want to know why."

"Doctor Holroyd, you are being paranoid. I think today's demonstration involves people believing you are engaged in tomb robbing and trying to steal ancient artifacts. We are looking for an ancient document that could tie in with your research, so it is not a great leap to believing you are trying to steal it. Especially if someone told them that's the reason behind your search."

"Someone? Who?"

"That I don't know. Perhaps a buyer or seller of artifacts or someone acting to ensure such artifacts remain in China. Nor do I think this is the time or the place to discuss this. I think we should head home and change."

Holroyd recognized the wisdom of Wendy's advice and allowed himself to be led away. But he was not so easily deterred from trying to get answers.

"Who knows we stumbled upon tomb robbing? I doubt anyone from the village would have reported us, and the only person with whom we discussed robbing tombs was Ding at last night's supper."

"Either someone from the village made a report, or Ding Qu Wan or one of his acquaintances knows of our interests and is unhappy about your research. Ding or anyone he talked with could have spread the word to these people. Organizing a demonstration is not difficult if it's sanctioned from on high. Perhaps we are close to something some person does not want us to see. Perhaps, in this case, that someone told the police not to get involved."

"So, whoever this someone might be, he or she is a person of influence if not of power."

"It is possible."

Oh, wonderful! Holroyd thought, looking at her. *I've been attacked by Asians working for people I don't have a clue about. I've been hindered and warned off by the Americans and now by Chinese power brokers. Well, let's see if there's anyone I can turn to.*

"That's enough. If those hooligans have dispersed, we are going straight to the police station. I want to get to the bottom of this right now."

"Why go to the police? As you noticed, the police did nothing."

"I noticed one policeman did nothing. Besides that, let's not forget someone took potshots at us in the park, and that motorcycle maniac tried to push us into the void. So, I think it's time we got the police involved."

"You don't know for sure we were the targets in the park, and as I told you, the motorcyclist could have been expressing his displeasure at our visit to the village. Yes, it is plausible that you or we are targets, but other than suspicions, what proof can you offer the police?" She paused to let Holroyd answer. When he said nothing, she continued.

"They will listen politely, give empty promises, and do nothing without proof. They might instead view you as a troublemaker and start making sure you don't cause any more problems."

"One or even two such incidents might be dismissed but look at all the others. Dejection Island will confirm the attack on me, and that would be proof."

"Do you seriously believe anyone will call Dejection Island? Why would any Chinese official even want to make an international call unless it was cleared through Beijing? And before you comment, let me tell you that getting official approvals from Beijing is neither easy nor quick. But in the meantime, you will have the local police becoming very interested in your mission and your activities. I think you would want that even less. " She stopped.

"Don't even think the local police will be eager to help you."

"Are you suggesting or telling me the whole police force is in on this?"

"No, I cannot suggest that." Wendy looked at him and then sighed in resignation. "All right, let's go to the police station as you wish," she said, then hailed a passing taxi.

On arrival at the police station, and after a wait of some forty minutes, a uniformed policeman escorted them into an office where two other policemen were waiting. The officers introduced themselves as Inspector Fang Wei and Lieutenant Wu Shi Ming. The two officers scrutinized Wendy and Holroyd with suspicion.

"How may we help you?" Fang Wei asked.

"There are two reasons we came here. The first is to report an incident earlier today," Holroyd said. "A group of hooligans attacked Miss Liu and me. A nearby policeman did nothing but stand there even though we called for help. The second reason is we would like to ask for your help in locating a missing man."

Fang Wei leaned forward and held out his hand. "May I see your passport?"

Holroyd was taken aback by the lack of comment other than this bureaucratic and unrelated request. He pulled out his passport and handed it over.

Fang Wei looked at him with what Holroyd could only interpret as unfriendliness. After a moment, he scrutinized the passport page by page. He rubbed each page between his fingers to ensure it wasn't fake.

"This is your first visit to China?"

"I'm sorry, but did you understand the reason for our visit? What bearing could any previous visit to China have on replying to the attack this morning?"

"Please answer my questions when I ask them."

Holroyd sighed. "No, I was here many years ago as a student."

"I see no record of a previous visit."

"No, you wouldn't. We renew British passports every ten years. The record of my previous visit would be in an old passport."

"Where are you staying?"

"The Auspicious Friendly Hotel."

"I see! The Auspicious Friendly Hotel. Why are you here?"

"I just told you we want to complain about being attacked this morning."

"Mister Holroyd, you would be wise to cooperate and not take me for a complete idiot. Why are you in China, and more to the point, here in FujinHaiZhou?"

"I'm doing some academic research."

"Yes, I can see that you have a visa that allows you to stay for academic research, but you have visited no university."

"No. At this point in my research, I need not contact any university. I'm looking for records that might exist in the library."

"Why would you think so?"

"Someone informed me that there was a document in the library here that I might find interesting."

"What is this research?"

"May I ask why you are so interested?"

"It is my duty to ensure that you have not entered China for fraudulent reasons. This morning I received a complaint that you were engaging in criminal activities."

"What criminal activities?"

"That is a question we need not answer at this point. However, we received a report that you were engaged in activities that abuse our hospitality."

"May I ask in what way I'm supposed to have abused your hospitality?" Holroyd was becoming irritated, and he felt Wendy shift as if she were worried.

"I ask the questions. Please cooperate and answer." Fang Wei looked at Holroyd, his voice conveying officialdom in full un-cooperation mode.

Holroyd realized that Wendy's predictions were proving true. He also realized he was getting angry and would be better off to mollify the inspector. Before he could say anything to defuse a possible confrontation, Wendy meekly addressed the inspector in Chinese, and from then on, Holroyd became a bystander.

As the conversation continued, he sensed the inspector's attitude change. The only problem was that he could not determine whether the change was favourable. Finally, Fang Wei turned to Holroyd and handed back his passport.

"I see no reason to proceed further at this time. Please ensure you follow China's laws when you come across ancient items, especially ancient documents." He paused. "You said there were two reasons for your visit here."

"Yes, inspector, the first is to ask what you will do about this morning's incident."

"What incident?"

Holroyd stared at him. "We came here to report that hooligans attacked us. Look at my clothes. Some brats threw eggs and rotten vegetables at us, ruining my suit."

"Brats? Please, what are brats? Some form of an animal or a bird?"

"Inspector, I do not think this is a laughing matter. They assaulted us, and a nearby policeman did nothing to help even though I called him."

"Yes, so you said. Wait a moment." He picked up his phone and hung up after a few moments of conversation. "I just spoke to the officer on duty at the library, and he said nothing unusual happened.

He saw no group of people or any demonstration, but he saw you and Miss Liu leave the library. Who should I believe?"

"Then how did I get egg all over my suit?"

"Perhaps you spilled your breakfast this morning."

Holroyd lost it. He lost it beyond redemption. "Fuck this!" he yelled in a voice that, in the back of his mind, sounded more like a primeval scream.

He continued in what a bystander might classify as a strident yell. "Are you really dimwitted or just incompetent? Is this how you treat everyone, or are we the only lucky ones?"

Deep down inside, he knew he was being utterly unreasonable because this was a police station, and as a guest of the country, he entirely depended on the goodwill of his hosts. But he was beyond caring. The two police officers looked thunderstruck. No one moved.

Wendy reached out and grabbed his arm. "Doctor Holroyd, please calm down." She sounded horrified and embarrassed, if not afraid. He felt himself deflating and, with that, also felt helpless and embarrassed.

This was not England. This was a country where, as reports would have it, people disappeared at the whim of nameless local functionaries. He thought such reports were sensationalized but did not want to discover the truth at that precise moment. He took a deep breath and tried to appear contrite.

"I apologize, gentlemen. The morning's events were stressful, even with no eggs for breakfast." The lieutenant smiled fleetingly, and Holroyd could almost feel the tension ebbing out of the room.

"We will look into the matter again. However, I cannot promise anything. You mentioned a second reason for your visit to the station."

"Yes, I wonder if you may know something about an American professor who was here. Someone told us his name was Nicholson and he was staying at our hotel."

"And? Did you ask at the registration desk about him?"

"Yes, and they told us he was not, and never had been, staying there."

"Perhaps you had the wrong hotel."

"Our informant was very definite."

"Are you related in any way?"

"No."

"Then, what is your interest?"

"We, or rather I, am trying to get in touch with him."

"And why is that?"

"He is supposedly engaged in the same field of research as I am. I have never met or even heard of him until a few days ago. But I'm wondering how I may have never heard of this man who people tell me is an expert in my academic field."

"Do you know, or have you heard of, everyone who works in your academic field?"

"No, but this field is narrow, and I believe I would know anyone who is an expert."

"Then it is possible that this man is not what he pretends to be. That is not always a crime. Do you know of any reason we would know something of this man?" Wu Shi Ming asked.

"The police register the whereabouts of every foreigner, Lieutenant. Surely you would know where he is or might be?"

"Doctor Holroyd, what the police may or may not know is not always available to citizens of China and, therefore, certainly not available to a guest of China," Fang Wei said.

"I agree, inspector, but there would be a crime if, by pretending to be an expert, he got a valuable ancient document."

"Has this man committed such a crime?" Fang Wei looked at Holroyd with what Holroyd took to be feigned interest.

"Perhaps. The library permitted him to take an ancient and very rare book from the library. So far, he has not returned the book, and no one knows where he is."

"You say they permitted him to take out the book? So, I do not see that anyone committed a crime. If the book's owner reports its loss, we may try to recover it and punish the person who stole it. Until then, we can only assume that this American will obey the laws of China regarding borrowing ancient documents. You are free to make a formal complaint." He turned to indicate Wu.

"Lieutenant Wu, here, can give you the forms, although they are only available in Chinese. I should warn you, however, that making a false declaration and wasting the time of the police in working on your complaint is a serious offence. You could end up in jail or at least be encouraged to leave China." He paused to let the message sink in.

Holroyd realized he was being warned, but before he could react, Fang Wei continued, "As you can imagine, we are very busy with actual crimes and crime prevention and do not wish to spend our time on imaginary cases. Please, remember you are a guest here. Do not make us regret the hospitality we offer you."

Holroyd was about to retort when Wendy touched his arm. "Thank you, Inspector. Please excuse us for troubling you."

"Not at all. However, since you are here, perhaps you would be kind enough to answer some questions we will ask other foreign visitors. First, may I ask where you were two evenings ago?" Holroyd was prevented from answering by Wendy.

"Oh! We went window shopping," she said.

Fang Wei frowned. "Shopping for windows?"

"No, no, Inspector, it means looking at what is displayed in the windows of shops." Holroyd managed to chuckle.

"So, you were not in the hotel that evening?"

Holroyd and Wendy shook their heads.

"As you looked at windows, did you also stop at Serenity Lake? Perhaps to see the light show or enjoy some small foods?"

"No."

"Are you quite sure? You see, there was a report of some shooting, and witnesses told us a foreigner accompanied by a Chinese female left the scene."

"It wasn't us, and I can't think of who it could have been."

"Not us," Wendy confirmed.

"Now another matter where you might be able to help us. You are staying on the twelfth floor of your hotel. Did you hear anything unusual two nights ago? A noise? A loud noise such as a firework or a shot?" Both shook their heads in unison.

"No! nothing like that," Wendy said.

"And another question. Have you met any other foreigners also staying at your hotel?" Holroyd looked at Wendy, and they both turned to the inspector. She shook her head. "No."

Fang Wei looked at them in silence. "Thank you. Please do not forget to call us if you remember anything." Holroyd and Wendy were about to leave, but they stopped when the door opened, and another man entered the room.

Fang Wei stood up with an attitude that, in Holroyd's Navy days, he would have described as dumb insolence.

Holroyd's first impression of the man who came in was unfavourable. He sensed a rather dissolute character who exuded self-importance. The man looked askance at Fang Wei, who stepped forward. "Doctor Holroyd, may I introduce you to the Commissioner of Police, Fu Li."

Fu Li approached, exuding a cloying obsequiousness and insincerity that left Holroyd queasy. To say the man's appearance surprised Holroyd would be a gross understatement. He may not have warmed to Inspector Fang Wei, but he respected him grudgingly. This man, however, only encouraged contempt. Still, one could never be sure about appearances, especially in China.

"I regret I could not greet you on your arrival, but I'm sure you understand that police matters detained me. However, as you English like to say, better late than never."

Holroyd wanted to say he never used that expression, but he held his tongue.

"I'm delighted you have visited our small town," Fu Li continued. "It is an honour you have chosen us for your research. I'm sure Director Ding at the library will assist you in any way he can." Fu Li paused as if to catch his breath. "Please accept our apologies for this morning's uncivilized behaviour by some of our citizens. I hurried over to make sure you were safe and not injured."

Holroyd thanked him while assuring him that he and Wendy were both in good health. He noted no sympathy for his ruined suit.

"Please know we will do our utmost to apprehend the culprits and ensure no one treats you in such an impolite manner again."

Holroyd nodded.

"We want to make sure our honoured guests enjoy their visits. I need not remind you to exercise care when walking, particularly in the dark, as, unfortunately, criminal elements will try to take advantage of visitors." Holroyd gave a nod of gratitude, though he took those words as a veiled threat.

"Should you have questions, or if you have anything you wish to tell me, here is my card. Call me; I'm always ready to hear from you. If for any reason I'm not available, please call upon Inspector Fang Wei." Holding it in both hands, he offered Holroyd his business card. He bowed, and with a peremptory gesture for Fang Wei to follow him, Commissioner Fu Li departed.

Fang Wei looked at Holroyd in a manner that suggested the interview had been adjourned. Fang Wei followed the Commissioner while Wu Shi Ming escorted Holroyd and Wendy to the front door.

"I think the Commissioner's arrival was curious," Wendy remarked upon leaving the station. "Why would he countermand the version of events that the inspector gave us? What does he have to gain by making Fang Wei lose face?"

"Yes. That was strange. But let's get back to the hotel. I really must change and see if I can salvage this suit. God only knows how much cleaning will cost and if cleaning will be enough." Fleetingly, he wondered whether he could charge its replacement to expenses.

Wendy hailed a taxi.

"It's been a most instructive day," Holroyd said once they were inside, "but I can't remember ever making an outburst like that."

Wendy said nothing, so Holroyd continued. "Wendy, getting back to the Commissioner's handling of the demonstration, I wonder if I missed something. People know that we're sniffing around the tomb-robbing pipeline and suppose the police are also hot on the trail, so could the Commissioner be trying to discredit Fang Wei to make sure we never trust him enough to exchange information?"

"Doctor Holroyd, once again, you are being overly fanciful. You give the Commissioner and the Inspector far too much credit. Do remember, this is provincial China. Junior people like Fang Wei often do not know what a senior person knows. You must read between the lines. They have now told you that senior and probably influential people are watching your every move but that no one will become officially involved at this stage. You are on your own."

How very comforting, he thought. *Who is this "they"? Oh, yes! As Wendy said, I am on my own. She failed to add that I am very much out of my depth and, with people taking shots at me, I feel like a fish in a barrel. Hardly the position a respected academician should be in, but that was precisely where I am, and I see no clear way out short of giving up. But not yet! No bloody way!*

28

Holroyd was woken by the telephone. "Peter, old boy. Trust I didn't wake you, but I have some sad news." It was Merry.

"They pulled your friend Rostwick from the Thames. From the looks of his body, someone treated him badly before he died."

Holroyd felt as if he had been sucker-punched. Rostwick dead? Suddenly, all his fears resurfaced. In addition to everything that had happened to him, he realized that he could be implicated and even a convenient scapegoat in Rostwick's death.

"What's terrible," Holroyd said, "but why would anyone want to kill him?"

"We were wondering if his death had anything to do with that document you asked him to look at," Merry   said,
"He wanted to give it or discuss it with me, but then he vanished until we found him in the river. Looked very hard, but we can't find the document in question."

"I can't help you there, I'm afraid," Holroyd said, "but is there something else you want from me?"

"It may have nothing to do with your task, but as you were in touch with him recently, perhaps there is a tie-in. We want to know why anyone would want to kill Rostwick if the document is the key," Merry insisted. "Can you remember anything about it at all?"

"Not really, other than it was written in Japanese. But I have wondered about it, and I suspect it had something to do with constructions the Japanese might have left behind on the Island. I was going to call the Island and see if anything could confirm that."

"I see. Interesting. I think I'll ask around. There may be something hidden in the files. On another matter, we got a call from our man in Beijing. Tells me that the Chinese are getting restless. Something about your robbing tombs, stealing ancient artifacts, attacking fellow guests, and waking sleeping dragons. Anything to the story?"

"Are you serious? That's ridiculous?"

" 'Fess up, old boy! Have you been ruffling feathers over there?" Holroyd was horrified. Was Merry accusing him, concerned, or joking? That was often the problem with Merry; one could never be quite sure where he was coming from.

"No! Of course not! What makes you think so?"

"The Chinese are getting uppity, being quite rude, in fact. Talked of arresting you if you don't behave. Have you been misbehaving, old boy?" Holroyd thought he detected a hint of menace and decided confrontation was the best response.

"Not at all. Merry, I'm rather miffed you would even ask, but I'm not surprised. I think people are trying to interfere with my mission. I just don't know who or how many."

"Look, Peter, old boy. It's becoming more complicated and may blow out of proportion. The Americans want to barge in with some sort of scientific team and may do a Grenada on the island. Very rude, really. To cap it all, the press is sniffing around. Did you talk to anyone when you were on the island?"

"No, other than the governor and one of his councilmen. Why?"

"Not to any woman, by chance?"

"No, why?"

"Some woman by the name of Elsie Watson has been writing to MPs and the press. She's claiming we're selling the colony down the drain. She mentions your visit as an example of our underhanded conduct." He paused and Holroyd thought he heard the sound of a glass being filled.

"The Opposition is having a field day, and you are not the flavour of the moment. It's getting warm to admit even knowing you as a friend. One of your colleagues at the university is expounding on what a cad you are and prophesying your imminent demise."

"Oh, hell!" Holroyd was appalled. How could matters have gotten so completely out of hand?

"I'm telling you all this, so you know more about what's in play." Merry's tone became more conciliatory. "But you are our man on the spot, and we rely on you. Just soldier on; you have my complete support."

"That's very reassuring, but honestly, I'm beginning to feel like Typhoid Mary with so many bodies turning up near me. I think there's more to all of this than I expected."

There was a pause, and then Merry became serious and cautious. "Alright, I'll bite. What bodies, and what's been happening?"

Holroyd could hardly remain calm as he gave Merry the details.

"I say, that's far from what we expected when we asked you to join in. But if you need anything, I might be able to help."

"That's decent of you, but what do you have in mind?"

"Just let me know! Any idea how much longer you think you need?"

"That depends on what happens next. I don't think I've hit a wall yet. I'm following some possible leads, but if they don't produce results, I'm not sure about my next move."

"I see. Well, soldier on, old boy." With that, Merry hung up.

A fat lot of help Merry is. Dammit, I'm a university professor, but I've just been sent up an alligator-filled creek without a paddle.

*****

Although it was still dark, Muramori was sitting at his desk when the phone rang. He listened in silence before making a non-committal noise.

"You have retrieved the map, and is it what we needed?"

"Yes, Muramori san."

"Have you examined it?"

"Yes."

"And?"

"The location is where you told us."

"Signal the ship's Master and inform him that he may now proceed as instructed. Encrypt the information and send it to him."

"Hai!"

"Anything from our agent watching the English professor?"

"There has been no change in the professor's activities. He continues to search for some book or document on early Chinese voyages."

Muramori grunted an acknowledgement and then cut the connection. *Now that I have retrieved the map, I don't think I need to follow Holroyd anymore. But what is he doing? My people on the island informed me he was asking about the early settlers. Why would he do that? And why would the British and maybe the American government be involved? Could he be part of a rumoured move to give the island away? If so, he could prove meddlesome and threaten my plans. Perhaps it's too soon to ignore this academic. Maybe he should be delayed. Now that I'm so close to success, nothing or nobody can be allowed to stop me.*

He picked up the phone and gave instructions.

*****

In his office, Li Wen Yao listened carefully to the report. "Please confirm Holroyd arrived in FujinHaiZhou with his assistant and visited the library and went out to the countryside. Do we know where he went or why? No? Try to find out and then report back." He hung up and then sat back. *I think it's time for me to get closer to Holroyd. Just what is he looking for and why?*

Deputy Director Ting grudgingly approved Li's request to go to FujinHaiZhou.

29

Holroyd left the hotel and wandered across the street to where workmen were cleaning up after some roadwork. Out of curiosity, he went over to see what they were up to and observed signs of a traffic incident.

He asked a workman what had happened. The man looked at him and shrugged. "Traffic accident. Someone got run over."

"Who?" Holroyd asked, and was met with resistance.

After a surreptitious exchange of money, the man grudgingly admitted it was a foreigner. "He's now in the hospital."

Holroyd looked away and thought *Another person met a life-threatening accident while I'm around. I'm beginning to feel I'm trapped in a spider's web of which I had no inkling.*

He casually surveyed the ground and noticed a piece of partially discoloured paper with Western writing. His curiosity was aroused because such rubbish would normally have Chinese writing.

He picked it up and saw that it was part of an airline boarding pass, but the passenger's name had been torn off. He took a closer look and scrutinized the discolouration, which had a reddish-brown hue. *Blood? If so, the scrap's owner and the traffic victim were likely the same person.*

On the back was written "Holro" and "Auspic." Holroyd was completely taken by surprise. *What the hell is this? "Holro" could refer to me and "Auspic" to the hotel. Who would be interested enough in me to write down my name and hotel and why? This person flew in from somewhere to do… what?*

He put the stub into his pocket, then went back to the hotel and ordered a coffee while he thought about the implications of what he had discovered.

Wondering who could have an interest, he remembered the three Americans in Singapore who had tried to warn him off his task. Could this be one of them, or was there yet another player of whom he had so far been ignorant?

Could this person have been the shooter at the lake? If that person was the victim of the accident, was he deliberately run over? *Or was I the intended victim, and the attacker made a mistake? I need to talk to this person if he, or she, is still alive.*

As he sipped his coffee, he realized he had too many questions and too few resources to get the answers. *How, for instance, can I find out about and get access to the victim?*

He decided that, based on the Commissioner's offer to help, he should visit the police with the stub. But he thought his visit should be to the inspector using the excuse that the scrap of paper might further the search for Nicholson. After trying unsuccessfully to get in touch with Wendy, he set off on his own.

Once at the police station, Holroyd was told to wait. After a long while, a constable ushered him into Fang Wei's office.

"Thank you for agreeing to see me, inspector."

"How can I help you this time?"

"You will remember, I came to ask about an American professor."

"Yes, and I said there was nothing we could do without an official complaint, which, I notice, you have not submitted."

"Yes. I did not submit one because I have nothing to officially complain about."

"I see. Then may I ask the reason for this visit?"

"I believe there was a traffic accident just outside the hotel and that the victim was a foreigner." Holroyd took the stub out from his pocket. "I found this scrap of paper at the scene of the accident." He handed it over.

Fang Wei examined it closely. "And?'

"This looks like an aircraft boarding pass. Looking at the discolouration suggests to me that the blood on this stub belongs to the victim. Furthermore, as you can see, the writing on the back links the owner to me and my hotel." Fang Wei examined the stub again.

"I see no proof that you found this where you say you did, nor do I see any proof this stub belonged to the traffic victim. It could have belonged to anyone. As for the writing on the back, I see words that I do not recognize, but then my knowledge of foreign languages is poor."

"Inspector, as far as I know, no other foreigner in FujinHaiZhou would have an interest in me and where I'm staying. Therefore, I believe this traffic accident victim could be Doctor Nicholson, about whom I came last time." It was a lie, but Holroyd hoped the inspector would not question the reasons behind his belief.

"Why do you assume this belonged to a foreigner?"

"I found it at the scene where I was told a foreigner had been in an accident. I think it's highly probable that this airline boarding pass belonged to the victim."

"That is your thinking, but that does not mean you are right. But let us accept your thinking for the moment. As far as you know, no other foreigner in the city has an interest in you, but could you perhaps not know enough to say that?"

"Are you suggesting my reasoning could be wrong?"

"Let me just say I see no proof to support your suggestions."

"I see. Would you allow me to question the traffic victim once he recovers?"

"Why do you think he will recover? What do you know about this person's injuries?"

"I don't. All I know is that he was taken to a hospital and, therefore, is not dead."

Fang Wei looked at him in silence before looking at the stub again. "All I see is a piece of paper that you say you found at the site of a reported traffic accident." He stopped and looked at Holroyd in a manner Holroyd thought would have fitted an interrogator during the Spanish Inquisition.

"But let us consider that you may be right," Fang Wei said, "That raises the question of your interest in this possible victim who you think might be Doctor Nicholson, and who you told us you are looking for. You told us that you are not a relative and do not know each other from your work, so I'm at a loss as to why you are so anxious to meet him."

"As I told you I believe he may have stolen a valuable book."

"Yes, you did tell me that. But as you also told me, you have no proof there has been a theft, which means nothing has changed. But let us say you are correct that this stub belonged to the victim. That does not mean the victim has any interest in you."

Fang Wei looked at the stub again, put it in a desk drawer, and then looked at Holroyd. "So, if the victim recovers, why do you need our permission to seek and interview him? You can do that once we are satisfied with the details of the accident, and he has been released from the hospital."

"If the person is indeed Doctor Nicholson, an interview would allow me to discover what he has done with the Dong Xi Yang Kao."

"Ah! But you have no proof the victim has done anything with that document. As I pointed out to you when you brought the matter to my attention, the owner has not reported the book lost, so nothing can be done until a formal complaint has been made."

"So, you will do nothing?"

"We will do what our duties require us to do." He paused and looked at Holroyd. "I should advise you that such duties do not involve you, and I hope you will respect that advice. Of course, it may happen that we will need to contact you again, but until then please continue with your academic research, and avoid distractions such as police matters."

"Then I apologize for wasting your time." Holroyd stood up as if to leave when Fang Wei continued.

"I said I see no proof. But that does not mean there is no proof to be found. I will consider this and will get in touch with you if necessary. Now I must excuse myself as I have duties to perform. Good day, Doctor Holroyd."

Holroyd left the station. *He's hiding something. It looks as if Wendy was right, and the police are involved. What's my next move? Oh, yes, a call to David on the Island to ask about Japanese constructions. And after that? The librarian again?*

He headed back to the hotel to find Wendy and plan for another visit to the library. On arrival, he called Wendy and gave her a brief report on his morning's visit to the police.

"Doctor Holroyd, I have warned you several times not to approach the police, but if you insist then I must ask that I accompany you."

"I don't think that will be necessary for the moment, but there is something I would like you to do. Find out where the traffic victim is being treated and see if you can arrange to let me visit him.”

“May I know the purpose of this visit?”

“I believe he might be Nicholson.” He heard a sharp intake of breath.

“Oh! Well then, a visit makes perfect sense. Let me arrange it.”

*****

“You have a visitor.” The constable stood aside as another man entered.

Fang Wei looked up at him. “Yes?”

“Good afternoon, Inspector. I’m Li Wen Yao from the Beijing Office of State Security.” He showed his identity card. Fang Wei stood up attentively.

“I’m here in pursuit of a criminal, and I believe you can help me in my inquiries. As it is a state matter, I require your cooperation and assistance.”

“Of course, I will be only too happy to assist. Perhaps I should call my assistant, Lieutenant Wu Shi Ming, to join us.”

“As long as he is cooperative, do so.”

30

With no other options readily at hand, Holroyd decided to follow up with a visit to Ding even though he was still determining how to proceed once there. On arrival at Ding's door, he knocked sharply and entered.

Ding was behind his desk, poring over some papers. He looked up with a frown. "Yes?" he asked peremptorily.

Holroyd entered but before he could say anything, there was another knock on the door and two police officers entered. Holroyd had met Wu before, and the other one seemed familiar.

Both officers stopped when they saw Holroyd.

"Doctor Holroyd, this is a surprise," Wu said. "However, while we apologize for this interruption, our business cannot wait."

"Oh, don't apologize. My business with Director Ding can wait. I'll come back another time."

Wu stood aside as if to allow Holroyd to depart, but the other officer stopped him.

"I think we should ask Doctor Holroyd to stay." Both Wu and Holroyd looked surprised. Wu turned to Holroyd and Ding. "Let me introduce my colleague, Li Wen Yao from the State Security Bureau in Beijing."

Li smiled at Holroyd. "We have met before. You will remember we had a delightful dinner together in Beijing." Li proffered a business card with both hands.

"Yes, I remember. But this isn't the same card you gave me before, and you weren't with the police when you introduced yourself." Holroyd looked attentively at the card.

Li continued to smile. "My job is to pursue criminals who have committed what you would call white-collar crimes. I do not usually identify myself as such."

"Are you thinking I might have committed a white-collar crime?" Holroyd asked facetiously. Remembering Merry's warning about getting arrested, Holroyd tried to look innocent.

"Oh no! At least, not yet." Li smiled mirthlessly before turning to Ding and, reaching into his pocket, showed his official identity card.

Ding turned pale and shifted nervously in his chair. "How can I be of help?"

"I'm investigating a criminal matter that may also involve a foreigner. And, to my surprise, that foreigner is here right now." Li paused. "I think it will be useful for him to be present, as he might be able to contribute to our inquiries."

A look of wariness crossed Ding's face, and Holroyd felt nervous about what might come next.

"A criminal matter? Involving foreigners?" Ding looked alarmed.

"I'm involved in a criminal matter?" Holroyd sounded surprised but suddenly felt very vulnerable. *Was this Li fellow following up on tomb robbing when he learned of my interest in the missing document or my visit to the village?* He decided to brazen it out.

"Well, I'm not sure how much I can help. I assume you will conduct your business in Chinese, and my knowledge of the language may not be sufficient."

"We will use English so that you do not miss anything." With that promise, Holroyd sat down.

Li turned to Ding. "You said 'foreigners,' although I only mentioned one. However, Doctor Holroyd has earlier expressed concerns to my colleagues about an American named Doctor Nicholson, so perhaps there are two. Let us first focus on this Nicholson. I understand his passport was in order and had a researcher's visa. His entry stamp was from Zhuhai. He claimed to be from a university in Mississippi specializing in Ming and Qing Dynasty history."

Ding nodded in agreement.

"Doctor Holroyd, can you add anything?"

"I have never heard of him, which is strange given his claims. I ran a check but found no mention of him."

Li nodded and turned back to Ding. "Did you check any of this information?"

"No, why? His passport and visa were in order."

"How did you learn of his arrival?"

"I received a call from the regional party secretary informing me that a distinguished foreign research professor was coming to the library. He asked me to assist him in every way possible."

Holroyd stirred. Was this revealing links to higher-ups and proving what Wendy had warned him about?

"Is it usual for the regional party secretary to call and ask you to cooperate with a visiting academic?"

"No."

"Do you know this party secretary personally?"

"Not at all."

"And yet he called you?"

"Yes."

"Did the Secretary inform you of the purpose of this visit?"

"No."

"Did he pass on the academic's name?"

"No."

"Did you ask any questions?"

"No."

"And the party secretary gave you no other information, such as where he received his instructions?"

"No."

"Did this not seem strange to you?"

"Honourable Li, surely you can understand that when someone like the party secretary calls to ask for cooperation, it is unwise to do anything other than obey."

Li and Wu both nodded.

"Researchers are welcome if they have the relevant permissions. I do not question how they get such permissions. I just make sure they are in order." Ding was obviously becoming more nervous.

"So please give us the details of this visit," Li continued

"Let me call my deputy. She might be able to help if I miss any details." After a short wait, there was a knock, and the door opened.

"Director Ding, you sent for me?" Pearl entered but then stopped "Oh! Doctor Holroyd, how nice to see you again." She smiled.

"This is Shao Yao, my deputy."

"I'm honoured to meet you, sirs." Li nodded as Pearl inclined her head in a small bow of acknowledgement.

"Chief Inspector Li is from Beijing and wishes to know about the academic researcher, Nicholson."

"How may I be of help?" Pearl looked suitably impressed.

"You worked with him, so tell me what he wanted!" Li used his authoritarian voice to impress Pearl on the importance of his question and her answer.

"He told me he was a professor from America and wanted to research historical travels in the South China Sea. He asked to examine one of the books in our collection, the Dong Xi Yang Kao."

"What happened after he examined it?"

"I don't know because he didn't examine the book here but borrowed it. He took it with him."

"You permitted that? Did you ask for approval?"

"Oh, no! I would never allow anything that valuable to leave the library. Only the Director has that authority."

Holroyd tensed. *That's interesting, I think Pearl just sold Ding down the river. I wonder if that's worth pursuing.*

"Are you telling us Director Ding loaned a valuable historical document out to a foreigner?" Wu asked. "On what surety?"

Pearl looked miserably at the floor but said nothing. Ding sat immobile while Holroyd sat silently thinking, *perhaps there is an opening here, but for now, I am no further ahead.*

"And was Doctor Holroyd looking for the same documents as this Doctor Nicholson?" Wu asked.

"Oh, not quite the same! Doctor Holroyd was interested in the Dong Xi Yang Kao but was particularly interested in another document."

"What document was that? Please fetch it, so I can see what it was about," Li said.

"But that has gone missing."

After Pearl reported what she knew, Li turned to Holroyd. "Well, Doctor Holroyd? What about this missing document?"

"Since I never saw it, and it is missing, I cannot tell you anything about it."

"And yet you have a particular interest in it. Why?"

"I believe it may be relevant to my research."

"Ah! Your research. I'm sure we will want to discuss that again but not now."

"Where did you get this document? Why is it missing?" Wu turned to Ding

"Well?" Ding turned to Pearl

"It was given to us by a student researcher who told me she got it from someone in her village."

"You mean possibly from tomb robbers?"

Pearl, almost in tears, nodded miserably.

"Tomb robbers? Did you report them?" Wu asked Ding.

"Lieutenant, we could only surmise they had stolen the document from a tomb." Ding seemed to come out of a trance. "We had no hard evidence we could report." He seemed almost to be pleading.

"Doctor Holroyd, do you know anything about robbing tombs?" Wu asked while Li looked hard at Holroyd. Holroyd shook his head deciding not to volunteer what he had learned at Wang Tang Cun, deeming he might need that information on some future occasion.

With no response from Holroyd, Wu turned back to Ding.

"But surely it is your responsibility to determine the provenance of objects you receive into the library's collection. And do you not report if an item appears as the result of a tomb-robbing activity? Your job is to notify the authorities even if you only suspect a possible theft. Then they will determine whether it was a theft."

"I mentioned it to the Commissioner of Police." Ding sounded agitated. "He asked me for details, and when I told him I knew nothing more, he dismissed it. As I'm sure you remember during the Cultural Revolution, Guards broke into the library, stole many of our rare books, and burned them in a public display. It was such a terrible, terrible waste and destruction of our heritage. I assume that's when it went missing."

"Please excuse me," Pearl said, "but you must be mistaken. We received the document we refer to long after the Revolution. We kept it next to the Dong Xi Yang Kao."

Li turned to Ding, who had turned a grayish shade of green.

"Well, Director? Please explain how this document that may bear on Doctors Holroyd's inquiries has disappeared. I'm beginning to question your competence."

As Ding shook his head, Holroyd noted Ding's face carried a sheen of sweat, and wet stains had appeared under the armpits of his shirt. Holroyd became very attentive. Here, at last, he might get the information he so desperately needed.

"I think we will discuss this again very soon, Director Ding," Li continued. "I believe you will find it helpful to answer our questions fully and truthfully when we do so."

Ding said nothing.

A wave of contempt washed over Holroyd as he sensed Ding was ready to cry. *The man seems*

Holroyd could not quite see a pattern but wondered if the policemen would arrest Ding and Pearl or whether they would just keep an eye on them. They would not try to flee because they had nowhere to go.

"I would suggest, Director Ding and Shao Yao, that you keep yourselves available should I or my colleagues require further information." The threat in Wu's voice was unmistakable.

Li looked up. "Doctor Holroyd, do you have anything to add?"

"No."

"Then please keep us informed if you change your plans."

With that, they got up, left the discomfited librarians, and went their separate ways.

Holroyd followed them out, pondering what he had heard. The only new information was that the regional party secretary and the police commissioner might be involved in the disappearance of the two documents he sought. Did that mean they were in the loop for selling artifacts recovered through tomb robbing? At the dinner, Ding had implied he was personally involved, but had he now provided a couple of further links? If so, how could Holroyd follow up?

He decided he would need to see Ding again, perhaps alone and in a different environment. As for Pearl, well, she was pretty and probably competent, but—as so many good people in China were—she was also submissive to authority.

She would never question her superior's actions openly, but Holroyd thought she would not take part in anything she considered wrong. He suspected that the library was efficient because Pearl was efficient. But perhaps she might be willing to be more open in an informal setting.

31

As he sat in the taxi on the way back to his hotel, Li pondered his next move. So far, nothing he had learned helped to further his inquiries. He could not even hazard a guess at how Holroyd's research might lead to Xiang, but it remained the only lead worth following at that point. Li realized the complexity of his problem might have increased by the intrusion of the elusive Doctor Nicholson. *Why is everyone so interested in this man, and what is his role*? *Is he stealing this book to sell, or does he have another reason? Strangely, no one seems to know much about him or his whereabouts.*

Unbidden, a verse from an English book he had read clandestinely while at college popped into his mind: "They seek him here, they seek him there, those Frenchies seek him everywhere. Is he in heaven, or is he in hell? That damned elusive Pimpernel." Perhaps Doctor Nicholson fitted the role.

He put the passage out of mind and returned to the matter of Nicholson's motivation. If Nicholson aimed to steal and sell this copy of the *Dong Xi Yang Kao*, the reasoning was obscure unless something made this copy special, like a handwritten annotation or a signature that other copies lacked.

But if this copy were special, its acquisition would surely have been completed less conspicuously given the risks in stealing. Ding was useless, but perhaps his deputy could be of help. *Pretty woman, that one*, he thought.

Then it occurred to Li that two people engaged in the exact search seemed too coincidental. But perhaps although Holroyd and Nicholson were searching for the same book, their respective purposes might differ. Maybe Nicholson was searching on behalf of some collector and Holroyd was researching for academic purposes. Nothing suggested that Holroyd had any reason other than a possible link to Xiang.

Did Xiang want both documents? Li changed his mind and headed for Fang Wei's office to discuss the next step.

"I know the foreigner, Holroyd, came here with his lady companion to ask about this Doctor Nicholson," he began after the customary greetings and the obligatory tea. "Were you able to help?"

"I saw no reason to get involved," Fang Wei explained.

Li thought for a moment. "I believe they also reported being mistreated outside the library."

Fang Wei shifted nervously but nodded.

"And the result?"

"Nothing yet. The initial reports were confusing and so we have only just considered it."

This was not strange, but Li wondered if, in this case, such indifference was not part of a pattern. From his own experience, Li knew the overworked but understaffed police often ignored reports that they considered unimportant.

They also occasionally delayed an investigation due to a so-called "suggestion" from a superior. An amusing euphemism, he thought, having heard it used many times when "order" was more apt. As a superior had once told him, "It's only a suggestion, but let's not forget who is making it."

"Maybe two foreigners looking for the same disappeared items in the same library and registered at the same hotel is not coincidental. I'm wondering if all this is perhaps more serious than was apparent at first."

Fang Wei looked surprised.

"How could they not be coincidental? Perhaps the foreigners are searching for the same document but are unaware of each other. Coincidentally, they arrive at the same place at the same time. That would not be so strange." He paused. "But I wonder if this Nicholson exists or if that is his real name."

"Exists?" Li was surprised "You have questions about his existence or his identity? Why is that?"

"We cannot locate him. At least we cannot locate him under that name. Maybe he has left town, or, possibly, he is now lying on a hospital bed but under a different name."

"Hospital bed? How is that relevant?"

"I'm only guessing at this moment, but there was a traffic accident, perhaps a fatality, outside Holroyd's hotel involving a pedestrian and the *fuerdai* son of a prominent businessman named Xun Fan Ting. The kid was drunk while driving and ran over a foreigner.

"The Commissioner asked me to lose the case. Unfortunately, a journalist was present, and the matter is all over *weibo* and *weixin*. As is often the case, I believe the father, or more likely the mother, who is highly connected in the Party through her father, has told the Commissioner to close the case." He stopped to look at Li.

"Perhaps you have heard of Xun?"

"No, but there may be a file on my desk about him."

"Perhaps, perhaps not. He also has connections with the Commissioner and other high Party officials."

Li Yao fully understood the implication. "But you were saying there was a traffic accident."

"Holroyd brought in part of an airplane boarding pass, and we found the other part in the victim's pocket. The name on the stub is Brugge. Earlier, we received a call from the hotel that there had been a murder in a room registered under the name of Brugge."

Fang Wei described how the inspection of the room where the murder had supposedly taken place showed no evidence of murder nor of any recent occupancy.

"You're telling me this supposed murder victim is now lying in the hospital after being run down? Strange! I was unaware that murder victims were capable of such feats."

"The curious thing is the hotel manager who reported the murder could not find the registration documents. Also, the manager's description of how Brugge's body was dressed does not fit how the traffic victim was dressed, so assuming there was a murder, two people were involved, the murder victim and the accident victim.

"But we are unable to answer how the supposed murder victim reappeared as a traffic victim unless the traffic victim was carrying a false identity. If that were so, the traffic victim could have murdered

Brugge, stolen some things, including the boarding pass with the name 'Brugge' on it, and got run over as he left the hotel. If all that is true, our hospital patient could be this missing Nicholson." He paused.

"Just a thought, you understand."

Li nodded, considering this. "Interesting. And how did you come to this… thought?"

"Instinct and maybe a sense of coincidence."

"And just what is coincidental?"

"There is a possible tie between the traffic victim and Holroyd."

Li waited as Fang Wei recounted Holroyd's visit and the writing on the boarding pass. Li thought for a moment and decided he would try to steer Fang Wei toward a more relevant line of inquiry.

"Hmm… Let us for the moment consider that the traffic accident victim did indeed murder Brugge and take pieces of identity off the corpse. Where did Brugge's body go? Did the traffic victim dispose of the body and clean the room all by himself? That seems far-fetched to me and suggests that would have required resources and good organization. Is there any suggestion that Holroyd has the resources or is supported by such an organization?"

Fang Wei shook his head.

To save his colleague's face, Li continued. "But what else might tie this non-existent murder to Holroyd?"

Fang Wei thought for a moment. "It is supposed to have taken place on the same floor where Holroyd is staying. And we got a report that a female—who, my sergeant reports, could have been Doctor Holroyd's companion, Miss Liu, though her hair was of a different colour—asked at the front desk for a foreigner's room, but the receptionist in question is away on a sudden family matter." He stopped and then added: "I suppose she might have been nothing more than a local prostitute visiting for an intimate commercial meeting.

"Go on."

"I have asked that the staff member who gave the report be given a quiet opportunity to identify if it was Miss Liu. If it was Miss Liu, we should ask which foreigner she visited and why she disguised herself."

"You may be right, and there may be a link, but it's all circumstantial. What about the other foreigners staying there?"

"Aside from Holroyd and a Mexican businessman, we only have reports that Nicholson and Brugge stayed there."

Li became very attentive. *Mexican? Xiang worked with the Mexican cartels. Is this Mexican linked to*

Xiang? If so, does that mean Xiang was so interested in the book he organized two independent searches and a murder? What is so important about the book that so many people are after it? That again raises the question of whether academic research is Holroyd's real reason for getting the book or whether he has a different reason.

"What do you know of this Mexican?"

"Only that he registered at the hotel, stayed a few days, and then checked out to the airport."

"When was that?"

"The morning of the reported murder."

"Are you sure he left?"

"I don't know. I'll have to check."

"Please do. And see if you can discover what he did while he was here."

Fang Wei gave him a puzzled look but said nothing.

"What do we know about this Miss Liu?"

"Very little. Her papers are in order, and she is not on our list of criminals, but her *Hukou* details are incomplete. We know nothing about her parents or where she received her early education. We know she studied in England and now works for Holroyd and Holroyd's employer."

"Ah! Holroyd's employer! Perhaps Miss Liu has information on Holroyd's employer. I want to look closely at Miss Liu."

Fang Wei sat silently, waiting for Li to give instructions. When Li remained quiet, Fang Wei continued with a touch of diffidence.

"Perhaps I should ask my assistant to invite the librarians to confirm if Nicholson and the traffic victim are the same person. If not, perhaps this Brugge is another player in this game." Li nodded his agreement, and Fang Wei made the arrangements.

Li gazed thoughtfully at a picture of the Party Leader hanging on the wall. "Perhaps if we knew what was in the documents Holroyd and Nicholson were searching for, we might come closer to the answers we seek."

"Yes, that is a possibility. Nicholson is not available now, but Holroyd is."

He was interrupted by a phone call. After listening, he gave instructions before turning back to Li. "Matters have just become more interesting. Miss Liu tried to get access to our patient and became very demanding when told all access was restricted. What is curious is that the guard reports she acted as if she had unquestionable authority like a state security officer might act."

Li allowed a fleeting grin to cross his face and hoped Fang Wei hadn't noticed. "The guard had to restrain her physically."

Unaware of Li's grin, Fang Wei continued. "I wonder what lies behind her action."

"I suggest another discussion is needed with our esteemed Doctor Holroyd. Perhaps he can tell us more about why he is here and about our traffic victim."

Fang Wei nodded and called for his sergeant to bring Holroyd in for questioning.

32

Once Holroyd arrived, Fang Wei greeted him and motioned him to sit. "Doctor Holroyd, thank you for agreeing to come to see us."

"It's not as if I had much choice."

Fang Wei smiled mirthlessly as he opened a file folder on his desk and looked over his notes.

"You came here earlier with a piece of paper you found near a recent traffic incident. That piece of paper had writing that could refer to you, although you say you have no idea why. Let me suggest that you do know why."

"What? How did you come to that idea?"

"Perhaps you and the traffic victim were after the same thing, whatever it is or was."

"I have told you what I'm looking for, but I have no knowledge what the victim wants or why he is interested in me."

"Let's see if I can help you to get an idea. A few days ago, you came in complaining about an attack outside the library. I understand the demonstrators accused you of wanting to steal valuable artifacts looted from ancient tombs. Is that correct?"

Holroyd nodded, suddenly very cautious.

"Now, why do you think the demonstrators would accuse you of such a deed unless they had some reason to believe you were doing that?"

"I have no idea."

Fang Wei looked at him in silence.

"Today my colleague and my assistant interrupted a meeting between yourself and the library director. As we now suspect, the director may be involved in tomb-robbing and selling valuable artifacts recovered from such a tomb. With that knowledge, I will ask you why you met him."

"I was there to see if I could get more information about the missing document."

"And that was the one document you were most eager to get. Am I correct so far?"

"Yes."

"Why was that document of such importance to you?"

"I'm sorry, but I don't know its contents, so I can't answer that."

"Then allow me to suggest a reason. You went there to acquire an ancient document recovered by tomb robbers. I further suggest that you want to acquire it not, as you have claimed, for reasons of academic research but so that you can smuggle it out of China and sell it for a profit."

"That is an outrageous suggestion." Holroyd suddenly realized he was skating on ice that was giving off loud cracking sounds. "You can check my credentials, and you will find I have never engaged in such activities."

"We have, and I agree, your credentials are respectable, but that does not mean you are incapable of engaging in, shall we say, less respectable activities."

There was silence as Holroyd began to take in what he was facing.

Li broke the silence. "Doctor Holroyd, let us leave aside for the moment my colleague's observations and discuss a different matter. I know you met and accepted a task from Xiang Jin Leng in England. Is he the one who wants to get this document?"

Holroyd was surprised. *Where is Li coming from? I think I'm being set up as a dealer in stolen artifacts!* He began to sweat and decided to stall.

"Mr. Li, I don't know what Mr. Xiang wants exactly. He never mentioned a document or any other object for that matter."

"Then what is your task?"

"I'm looking for reports of Chinese voyages during the late Ming and early Qing Dynasties in the South China Sea area."

"So, you say. And were it not for the demonstration at the library and your meeting with Director Ding, I would be inclined to accept your word. However, the demonstration and the meeting both took place, and we want to know if the demonstrators had a valid reason for their actions."

"Look, I don't know where this preposterous idea is coming from that I'm engaged in tomb-robbing or stealing ancient artifacts."

Li leaned forward. "Doctor Holroyd, I'm informed you visited Wang Tang Cun. What was your reason for going there?"

Fang Wei looked surprised.

Holroyd was also taken unawares. "I went there because I was told the document I'm looking for came from there."

"And when you got there, did you find this document?"

"No."

"So, you were unable to obtain it?"

"I can't obtain something I can't find"

"Kindly just answer my questions. Did you try to make arrangements for it to be delivered or shown to you?"

"No."

"Were you told where you might find it or at least get further information as to its location?"

"No."

"I do not find your denial convincing." Li looked at Holroyd thoughtfully. "First, you have been visiting the librarian and not, as you stated was your original intention, visited the university. Then you went to some village that may be engaged in tomb robbing. Next, you were accused by demonstrators of tomb robbing and trying to sell stolen artifacts, and now, as we learned, the librarian you were visiting appears to be deeply involved in those activities. What are we to conclude?"

"I don't think you can conclude anything. It's all circumstantial and were you to charge me, it would never stand up in court, not even a Chinese court." Despite his show of defiance, Holroyd was becoming very afraid of where this could be leading.

"I sincerely hope you will not have to discover what does or does not stand up in a Chinese court," Li observed drily.

Holroyd hoped his fear did not show.

"What is your connection to Mr. Brugge?" Fang Wei asked, taking over the questioning.

"Who? I have never heard of him."

"Oh! Did I forget to mention the name? He is lying in the hospital, the victim of a traffic event that may have been accidental or deliberate. Perhaps you have not heard of him, but as shown by the boarding pass you brought to my attention, he seems to have heard of and be interested in you. If his injuries resulted from a deliberate act, you, Doctor Holroyd will have some further questions to answer, and answer you will."

Holroyd began to sweat. "But isn't that man Nicholson?"

"You suggested he might be Nicholson. I wonder why. Could it be that you learned Nicholson was interfering with your activities, and you wanted to remove him? If so, perhaps you even arranged for the traffic accident, if an accident is what it was."

"What are you saying? Are you accusing me of attempted murder? Who do you think I am?" His voice rose, but he hoped his rising panic was not evident.

"We are trying to determine who you are."

"I have nothing to hide!" Holroyd protested." I came here with an academic visa to do some research."

"So, you say, but you seem to attract accidents and losses of documents faster than shit attracts flies. Perhaps your stated purpose of doing research hides another purpose, and you discovered a competitor such as Brugge or Nicholson or whatever his real name is."

"I really think you're being fanciful. I told you why I thought the man might be Nicholson, but of this Brugge, I have no knowledge."

"Really? Then why was your assistant, Miss Liu, so eager to visit Brugge?"

"What? I asked her to find out where Nicholson was being treated."

"Is that so? Well, we will discuss that later. Meantime, I will remind you again to respect the laws here. And please remember your visa can be revoked in an instant."

Holroyd was taken unawares. "You… you wouldn't do that!" As he said it, Holroyd realized he had just blundered.

Li leaned forward. "Are you so confident that we wouldn't do that, Doctor Holroyd? Please be careful in challenging us. As of this moment, we have serious doubts about your reason for being here. Under the circumstances, we cannot let you continue freely until we are satisfied that your reasons are as you claim."

Holroyd was so shocked he almost shouted. "If I can't continue freely, I might as well go home."

"Oh! If that is your intention you are free to do so. In fact, I think we will be pleased to help you on your way."

Holroyd realized the ice he was skating on was definitely cracking. Recognizing that resistance was futile, he calmed down and spoke with obvious contrition. "My apologies. I spoke in haste. I assume I'm not under arrest?"

"As long as you remain in the city and stay at your hotel, you are not. But if there are any more disturbances, you will be arrested and escorted to the airport and leave China. I trust we understand each other?"

Holroyd left feeling very shaken. His whole mission was now threatened. Restricted access might still allow him to finish his task, but now he was under the watchful eye of the police, and Wendy had warned him that the police might not be on his side. He felt his mission had just become much more difficult.

The two officers sat silent for a moment. Finally, Li spoke. "I'm not inclined to believe him. Although his story has been consistent, he refuses to tell us the complete story, and I'm not convinced he is telling the truth when he says he knows nothing of Brugge."

"I agree. Should we arrest him?" Fang Wei asked.

"No, at least not yet. In the meantime, I want to know more about this Nicholson and how he may be involved in my inquiries. I wonder where we can find Nicholson?"

"I've asked both the librarian and his assistant to see if this Brugge is Nicholson," Fang Wei reminded Li.

"That would make matters simpler. If he's not the same, we must find out what links exist between Holroyd, Brugge, and Holroyd and Nicholson. But if they are the same, we may have just the one link to Holroyd, but are we any further ahead?"

"Perhaps not. But regardless of who is lying in the hospital, we should not forget that he may have been deliberately run over," Li said, "But if the act was deliberate, why? And what is the role of the driver? This son of the local businessman?"

Fang Wei said nothing but looked up at the ceiling. "I'm still curious about the reported murder at the hotel."

Li frowned. "Are you sure it might have a connection to our inquiries? I would not want to waste my time here by addressing some circumstantial and possibly irrelevant issue."

"If for the moment we accept that there was a murder, but the evidence was somehow removed before we got to the scene, is it possible that the victim was another person trying to get the documents Holroyd is so anxious to obtain?" Fang Wei asked. "If so, did Holroyd somehow arrange for the attack? Or did the attack come from somewhere else?"

"The murder victim's name was Brugge, which was the name on the boarding stub. Unless murdered corpses can get up so as to get run over later, I would have to conclude there was no murder."

"But what about the call from the hotel?" Fang Wei asked.

"Yes, that puzzles me," Li conceded.

"Let us consider that there was a murder and that for some reason Holroyd arranged it. If that is so, and if the traffic attack was arranged by Holroyd, we must ask if Holroyd could have arranged two murders to eliminate his competition. If so, how is Xun Fan Ting's son involved? Are Holroyd and Xun working together?"

"But why this book? What's so special about this book? It's not an original. "

"I don't have that information, but I will check." Fang Wei made a note on his file.

"Given that Holroyd is engaged by the British government and the criminal Xiang Jin Leng, I could see Xiang wanting a book, but then how is the British government involved? That brings us back to Holroyd's reason for searching for the book."

"I agree. But there is another question. Why did Miss Liu try to get access to Brugge? Holroyd told us her instructions were only to locate him, so either Holroyd is lying, or Liu had some purpose of which Holroyd is unaware. Was she trying to get some information from Brugge that she may not want Holroyd to know?"

"So, Miss Liu might not be the assistant Holroyd thinks she is. Have we found how she came to be employed by Holroyd? I think Miss Liu might be a better source of information than the uncooperative professor."

"Honourable Li, we are not making progress at this moment. Let's go eat, and we can continue to work later."

Li nodded, and they headed out the door.

Over a lunch of noodle soup and beer, Fang Wei and Li avoided discussing the case. Instead, they chatted about their families, the perfidy of many western nations, and beautiful places they had visited. At one point they thought they might have a distant relationship by marriage.

They compared working conditions but avoided any mention of specifics or matters that someone might later construe as criticism. A guarded trust burgeoned that thawed the traditional ice between conflicting jurisdictions.

Having eaten, the two policemen relaxed.

"Why do we let Holroyd loose when we're not sure how he's involved?" Fang Wei asked.

"Interference in his work could close my only leads to Xiang Jin Leng, and I'm not ready to do that just yet."

Just then Fang Wei's phone rang. He accepted the call and listened for a moment. "Is he certain?" He listened further and then hung up.

"That was Wu Shi Ming. The librarian confirmed that the patient is Nicholson. So, now we have the questions of why Nicholson was run over and why he had a boarding stub with the name 'Brugge' on it.

And perhaps why the hotel staff reported Brugge had been murdered."

"But you said there was no proof there was a murder victim."

"True, but the people who brought it to our attention were certain, and they know the penalties for misleading the police. I'm inclined to believe them for the moment even if there is no evidence."

"Curious but not perhaps relevant to the matter at hand. But let me return to the identity of Brugge, who the librarian confirms is Nicholson. Only the librarian confirmed it? Was the deputy not also called to view the body?"

"She was not available."

"Here I think another confirmation would be advisable. Somehow, I do not feel confident that the librarian has been fully open and truthful. Please have the deputy verify the librarian's testimony."

And with that, lunch was over.

33

Left to his own devices but now conscious he was under the watchful eyes of a suspicious police force, Holroyd decided to try his luck with Pearl. Perhaps with some encouragement she might be prepared to open up a little more. He managed to reach her.

She declined the invitation to be his guide, but to his delight, she invited him to visit her apartment after work.

Pearl lived on the fifth floor of a three-unit six-story working-class apartment block that had no lift. The drab concrete stairwell could have profited from a wash, a coat of paint, and light bulbs on each floor.

The apartment was small by Western standards. Inside, a small bedroom and a smaller sitting room adjoined a bathroom with a small hand basin, a single pipe mounted on the wall for showers, and a squat toilet that also served as the drain for the shower.

Personal belongings cluttered the otherwise scrupulously clean spaces. On arrival, Holroyd was greeted with a smile. After he was seated, Pearl offered a plate of sunflower seeds, tiny biscuits, and tea.

Holroyd leaned forward. "Pearl," he said encouragingly, "you have told us what happened to the Dong Xi Yang Kao and even something about the missing document. But perhaps you know more but are reluctant to tell anybody." Pearl looked at the floor.

"Pearl, I believe you are a competent librarian trying to fulfil her duties in the best possible manner. But maybe you are not entirely free to do as you think you should." Pearl remained silent.

"I can see you are very loyal to your colleagues. But you must put your loyalty to your colleagues behind your loyalty to the people of China. If you are loyal to anyone who does not deserve such loyalty, now is the time to tell someone."

Pearl began to cry. Holroyd thought to reach out and comfort her, but he hesitated. Finally, her voice choked by tears, Pearl spoke. "I think it is terrible that there are people who steal the national heritage and treasures that belong to all our people. We should stop such people and punish them."

"I agree, but why not tell the authorities?"

"Which authorities, and who would believe me?"

"I'm sure there are people who could help, but—"

"But I think I can trust you, and I hope you may help us," she said teary-eyed.

"Us?"

"The people of China, the Party, future generations."

"And how can I help?"

"I think I can suggest who might have the missing document."

His heart beat faster. If Pearl's information turned out to be true, then the object of his quest might be within reach. "Who is he?"

"His name is Xun Fan Ting. He is a rich businessman here in FujinHaiZhou."

"Why do you think he has the document?"

"Something Librarian Ding once said when he thought I could not hear. He was on the telephone with someone discussing the value of the Dong Xi Yang Kao. They were arguing, and finally, Ding said they should let Xun Fan Ting decide. I did not think much about it then, but later I wondered what Xun would know about the book and why Librarian Ding would let him decide its value." She reached for a tissue to wipe away a tear.

"Then I remembered that people say Xun owns a marvellous collection of ancient Chinese things. No one knows how he gained this collection, but I do not think his business would provide him with the means to buy the items.

"The government controls the purchasing of ancient Chinese things, so even if he has enough money, collecting things would not be easy. I know this is not enough for you to believe me, but you are the only person I think I can trust."

"Thank you for your confidence, but why not go to the police?"

"The police?" Pearl could not keep a mocking tone out of her voice. "Who can trust the police these days? I have no faith that by going to the police I would achieve anything except losing my job and my apartment. There is talk in the courtyards that the respectable Commissioner of Police, Fu Li, is engaged with criminal elements and revenges himself on anyone who dares suggest that his police force is anything but a model law enforcement organization. I have no real proof, and without proof, I could get into trouble. I may have little, but I do not wish to lose what I have." She waved her hand over the cluttered apartment.

"The Commissioner is a close friend of Xun's, and I don't know how many others are also corrupt. I do not trust the police." Her lower lip quivered, and for a horrible moment, he thought she might start to cry again. However, she reached for another tissue and wiped her eyes

"Thank you for confiding in me, Pearl. I'm not sure how I can respond, but perhaps there is a way. Please leave this with me. I will try my best. But thank you for having so much faith in me."

"I can think of no one else to whom I could turn," Pearl mumbled, and he thought she might cry again. She pulled out another tissue and dabbed her eyes. "Must be the dust or the pollution." She smiled bravely.

"Yes, I'm sure it is." With that, he thanked her and then got up and left.

Holroyd mulled over Pearl's information and wondered if Ding could be made to admit where the missing documents might be found. Presumably, Ding had sold them, perhaps to Xun Fan Ting, but that only raised the bigger question of how to approach Ding and Xun.

He decided he could pose to a trader as a buyer in stolen artifacts. He would ask no questions about provenance but would offer a substantial amount of money.

Mr. Xiang and the American general, he reasoned, had said they would cover all expenses, and if they demurred over this item, Holroyd could still fall back on his £100,000 fee or perhaps even the resources of Her Majesty's Exchequer. *I'll have to ask Wendy, and at the same time, I should ask what she discovered at the hospital about Nicholson.*

Back at the hotel, he asked Wendy about her attempt at seeing the patient, but Wendy refused to reveal any details. Holroyd was surprised and annoyed but decided to discuss the matter later, asking her about Xun Fan Ting instead.

Wendy knew quite a bit, enough for Holroyd to ask Wendy to pursue the contact. Wendy did not seem keen, nor did she think Xun would refuse to help. Holroyd did not care about Wendy's misgivings. She had corroborated most of the information Pearl had given him, and that was enough for him to insist.

Wendy duly arranged a meeting.

*****

Li was pondering what his next move should be when the phone rang. Deputy Director Ting came straight to the point, and his voice did not sound friendly. Li groaned inwardly, wondering what his leader wanted now.

"This man, Holroyd, is disturbing our leaders. We received information that he is abusing our hospitality by stealing ancient artifacts and attacking other foreigners. He seems to attract crime like honey attracts wasps. Holroyd may have hidden his real purpose in coming here and involved himself with criminal elements. That possibility upsets the Director, and he is eager to defuse the situation before anything else alarms our leaders. Let the local police handle Holroyd. I need you here to keep an eye on developments."

Li thought for a moment and then tried placating his superior. "I think I may be able to help reduce our leaders' worries."

"How?" Ting asked.

"I need to make further inquiries before I can brief you fully, but I'm making progress."

"This is not some lame excuse to delay your return?" Ting asked, resuming his attack. "And can you assure me that this distraction will deflect the possible annoyance of our leaders at what Holroyd is doing?"

"I believe so, Deputy Director."

"How much time will you need before you can return?"

"Forty-eight hours, but I think probably less."

"You have your forty-eight hours." Li fully understood the not-so veiled menace in the deputy director's approval.

34

Fang Wei and Li sat on a bench where no one could overhear their conversation. Fang Wei's phone rang, and he answered it, listening but saying nothing. After a few seconds, he hung up. "Shao Yao is ready to view Brugge."

"Why not accompany her?" Li asked. "We can provide transport." Fang Wei nodded, and they went to collect Pearl.

At the hospital, the three looked at the recumbent figure. "Well, Shao Yao? Is this Doctor Nicholson?"

"Oh, no! This man is younger and has blond hair cut short, but Doctor Nicholson was older and had darker skin, He also had black or very dark brown hair that was much longer."

"Are you quite certain?"

"Oh yes. Quite sure."

The officers sent Pearl back in a taxi. As they watched her leave, Fang Wei turned to Li. "Our distinguished librarian has some explaining to do as to why he was so confused."

"Are you sure that Shao Yao is correct?" Li asked. "Or could she be mistaken?"

"It is possible," Fang Wei admitted, "but she seemed certain, and if asked about who is telling the truth, I choose Shao Yao over Ding Qu Wan."

Li nodded. "I agree." He stood there, thinking. "Is it possible Brugge was attacked as the hotel staff maintain and that his body was thrown in front of a car to suggest he was run over? If that was how it happened, then the attackers might be concerned that Brugge did not die and might try to finish the task at the hospital."

"Holroyd's assistant, Miss Liu, tried to get access to the patient," Fang Wei exclaimed.

"That puts Miss Liu and Holroyd in an interesting position and not one that fits an academic and his assistant simply doing research."

"But that still leaves Nicholson," Fang Wei said. "How did Shao Yao describe him? Older with black hair?"

Li thought for a moment "Black hair among foreigners is often a characteristic of Central Americans. I'm wondering if the Mexican at the hotel could have been Nicholson. He might have registered using his real name but used a false one at the library. That would explain why you could not locate him." He turned to face Fang Wei.

"Perhaps you might show the librarians the Mexican's registration or passport photograph and see how they react. If Shao Yao identifies him as Nicholson, we can check with Immigration to see when he left and where he went. That will solve his whereabouts." He stopped.

"I may not be able to stay and help much longer. My superior has called me back to Beijing. Let's see if we can close this case before I have to depart."

"That would be fortunate," Fang Wei said, also hoping they could close the case quickly.

"Holroyd is looking for ancient documents and seems to be focused on two that have gone missing. I wonder why. One document, a book, we know was taken from the library, but copies exist in Beijing. The other went missing after an illegal recovery from a tomb. I think that is the one we should focus on for the moment. If the librarian is telling the truth, we may now have a direct link from the tomb robbers to Fu Li."

"The librarian may be lying, but even if he did tell the Commissioner, the Commissioner may simply have been dismissive."

"What we would need is a link from Fu Li to the final buyer or buyers."

Fang Wei thought for a moment. "Perhaps we do have a link between Fu Li and a possible buyer. Xun Fang Ting was in the Red Guards together with Fu

Li and Xun is reported to be a receiver of ancient artifacts looted from tombs."

"That could establish a link, but is it enough to tie Xun to the missing book and the document? We need to find either one or both in Xun's possession, or get an admission that he got them from Fu Li. I don't hold out much hope for that." He paused.

"But perhaps we can get at it from another angle. Brugge had Holroyd's name and address written down, Holroyd is interested in stolen documents, and Xun's son ran over Brugge. Perhaps Holroyd engaged Xun to remove Brugge, and Xun used his son as the means. It's rather weak, but I can see possibilities."

"I agree. But who directed these developments if there's no link between Holroyd and Xun?"

The two officers looked at each other and then answered the question in unison. "Commissioner Fu Li."

Li looked up at the sky. "We have been told he knew about the book," he said pensively, "but we don't know if he got it, kept it, or sold it, and we still don't know why Doctor Holroyd is so interested. Nor does it bring me closer to Xiang Jin Leng."

"Because of your impending departure," Fang Wei said, "I don't think it would be wise to wait for Brugge to come out of his coma. He may never tell us anything; even if he does, he may not know anything useful. Perhaps we should look in a new direction.”

“Which direction do you suggest?”

“I don’t think we have enough evidence to challenge Fu Li on the missing book or any other artifacts. But is there any other reason we would want to meet with him? Or better yet, any reason we should not meet with him?”

“Whispers from the courtyards suggest that we both should and should not. I think if we go, we should be careful. A wrong step could land us deep enough in manure we may never escape the stink.”

“True, but are you afraid?” Li asked in a tone that suggested Fang Wei might lose face.

“No, I do not think I am. I think I have been waiting a long time for an opportunity to clean out this cowshed.”

“What approach do you suggest?” Li asked, feigning ignorance to give his colleague face.

“Why not be direct? Together, we ask Fu Li why he directed me to drop the DUI case. We can suggest that someone in authority or at least with guanxi is trying to influence the course of justice. We can imply that we suspect the said person is him. With you in attendance, we can suggest that we might want to extend a *shuanggui* invitation.[3] If nothing else that should worry him."

"Ah, good. Using guanxi to get preferential treatment. Excellent suggestion."

"Once he has become nervous, we can ask why there are rumours he owns stolen artifacts." Fang Wei was warming to his theme. Li could see that the inspector was relishing the confrontation, and that satisfied Li very much.

"Then off to visit Fu Li we go," said Fang Wei.

But Li hesitated. "I'm not sure I agree. I see no link between Fu Li and my search for Xiang Jin Leng. I know that Xiang commissioned Holroyd to do research, and Holroyd is now interested in a document that Fu Li may have or may have had in his possession. If we now confront Fu Li, he will either deny he has it or will tell us he sold it but can't remember to whom. Of course, with time his

---

3 *Shuanggui* (双规) functions beyond the reach of China's criminal justice system and gives the Party the authority to summon any of the communist Party's 88 million members to account for allegedly ill-gotten gains at a "designated location at a designated time." Those summoned are deprived of liberty for days, weeks, or months, during which time they are repeatedly interrogated and reportedly sometimes tortured.

memory will improve, but I doubt it will before my departure."

"What do you suggest?"

"I'm wondering if we can use Xun's reputation as a questionable collector of antiques and his relationship to Fu Li to reveal if Xun was the buyer. If Xun does have the missing document, we might discover why Holroyd is so eager to get it. Once we know that, I suspect Holroyd will be more cooperative about where I can find Xiang."

"Do you think Xun will cooperate?" Before Li could answer, Fang Wei's cell phone rang. He answered and then hung up shortly after. "This case just got even more interesting. Brugge died without regaining consciousness. I suspect the news will not be welcome in the Xun household. However, it gives us an excellent reason to go visit our illustrious Xun Fan Ting."

"I agree. Now you can charge their son with murder, manslaughter, or accidental death. I'm sure the loving parents will be eager to save their son from a bullet or the warm welcome offered in our prisons by the guards and other prisoners. I'm told few people forget the experience."

Both officers grinned.

35

Holroyd and Wendy arrived at Xun's house and were led to the study.

"Doctor Holroyd and Miss Liu, welcome to my home. Please take a seat. May I offer you some tea? Something stronger? Filomena, biscuits." The maid nodded and departed. Xun sat behind his desk, steepled his hands, and regarded his guests, his face expressionless. After some polite small talk, Xun came to the point.

"They tell me you are interested in gaining some ancient artifacts. China has a long history of producing some of the finest pieces of ancient art. Many people come to China looking for antiques, but I'm curious why you think I can help."

"A respected source suggested that we contact you," Holroyd said.

"A respected source,'" Xun repeated dubiously. "Flattering though that may be, Doctor Holroyd, I'm curious as to why my name was suggested."

"They told us you have an impressive collection of Chinese antiques, and I wondered if you might be willing to part with any of it."

"I have to suggest your source is mistaken. Regretfully, I do not own such a collection. So, I'm sorry to say your visit is a waste."

"Ah! That would be a shame." Undeterred, Holroyd continued. "Mr. Xun, I'm looking for a document written during the late Ming or early Qing Dynasty by an official from Haicheng and taken from the official's tomb."

"Doctor Holroyd, as I have said—"

"We believe this document was at once deposited in the local library but may have moved elsewhere, such as into your collection."

"That is an outrageous suggestion. How dare you come into my house and accuse me of collecting stolen artifacts? I think you had better leave now." He got up from behind his desk.

"Mr. Xun, I have no interest in how you may have acquired this document. That would perhaps be a matter for the local authorities, but I have no desire to involve them." He let the implied threat sink in.

"Let me be quite clear. I'm most interested in examining this document and perhaps buying it. Naturally, I would not wish to buy the wrong item, but if it were to be the one in which I have an interest, I would acknowledge its worth."

Xun's eyes lit up at the suggestion of payment, but otherwise, his face remained impassive. "And you believe I may have this document?"

"It is possible."

"If I were to have such a document, I could hardly admit that to two strangers, regardless of their credentials. While I find your story interesting, I do not see how I could help."

"How very frustrating. They led us to understand that you might know of such a record."

"Doctor Holroyd, I'm sorry, but whoever informed you I could be of help is mistaken. I neither have nor have any knowledge of any records of early exploration. I suspect you will have difficulty locating such an item unless they exist in the National Archives or the National Museum in Beijing."

"We have looked there but without success. They informed us that people lost many historical records during the Cultural Revolution."

"Yes. Our Cultural Revolution was a terrible happening. Those ignorant and misguided young people destroyed so much of China's history. But I suppose they believed the destruction of the past and its signs was the way for a better future."

Holroyd froze, remembering he had heard the exact words from a young Red Guard when he had last been in China. But who had it been? Why did he have such a strong sense of *déjà vu*? Was it possible that Xun himself had been that Red Guard?

"Mr. Xun, may I ask a direct question?" Xun frowned but nodded. "I cannot help but feel that I know you. Had you been on film or television at one point many years ago?"

"Yes," Xun said warily, "I once acted on television."

"I don't believe what I remember was acting. I believe it was a documentary or a report. As I remember, the person, who may have been you, played a prominent part in an event near Nanjing during the Cultural Revolution. I noticed it because I had just left there on my way out of China. As I remember now, that person cheered and even led the destruction of books in front of the private house where I had been given shelter. I later heard the couple that lived there was sent to XinJiang and died there of starvation and deprivation."

"Oh no, Doctor Holroyd! I think you are confusing me with someone else. Unfortunately, there were many occasions where people engaged in what we now know were irresponsible and unforgivable acts. However, I was travelling on business and missed everything. I was lucky enough to escape that horrible experience."

"Mr. Xun, the Revolution lasted ten years. Surely you did not travel all that time?"

Xun remained silent, and after a moment, Holroyd persisted. "If you didn't travel all that time, what did you do?"

Mr. Xun did not answer, but Wendy spoke up. "I think Mr. Xun was active in the removal—or should I say theft—of historical artifacts that people later reported destroyed."

Xun looked at her reproachfully and spoke in Chinese.

"Mr. Xun, do not accuse me of being impolite," Wendy replied in English. "Thefts during the Revolution, even if sanctioned by the government of the time, do not sit quite well in modern China. Had you been honest with us, you might have had a point." Xun said nothing, and Wendy continued.

"I wonder what they would find if there were a thorough search of this house and its contents."

Xun was silent. "As private citizens, perhaps we might feel obligated to notify the relevant authorities of our suspicions." Wendy smiled in what Holroyd considered a guileless manner.

Xun looked at her in silence, then leaned forward. "Shall we be open with each other, Doctor Holroyd? I have no reason to help you."

"Not true, Mister Xun," Wendy said. "You can avoid scrutiny of your activities so many years ago."

"I hardly think my activities during those years will excite much attention. Many people were involved, many of whom now occupy positions of power."

"True, and perhaps you are right. But I think people would be very attentive if your activities were conducted to enrich yourself and not to further the political ideas of the time. You know how quickly matters can get out of control. Sometimes, a whisper in the right quarters is enough to start unwelcome inquiries."

"Wendy, stop that! I'm sure Mr. Xun knows what you're saying." Holroyd broke in. "So, why don't we start from the beginning and try a different approach? Perhaps by doing so, we can progress."

Wendy looked annoyed, but Xun looked relieved.

"Mr. Xun, I'm engaged to get or copy any records that can give detailed accounts of settlers moving into the South China Sea during the late Ming and or early Qing dynasties. If such documents exist, and if I can get them, or at least photograph or scan them, my employers will pay handsomely."

"So, you are interested in one particular item?"

"Not necessarily, unless that one item provides me with the information I need."

"And other than ensuring that the item is genuine, you would not be too concerned about how such an item found itself in a particular place or collection?"

Holroyd nodded.

"And you say the buyer or buyers can afford a high price, let me say a very high price?"

Holroyd nodded again.

"Any details of a possible sale will remain secret?"

"With the seller's cooperation, yes."

"Perhaps, with that undertaking, I may be able to assist you to some extent as long as we both understand your specific guarantees to avoid any unpleasant rumours about how I might have gathered my collection." Xun looked to Holroyd for some sign of agreement.

When Holroyd nodded, he continued. "Then, let us see how I may be of service."

He got up from behind his desk and, after pressing a hidden button, opened a door that led into an adjacent room. He waved for Holroyd and Wendy to follow. When they did, they feasted their eyes on the contents of Xun's treasure room.

Holroyd looked in amazement at the collection of priceless artifacts. Wendy remained silent. There was no way that Xun had legitimately gained any of the items.

Holroyd thought the collection must have ranked among the best in the world. It boasted porcelain, clay, jade, bronze, gold, and silk items. In one case, a caparisoned horse glazed with green and gold, waited impatiently for its rider. In another, merchants on camels were setting out for distant lands but now sat frozen in positions, suggesting their sedate movement across the desert sand.

Many items of jade and gold jewellery lay on shelves and in trays. Several large vases from the Tang, Song, and Ming dynasties showed off their craftsmanship and beauty. Three mannequins wore embroidered silks. In yet another case stood a complete set of armour. Antique chests and cupboards probably held more treasures. The collection was incredible.

"This is fabulous, Mr. Xun."

"Thank you, Professor. Coming from you such an appreciation is an honour. It has taken me many years and effort to gather these few testimonials on China's great past."

"Is that a real Ming vase?" Wendy asked, pointing to a huge vessel standing off one side. "It must be worth a lot."

"Yes," Xun said, smiling dismissively, "if any of these items were on the market, I'm sure they would fetch a good price."

Holroyd's heart beat faster as Xun went over to a glass cabinet and extracted a package, which he unwrapped carefully to reveal a traditional book of bound bamboo strips He stepped back and, handing Holroyd some cotton gloves, invited him to look. The book was a *jiandu* tied by a faded red ribbon. *This is what the old woman in Wang Tang Cun was talking about! We found it! Now let's see what it says!*

Xun gave gloves to Wendy and motioned her to examine the treasure. She unrolled the strips and quickly scanned several pages.

"It's written in traditional old Chinese, but the calligraphy is impressive. This is the diary of an official who held a position in the port of Haicheng. He may have been a collector of customs duties because I see many entries of money received from individuals, some of whom are ship owners. They could also have been bribes, but I doubt he would have recorded those. He could never be certain that imperial examiners would not demand to see his records one day."

Xun nodded and reached to take the book back but seemed to fumble and almost drop the priceless object. He managed to catch it in time by a quick manoeuvre as Holroyd stepped forward as if to help.

"Oh! Thank you. Luckily, we managed to catch it before it fell."

"Mr. Xun, did you just remove something from the book?" Holroyd asked. "May I see it?"

"It's nothing. Just a scrap of paper that should not have been there."

"Let me see it." Reluctantly Xun passed it over, and Holroyd carefully placed it on a nearby table. "Wendy, come and look at this."

Wendy carefully examined the scrap. "This is a note of several boats leaving with fisherman families bound for islands in the south but to the east of Vietnam and the west of the Philippines. The writer noted that they left without paying the required taxes and recorded the number of men, women, and children." She examined it further.

"He reminded himself of the departure because the people made it clear they intended to return, and he would need to collect taxes when they did."

"That sounds like an ancient Post-it note. It wasn't entered in the book itself because it was a reminder and not yet official. Anything more?" Holroyd asked.

"Not on the paper but perhaps in the book."

"Is there a date? Anything that tells us when these fishermen departed?"

"Please wait a moment." Wendy looked in the book again, turning some pages and mumbling in Chinese. "The sixth lunar month of the forty-seventh year of the Qian-Long Emperor." She thought for a moment before continuing. "That would translate into June or July 1782." She scanned further.

"Oh! Here's a note dated a year later that a trader brought back a shipwrecked sailor, a fisherman swept out to sea by a storm. He had been a member of one of the original fisher families. He reported they had landed on an Island and established a settlement there. When he left, the settlement was in good shape, and his family would be happy to see his safe return. A note is that any ship travelling in that direction should carry him home."

"Does it say anything about where this fisherman was to go?"

"No. It just says, 'to the south.'"

"So, it describes people setting out and founding a settlement to the south?"

She looked up. "Yes. I think we've found what you are looking for."

"I think we have. It doesn't give us precise locations, but I think it would stand up in court." *Eureka! We've found it! After everything I've been through, I've finally found it.* Elated, he wanted to jump for joy, but he managed to restrain himself by thinking how Xun and Wendy would react. However, he could not refrain from a gleeful grin. He turned to Xun.

"Mr. Xun, what price do you want for this document?"

"The items in my collection are priceless. But as a gesture of friendliness and goodwill, I suggest a million dollars would be appropriate." Holroyd thought for a moment and calculated that, at the present exchange rate, $1 million would work out to be £750,000. Rather above his resources but well within what he thought Mr. Xiang or Her Majesty would pay.

"Doctor Holroyd, look at this!" Wendy was pointing at another book displayed on a shelf in another case. Holroyd went over. "The Dong Xi Yang Kao! So here is where it is. Mr. Xun, may I ask how you got this book?" Xun was about to reply when the door opened.

"Xun Fan Ting! You fucking bastard!"

Holroyd looked up at the interruption. He saw a well-manicured woman who screeched as she projected herself into the room. "You son of a whore. You *shabi. Cao ni ma*!" Wendy and Xun flinched at the words, though Holroyd only discovered their true meaning later.

"What?" Xun was visibly trying to regain control of the meeting.

"Our son! They have charged him with causing a death. I told you to contact that useless Commissioner of Police."

"I did, and he assured me he would resolve the matter. He also suggested our son might enjoy an extended visit abroad."

"Well, it seems you did not persuade our honourable policeman enough to follow through." She stopped as if aware for the first time she was not alone with her husband. She stared at the two guests and then turned back to Xun.

"Who are these people? Get rid of them now."

Holroyd couldn't understand everything she said, but he sensed from her tone that Xun would unlikely be pleased. He looked at Wendy, who regarded the intruder with what Holroyd thought was a mixture of irritation and interest. What was this about?

"Doctor Holroyd, Miss Liu, my sincerest apologies. Allow me to introduce Zhu Mei Li, my wife. An unfortunate traffic accident involves our son, and though the police promised they would resolve the matter quietly and quickly, it seems perhaps not."

There was a knock on the door, and Filomena stood there waiting for permission to speak. Before she could, Li and Fang Wei brushed past her.

Both men stopped in astonishment when they saw the contents of the room. Holroyd's heart missed a beat. He understood the expression "being caught with one hand in the till." He had a vision of himself languishing in a prison cell rather than enjoying the comforts of his flat in London. He had little time to think further as the officers moved into the room, but he noted that Li was looking at him like a vulture looks at carrion.

"Well, well, well, what have we here? This looks better than a visit to the National Museum," Fang Wei said, looking at Xun. "Now, how did you get all these wonderful items?"

"And Doctor Holroyd is here!" Li's expression gave nothing away, but Holroyd sensed a coming confrontation.

There was a silence, during which Zhu Mei Li took out a cigarette and lit it with trembling fingers. She took a deep drag and exhaled into the air-conditioned room. Holroyd was horrified and started to protest, but Xun beat him to it. "Dammit, woman, put that cigarette out. You know enough not to smoke in here. Have you any idea of the damage cigarette smoke can do to the collection?"

"Oh, yes, I do." Zhu Mei Li looked at him and, with slow deliberation, stubbed her cigarette out on the nearest convenient surface, which happened to be the open document with its precious scrap of paper.

The centuries-old parchment burst into flames, and the book's surface blackened. Shocked by the turn of events, no one moved immediately. Finally, with a hoarse cry of despair, Holroyd launched himself at the burning mass to quench the flames, but he bumped into Xun, delaying the rescue by vital seconds, and the document curled up into a pile of grey ash.

Holroyd felt as if he had been punched in the gut and almost vomited as he realized his quest had gone up in smoke. A mixture of fury, sorrow, and despair washed over him, and for a moment, he refused to believe what had just happened.

He had found what he had been searching for, only to see it destroyed by a careless act by a stupid, self-important woman. However, he wondered if he might salvage his task based on the testimony of those present.

He looked around at the others and saw a grin of triumph on Zhu Mei Li's face. Xun had turned a sickly shade of yellow and was now looking at his wife with murderous intent. The two policemen had not yet grasped the import of the destruction and seemed unsure what to do next. He looked over at

Wendy, but as he did so she pushed over the Ming vase, which shattered utterly.

Distracted from his wife, Xun turned on Wendy. "You fucking *shabi* bitch! *Ni choubi!*" He launched himself at her, but Fang Wei grabbed him from behind and stopped him.

"I foolishly bumped into a vase and broke it. I apologize." Wendy sounded contrite but was not. Holroyd, already stunned at the loss of the document, could not grasp how the situation had degenerated so quickly into chaos.

"Everyone, stop!" Li said, taking command. "Xun Fan Ting, sit down in the corner on the floor! Now! Miss Liu, stop. You are destroying artifacts that belong to the whole nation. Zhu Mei Li, go sit with your husband." Holroyd was still shaken by what had happened but was relieved that, somehow, a semblance of order might be returning. Zhu Mei Li did not see it that way.

"I will not! How dare you give me orders? Do you know who I am?"

"Yes, I know exactly who you are. Do you know who I am?"

"No! And I don't care! You will pay for this!" Zhu Mei Li was white with fury. Suddenly, she screamed. Without warning, she launched herself at Li, hands outstretched, and raked her nails down his face.

Fang Wei moved swiftly to pull her away but could not prevent her from giving Li a nasty scratch, which immediately started bleeding. As Zhu Mei Li was pulled back, Li touched his face and considered the blood on his fingertips. Coldly, he looked up at the screaming woman and stepped forward, slapping her across both sides of her face. Zhu gasped and then sank to the floor, whimpering. Li looked at her dispassionately.

"I will not be paying for anything. But you will pay a lot and for a long time. Now sit down." Fang Wei grasped her by the arm and led her to the corner where her husband was sitting with his head in his hands, moaning softly. Holroyd stood watching it all in disbelief.

"Now, let's see what this is all about. Doctor Holroyd," Li began, "please explain what you are doing here."

"First, perhaps you would be good enough to tell me why *you* are here."

"As I informed you at our last meeting, I follow white-collar crime. Xiang Jin Leng, whom you know, is a person who interests my government. It is my responsibility to bring him to justice, and I have been observing your activities, hoping you would lead me to him. Instead, I find out you are meeting here with another person who will greatly interest my government."

Holroyd became very cautious, sensing danger.

"You were warned at our last meeting about your activities." Li smiled mirthlessly and looked around the room. "It seems you failed to listen to our advice. We have many questions, and we can start by asking why you are in a room filled with what looks like valuable ancient Chinese cultural objects. As a guest of China, I'm sure you will be happy to assist me."

"Someone told me Mr. Xun might have an item that interests me as an academic. That item was here, but that woman destroyed it." He pointed at Zhu Mei Li.

"Who is this someone, and what was this item?"

"It was a record of voyages during the early Qing Dynasty."

"How does that bear on all this?" Li waved his hand over the room. "I can accept that you might be interested in a document or a record, but I see few records or documents here. I see many items that would be of interest to an agent for a collector, or to a collector who also happens to be an academic professor supposedly conducting research. Which are you?"

"All I can say is that I was engaged to search for records of ancient Chinese travellers."

"Really? Engaged by Xiang Jin Leng? And why would he want such records? And where are these ancient Chinese travellers supposed to have gone?"

"Mr. Li, I cannot answer your questions." Holroyd was not in the mood to be cooperative.

"May I ask why?" Li went on relentlessly

"Because I'm not at liberty to disclose the answer. What I can promise you, however, is that my inquiries are not—or perhaps better said now, are no longer—related to criminal activities within or outside of China."

"I would not be so sure. With all due respect to your academic credentials, you can hardly determine what makes up criminal activities in China. On the other hand, we do know what such activities include, and I would have to say your presence here tells me you are or might be engaged in wrongdoing. Your scruples about confidentiality cannot influence what questions you will or will not answer." He looked sternly at Holroyd.

"This is not England, and you are a guest here. Until I'm convinced you are innocent and are not abusing the terms of your visit, we will have to keep you here until you give us the answers we want, and then we may help you leave our country— eventually."

"Eventually?"

"He means after interrogation," Wendy commented bitterly.

"Are you arresting me?" Holroyd could feel a rising hysteria. His voice went up an octave, and he almost shouted. "I came here as an accredited academic researcher, yet all that happened is I got bodies falling all over me, people have shot at me, I was almost run off the road, some mad woman destroyed valuable if not irreplaceable treasures, and now, on top of everything else, I stand accused of criminal activities?"

"Doctor Holroyd, you are not in the best position to complain. I do not know of all these events that you say have happened to you. But you may rest assured we will discuss them further. Meanwhile, you came to China to find a document, and from what I can see you think you found this document in Xun Fan Ting's collection." He looked over the collection in the room before continuing.

"However, I believe you were about to negotiate to buy that document and take it home, an action you know is illegal under the laws of China concerning the acquisition and export of ancient artifacts."

"Well, that possibility is no longer available because she destroyed the document I may have been interested in." Holroyd pointed at Zhu Mei Li.

"That point is irrelevant. You intended to acquire and export it, which is as good as doing so. An intent, even if the action was not completed, is also a crime. However, without further information, we do not know if you intended to acquire other items."

"I am, or rather I was, interested only in that document."

"I see. So you say. Somehow, I do not think you have answered truthfully or completely. Accordingly, I have no choice but to detain you until I'm satisfied with your answers."

"Are you arresting me?"

"Arresting you? Let's just say I'm offering you free accommodation while we detain you for questioning."

"And if I refuse your kind offer?"

"You may do so, but I hardly think that would be in your best interest. Nor would it stop you from enjoying what hospitality we intend to offer."

"Given I have no choice I accept your offer, but under protest."

"Your protest is noted, and you will receive our reply in due course. Until then…" Li let the rest of the sentence hang.

"I demand to see my consul," Holroyd said, trying to avoid the inevitable.

"We will, of course, notify the relevant authorities of your demand… in due course."

Holroyd alternated between fury and panic but managed to hold his tongue.

There was a silence broken only by the occasional groan from Xun. Zhu Mei Li was rocking back and forth, and tears mixed with mascara running down her cheeks, which were already showing signs of the slaps she had received. "You mean we could have sold that document for millions?" Everyone stared at her in silence.

Filomena appeared at the door and ushered Fu Li into the room. The Commissioner stopped when he realized there were several strangers in the room. He looked around and his mouth opened in a silent exclamation.

"Well, commissioner, this is an unexpected visit," Li said, looking amused.

"I came here to discuss the matter of Xun Fan Ting's son. That matter has become serious with the death of the victim. We are about to charge his son with murder, or at least with manslaughter. However, this is not an opportune time to raise the matter."

"Perhaps not that issue, commissioner. But your arrival may not be so inopportune. As you can see, we are standing in a treasure trove of great value. I'm most curious how Mr. Xun collected so many fine pieces. Maybe Mr. Xun has information about tomb robbing in this part of China. It is also possible that the late American helped in assembling this collection. However, I cannot help feeling this is your responsibility."

Wendy laughed.

"That's probably asking the fox to guard the chickens."

"Now that," Li said, "is a quaint expression that comes, I believe from England, Doctor Holroyd?"

"I believe so," he said, nodding.

"Excellent, then Miss Liu, would you be so kind as to identify who is the fox and who are the chickens here?"

"I think Miss Liu was speaking figuratively," Fu Li interjected. Holroyd glanced at Xun, whose face had turned a sickly yellowish-green colour, but he had ceased moaning. Fang Wei looked at his superior with great interest.

"I rather think not, commissioner." Li smiled at Fu Li, who was about to say something more but stopped. "I think Miss Liu has a great deal to tell us not only about who the foxes and chickens are but also about this chicken coop." He turned toward Wendy.

She looked defiantly at Li and then imploringly at Holroyd, who shook his head. There was nothing he could do for her. Li noticed her look. "Perhaps, Miss Liu, you can explain what you have been doing."

Wendy thought for a moment. "I assisted Dr. Holroyd in his research, which led me to contact him." She pointed at Xun, who was hunched in the corner, cradling his head in his arms.

"I knew of him as a leader during the Cultural Revolution, but I did not expect to find him to be a parasite stealing Chinese treasures. How many families suffered so this turd could live in luxury?" With that, she seized yet another case and threw its contents on the floor, where they shattered.

Xun Fan Ting looked up and groaned. A picture of defeat and misery, he sat on the floor staring vacantly at his treasures. He was beyond words. Holroyd could not believe what was happening and moved forward to restrain Wendy. But he was too far away, and Fang Wei got to her first.

"Miss Liu! Stop that now!" Fang Wei pulled her away from any other items she could destroy. Except for an occasional whimper from Zhu Mei Li, there was silence. Fang Wei turned to Li. "Perhaps,

Honourable Li, we have finished here. We should lock and guard this room and escort everyone to the police station to discuss these matters further."

"Yes, Inspector, I agree. Commissioner, may I ask you to make the arrangements?" Fu Li was only too happy to oblige.

36

Holroyd could not sleep. The cell was small and stank of sweat and urine. A bucket was placed against one wall to meet his needs. Next to it, some scraps of newspaper were heaped on the floor. There was only a small window high up on one concrete wall. Bright lights nestled in the high ceiling. *Definitely not five-star accommodation.*

The bunk was metal with only a thin blanket and a disgusting-looking stained pillow for comfort. Afraid of what might be lurking in them, he refrained from using either. Unless he wanted to squat on the floor, a metal bunk securely fixed to the floor was all he had to sit on.

He had failed just when success seemed certain. Everything he had done and suffered had gone up in smoke, literally, and all because a stupid harridan was furious her precious son had been arrested. *Well,* Holroyd thought, *I hope he rots in hell, her along with him.*

He alternated between rage, frustration, and fear. What had he done wrong? To whom could he turn for help? Come to think of it, how could he reach out for help? He was at the mercy of a provincial police force that so far had shown little sympathy for any of his problems.

What about Pearl? Would she be drawn into the net along with Xun, Xun's wife, and Ding? Who else might surface? What about Nicholson or Brugge or whatever his name might be? How did I ever get into this state of affairs? Perhaps more to the point, how will I ever get out of it and when? His thoughts returned to Pearl. *She helped enormously even if by doing so I'm in this cell. I would have liked to have gotten to know her better, but I suppose that's not going to happen.*

The morning wake-up call and the offer of a meagre breakfast of glutinous rice, overly boiled vegetables, and cold, weak tea did nothing to brighten his outlook. Looking at the rice and seeing small black things of doubtful origin among the kernels, he decided that hunger was preferable to any consequences of eating the food.

He wondered what the day would bring.

*****

Li Wen Yao and Fang Wei sipped tea on the floor above Holroyd's cell. Fang Wei flouted the rules and lit a cigarette. Li Wen Yao said nothing.

"I foresee a most satisfactory ending to our investigations, Fang Wei. I congratulate you on exposing the traffic in stolen treasures. Beijing will be pleased. I will have the pleasure of reporting your efforts to my superiors."

"That is generous of you, Li Wen Yao. But allow me to congratulate you on furthering your investigation. With Holroyd in our cells, you should be able to get a definitive lead to your quarry. I'm sure your superiors will be pleased."

"Perhaps. This, for me, has been a case of unusual interest. Holroyd will, I think, lead me to Xiang Jin Leng, but I did not expect the many other issues that we had to address. The discovery of Xun Fan Ting and his treasures surprised me. I'm happy we rescued so many valuable artifacts."

He grinned "But perhaps more satisfying is that you now can influence the commissioner. I believe you have wanted that for some time." Both officers smiled.

"Then let us finish our work. Let's see what our guests want to tell us. I'm sure, after a night here, the prospect of better living conditions will improve their desire to cooperate."

"Oh! I almost forgot. You remember I asked for more information about Miss Liu. I received a reply." Fang Wei opened a folder on his desk and took out a document. "Miss Liu is not in our records."

"That is strange! Are we sure she is a Chinese citizen?"

"Her papers say so." Fang Wei allowed a note of doubt to creep into his voice. "Perhaps she has another name. Now that she's in our cells, we can find out."

"Excellent. I think I can now delay my departure for Beijing until our interrogations are complete. I prefer FujinHaiZhou over Beijing, so our interrogations will be long and difficult." He paused as a thought struck him.

"Perhaps we can put the good professor and his assistant together in a room where they can talk, and we can listen without them knowing. Who knows what we may learn?"

Fang Wei thought for a moment, then picked up his phone and gave the order to put Holroyd and Wendy in a room together where they could be overheard.

*****

A policeman ushered Holroyd, dishevelled and unshaven, into the room where Wendy was already sitting. The room was small, the walls painted a drab green but with the occasional brown stain that suggested blood had sometimes sprayed. Bright ceiling lights were set back in the ceiling and reflected off the metal table and chairs.

Holroyd could smell stale cigarette smoke and noticed burn marks on the table's surface, suggesting that in that room, at least, the government ban on smoking was not always observed. Here, Holroyd thought, the parameters of acceptable interviewing techniques were more often observed in the breach.

Wendy looked tired, and her clothes were rumpled. Holroyd could not determine her mood. Was she defiant, satisfied, triumphant, contrite, afraid, or unemotional? Looking at her, Holroyd was not sure at first how to approach her, so he decided to play it by ear.

"Hello, Wendy. Are you alright?"

"That is a ridiculous question, Doctor Holroyd. How do you think I am, sitting in a Chinese provincial jail?" She snapped back.

Okay! She's taking the aggrieved approach.

"Well, we're in the same situation. Hardly the outcome to our task that I had hoped for." He grabbed a chair and sat down. Wendy said nothing.

Holroyd sat silently for a moment. "Did Xiang ever tell you why he wanted me to research the island's sovereignty?"

"Xiang? I have no idea what he wanted. My employer was concerned that you might find evidence to help China get sovereignty over the island. I was to stop you from passing it on, but I do not know why."

"Your employer? You told me that Xiang was your employer. Are you telling me you lied?"

"I never met or communicated with Xiang. I was told Xiang was a competitor. My employer knew Xiang had engaged you, so pretending Xiang had sent me to assist you was an easy way to get your confidence."

"Then who is your real employer, and what does he want from me?"

"Isayo Muramori of Muramori Industries employed me."

"Who is this Muramori, and why would you work for him? What's the whole story here?"

"After I left the service here in China, Muramori Industries offered me a good job."

"You were in the service here? What service?"

"That I cannot tell you."

"Did you have some form of military training?" A sudden flash of insight hit Holroyd. "That could explain how you were so cool and efficient under stress." He realized he had been set up. "I suppose you arranged for the attacks on me as well?" Wendy just looked at him.

"Oh, fuck it! You conniving little bitch." The uncharacteristic expletive was a sign of his feelings.

"Doctor Holroyd, there is no need for such offensive language."

"Oh, no? Here we are in jail, you admit to interfering with my task and even endangering me, and you have the gall to tell me how to express my feelings?"

"I did not arrange for all the attacks on you. For instance, I had nothing to do with the incident on the road from Wang Tang Cun or the demonstration at the library."

"Then who arranged those?"

"Probably Xun Fan Ting or his accomplices. Or someone else, who knows?"

"Really? That might follow because we were closing in on the illegal traffic of artifacts. But what of the other incidents? The body in my library, the attacks on the island, the shooting by the lake?"

"I assure you; you were never in danger. As for the other incidents, I was, how do you say it? Oh! Neutralizing the competition."

"What competition?"

"I don't fully know, but I believe it had something to do with finding a document Muramori was looking for."

"What document?"

"I don't know, but I was told to help find this document. I was given a contact, but I found him on your library floor."

"My library floor? I was right then, and I should never have believed you. Did you kill him?"

"No! He was Muramori's cousin."

"Bloody hell, I could have saved myself a lot of trouble if I had followed my instincts." He stopped. "Wait a minute. Was Muramori's cousin looking for that piece of paper the bookseller found in the Yongle Dadian? I think it may have been a map, perhaps of something buried on Dejection Island. If that's what Muramori is after, that would explain the attack."

"Yes, it was."

"I gave it to an acquaintance of mine who later was found dead, but he no longer had the paper."

"No, Muramori got it."

"But how did Muramori know who had it?"

"I was able to blackmail an English aristocrat into cooperation, and with his help, we recovered it."

"Blackmail? How?"

"He had gambling debts he could not pay and sexual preferences for good-looking Asian boys that he wanted to keep private. We offered suitable incentives and assurances, and he agreed to work with us."

"Which aristocrat? Oh, wait! This wouldn't have been Viscount Hantington?"

"Yes, that is his name."

"Hantington was helping you? Bugger him! Another swindling sod! And because you were with me and I reported back to Merry, everyone knew where I was and how far I had got. I was set up and never had a chance!"

Holroyd felt as if all energy had just been drained out of him. *One betrayal after another!* He collapsed on his chair feeling beaten and on the verge of tears, but then, with a weak spark of defiance, he vowed he would get satisfaction, although in his present situation, he was not quite sure how he would get it.

He took a deep breath to calm himself and then looked up at Wendy. "What happened to Nicholson?"

"Who? Oh, yes! The man in the hospital. I wanted to visit him, but as you know, I was stopped. I suppose he might have recovered by now."

"Given we found the Dong Xi Yang Kao among Xun's treasures, I don't think it matters much anymore. And what about the destruction of the treasures in Xun's vault?"

"That was part of my revenge," Wendy replied with a touch of triumph.

"What revenge?"

"Making Xun Fan Ting pay for what he did to my parents. Of course, he did not recognize me. I had another name then. But I'm not finished yet." Holroyd thought it wiser not to pursue this opening.

"Wendy, I think you owe it to me to tell me the truth about yourself."

"My parents were from near here. My mother came to China as a Japanese nurse at the same hospital where my father was a doctor. They met and they got married. During the Cultural Revolution, they beat my father and sent him to prison, where he died. The Red Guards humiliated my mother because of her ancestry by disfiguring her face in a vicious attack led by a local functionary. Xun Fan Ting was the leader of the gang that did all that."

At that moment, the door opened, and a policeman pointed at Holroyd.

"You! Come!" He led the way to Fang Wei's office.

*****

Fang Wei shut the loudspeaker off. The two officers looked at each other. "I would say that was a most helpful conversation," Fang Wei observed.

"I agree. Now let us see what else we can learn." Just then Holroyd was ushered into the office, and Fang Wei motioned him to sit in a chair opposite the two officers.

"Good morning, Doctor Holroyd. I trust our hospitality is to your satisfaction?" If Holroyd's looks could kill, they would have reduced Fang Wei to a pile of smouldering ash.

"Not the worst overnight accommodation in my experience, but I won't give it five stars," Holroyd said bitterly.

Fang Wei looked amused. "I must see what improvements they can make. In case you find yourself here for any longer."

"I have neither the intention nor the desire to repeat this experience. Why am I here?"

"Normally, I would not bother to answer that question, but in your case, I will make an exception. We wanted to be sure you would be available to answer a few questions we think you have the answers for."

"Are you charging me?"

"At the moment you are what you might call a material witness. We will see if we charge you with anything."

"And you felt it necessary to hold me overnight? Why not let me return to the hotel where I could get a decent bath and a shave?"

"I hope that will still be possible." Fang Wei let the threat sink in. "To speed that happy event, let's start with our questions." Holroyd could only agree.

"Let us start by discussing why that piece of paper was of such importance to you." Li looked intensely at Holroyd.

"Me personally? It was only of academic interest, but since I did not read the document, I can only conjecture its value. However, I believe that document had great significance to others."

"To whom then?"

Holroyd decided that in light of what he had just learned, his personal comfort and safety overrode the need for any further secrecy. "I believe the British and Chinese governments would have been very pleased for me to have it."

"Both governments? I don't see the relevance."

Holroyd decided that his hopes for a speedy release rested on cooperation, so he revealed the true reason behind his task and how Zhu Mei Li had spoiled the result.

Li Wen Yao could not believe the enormity of what he had heard. He wasn't sure he was closer to finding Xiang, but he had been close to resolving a problem he knew to be of great interest to the nation's leaders.

"Are you telling me you were tasked to find proof that China owned the island and thus the British claim was illegal?"

"Yes."

Li Wen Yao swore he would make every effort to make that stupid bitch who had snatched defeat from the jaws of victory rue her action.

"At least you have witnesses that you found what you were looking for," Fang Wei said, interrupting Li Wen Yao's thoughts.

"Witnesses?" Holroyd looked at him with sudden fury. "Do you really think I have witnesses? Who would be a credible witness, and what could they swear to? Did you read the document? No? I thought not. Credible witnesses? At a pinch I might be deemed credible, but as for the others, I'm not so sure. And even so, witnesses to what? Miss Liu and Mr. Xun could swear to its contents, but I think their testimony would be suspect."

Li looked at him thoughtfully. "Where is Xiang now?"

Holroyd shook his head. "I have no idea, but I think Miss Liu may be able to help you."

"Ah, yes! Miss Liu! Tell me, Professor, why did you want Miss Liu to visit Brugge in the hospital?"

"Brugge? I thought it was Nicholson, and I told the inspector why I wanted to make contact."

"Yes, you did. But we now know it was not Nicholson, but a man named Brugge, and we both know Brugge had some interest in you."

"You said 'had some interest.' He has none now?"

"Unlikely, because he died a short while ago."

"Oh, hell! I have no idea who this man is or was."

Li sat quietly for a moment before turning to Fang Wei. "Perhaps the good professor will be able to remember better and be more informative after he has seen the body. Please have him taken to the mortuary and report back."

Fang Wei nodded and picked up the phone to give the order.

"After Doctor Holroyd has seen the body," Li continued, "please return him to his quarters." Fang Wei nodded.

"Wait. Are you still keeping me?" Holroyd demanded. "I have told you what I know. What else do you want?"

"Yes, we are still detaining you, and we will question you again if necessary." With that, a policeman collected Holroyd and then left.

"Now let us question Miss Liu. Tell me again what you know of her."

Fang Wei pulled a file closer and opened it. "Strange, but we have no record of Wendy Liu at all. We cannot even verify her story about her parents, perhaps because we lost many records during the Revolution. Nor can we find any reference to her claimed service in China. But it's strange because there ought to be some corroborating evidence somewhere. To help me, I sent her fingerprints to Beijing, so let us see what answers we get."

A young policeman entered and handed Fang Wei a file. "Oh! How very convenient. This is an email from Beijing. They found her fingerprints on file." Li waited expectantly as Fang Wei read the message.

"It appears Miss Wendy Liu, under a different name, was trained to undertake special work for one of our departments but became unreliable and underwent corrective education. She escaped to take up unauthorized employment. We did not know who her employer was, but thanks to what we heard this morning, we do know now! I think we have lots of questions to ask Miss Liu."

At that moment, two beefy female policewomen escorted Wendy into the interrogation room, looking bedraggled but defiant. One policewoman told Wendy to sit after which Fang Wei opened the file that lay before him while Li Wen Yao looked impassively at the prisoner.

Fang Wei looked up. "Miss Liu, you are here because you destroyed valuable artifacts, knowing them to be the property of the people of China. That is a serious charge."

Wendy said nothing.

"You would help yourself by cooperating with us and answering our questions truthfully and completely."

Li looked at her impassively. "Who are you working for?"

"Doctor Holroyd."

"Ah, yes. But Doctor Holroyd is not your employer, is he? Your employer is someone named Muramori! However, he is not present, but you are. So, using another quaint English expression, a bird in the hand is worth two in the bush, and you, Miss Liu, are the bird now in my hand."

Li could see she was surprised that he knew of her relationship to Muramori.

"You listened in on the conversation I had with Holroyd, damn you."

"Yes, and that is why we want answers from you."

"I have no reason to answer any questions."

"Oh, but I think we might have some reasons. I suggest to you that defiance and uncooperative behaviour are not in your best interest." Wendy remained defiant.

Fang Wei leaned forward. "Let's start with something we do know. We know about your career in one of our departments, so we know you are quite capable of removing inconvenient people. Did you have anything to do with the disappearance of an American staying at the Auspicious Friendly Hotel?"

The question surprised Li Wen Yao, but he gave his colleague credit. Was it an inspired shot in the dark? At the worst, Wendy would deny any involvement. At the best, a loose end would get tied up.

"What American and what disappearance?"

"Brugge."

"Brugge? I have no idea who or where he is."

"But you went to the hospital and insisted you wanted to see him."

"Doctor Holroyd asked me to find Nicholson, not anyone called Brugge."

"I think Miss Liu knows very well that Brugge and Nicholson are not the same person," Li interjected. "I also think she knows a lot about both of them."

"Don't try to pretend you do not know Brugge." Fang Wei was losing his temper. "Someone saw you asking about a foreigner staying at the hotel. Not long after that, they called us to report a murder. What do you know about that? And, Miss Liu, cooperating with us now will help you later when you appear before a judge. Failure to do so might shorten your life expectancy by a considerable amount."

Wendy remained silent, but Li Wen Yao suspected something was worrying her.

"Why would I even think cooperation is necessary?" she asked finally.

"We think you possibly killed him."

"Possibly? I assure you if I did kill him, he would most definitely be dead, and I doubt you would find his remains."

"If that is so, that is a capital crime for which they will execute you."

"But proving it would challenge even you."

"I think not. As you well know, any case against you can be decided long before you appear before a judge." Wendy did not move and said nothing.

"Then let us consider the man Brugge," Fang Wei said. "Why did Xun Fan Ting's son run over him? Who organized that?"

More silence.

"Miss Liu, we know you were ordered to find some document for Muramori, which he got, and then delay Holroyd if he found proof that would help solve the island's sovereignty. What was Brugge's role, and why were you so keen to visit him?"

Wendy still refused to answer.

"If you will not cooperate, I see no reason to stop any of our investigations and leave you to your fate."

"Are you making an offer?"

"Maybe. We cannot promise what a judge will decide, but we will inform the judge of your cooperation."

Li Wen Yao shifted in his chair. "Excuse me, Inspector, but I have a suggestion. If Miss Liu is cooperative, you could lose the matter of the murder at the hotel and even any involvement Miss Liu might have had in the traffic accident."

Fang Wei looked at his colleague in amazement, but before he could say anything, Li continued. "Miss Liu has enough experience to know what is possible if she cooperates."

Wendy looked at him. "What are you offering?"

"We could dismiss the matter of the murder of this American for lack of proof. Miss Liu could avoid execution for a murder of which we would not know. The traffic accident can be blamed on Xun Fan Ting's son. Miss Liu would escape execution, but she would not escape a prison sentence because she will be punished for her actions in destroying valuable Chinese artifacts."

"If you can do that, why bother to question me further?"

"Because I think you can lead me to Xiang Jin Leng." Wendy remained silent. "No? Then please excuse my interruption, Inspector, and continue with your questions."

"Wait!" Wendy sat up. "Forget the American, and I will cooperate fully." Li Wen Yao looked at Fang Wei, who nodded. Li Wen Yao turned back to Wendy. "Please continue."

"As you know, Muramori wanted a document that he now has after getting it from Holroyd's friend and wanted to delay any transfer of sovereignty. I was ordered to stop anyone from interfering with Holroyd to make sure Muramori alone could control events. I know that Muramori believed Xiang was competition and that Xiang engaged Nicholson to recover any documents before Holroyd could. I was told to get rid of the man."

"Did you meet with him and if so, where?"

"Yes, in his room at the Auspicious Friendly Hotel."

"Did he admit he was working for Xiang?"

"No! He claimed he had never heard of Xiang or Holroyd."

"So, how do you justify his removal?"

"Justify it? To whom? He had taken some book from the library, and when I demanded he hand it over, he was less than cooperative. In the end, he admitted he had sold it to Xun. My conclusion was that he was just a thief stealing valuable Chinese artifacts. He got his reward."

"And just how did he get this reward?"

"He was persuaded to check out and leave immediately for home. I understand he did not get to the airport, but I don't know where he is now."

"I see." Li leaned forward. "Before you persuaded him to check out, did you inquire as to his identity?"

"No. I searched through his belongings and found several passports from different countries and with different names."

"Such as?"

"There was an American one with the name Nicholson, a Mexican one with a name that escapes me, and two others. I assumed all of them were false."

Li nodded and resumed a watchful attitude.

"And do you know anything about Brugge?" Fang Wei continued.

"I was told the American government hired him to watch Holroyd, but why that was so, I don't know. My instructions were to neutralize him."

"How did you do that?"

"He was incapacitated before one of my associates helped him cross the road just as a fast car was conveniently approaching. It was not my intention to kill him."

There was silence. Then Li looked at Wendy. "Telling Holroyd you were working for Xiang while working for Muramori suggests you know where Xiang is or will be."

"No."

Li looked intently at Wendy. "Miss Liu, be very sure of your answer. Unless you can convince me you do not know where Xiang can be found, I will have to conclude you are not being cooperative."

"I do not know. But I can tell you the name of someone who does know."

"And, of course, where can I find this person?"

"He is in England."

"Who is he?"

"As long as you do not reveal me as the source of this information, I'll give you his name."

Li nodded and sat back, thinking. "I cannot tell you how this will affect your case," he said, "but I will let you know when I have decided."

The interview was over, and Wendy went back to her cell.

The two officers sat thinking. Finally, Li Wen Yao turned to Fang Wei. "I want to know why everyone was so eager to ensure Holroyd failed his task. He told us he was looking for proof that the island should never have become a British colony, which suggests that Xiang, Muramori, and the Americans did not want that proof to be found. That would mean they wanted the island to remain British, but why?"

"Remembering that Xun's bitch burned the evidence, could she and he be part of the plan to stop Holroyd?"

"It's possible, but that tells me the case is far above my pay scale and is a matter for our leaders to investigate."

Fang Wei nodded. "If it's above your pay scale, it's so far above mine I'll never even be aware of it,"

"No, but you do have an important role by providing information on what happened here. Let me suggest what you might find helpful. I think your work will be less demanding if you file the case of the missing body under insufficient information to determine if someone committed a crime. After all, you don't have an inconvenient body that needs explaining. And anyway, we now know what happened." He looked at Fang Wei.

"I have no further interest in how Brugge came to die in a traffic accident, and unless you wish me to raise it with my superiors, I won't mention it. It is a local matter outside my jurisdiction. As to why Brugge suffered that fate, it is not clear enough to me to raise it other than as a crime that can be charged to Xun, in which case it's a local matter."

Fang Wei sat in silence for a moment. "I'm not sure I follow you. How do you suggest I handle it?"

"Based on what we have just learned, I think the incident was an accident as far as the driver was concerned, but it could strengthen our case against Xun if we were to ignore Miss Liu's contribution as to how Brugge happened to be in front of the vehicle at that precise moment. I think that can safely be laid at Xun Fan Ting's door, although, of course, he will deny it. But who will believe him?"

"Are you sure we need not pursue the matter?" Fang Wei persisted. "We haven't examined that hotel room, which is under renovation, to see if there is evidence of a murder."

"You are, of course, free to do so. But are you sure you were shown the correct room?" Li paused to let Fang Wei consider this escape before continuing.

"As we now know, the victim of that attack was incapacitated which could explain the blood. He was then thrown under a passing car driven by a drunk driver. Why investigate two incidents at a time when you are already overloaded with other cases?" Li waited for a reply.

"Might I suggest that your workload would be reduced if you were to dismiss any crime in the hotel for lack of evidence? I doubt the hotel staff will persist in maintaining there was a murder if nothing further was said."

Fang Wei nodded in agreement. "And Holroyd?"

"I'm inclined to accept that he is telling as much as he knows. We don't have a convincing case against him, and I'm not sure it would be in the state's interests to discover one. I think my leaders will be quite pleased with what he has done. Get him to write down everything, and then I suggest he be returned to the hotel. After that let's put him on a plane out of China."

Fang Wei nodded in agreement.

"I'm curious why Muramori went to such lengths to get that first document," Li continued. "If I understand the matter, the document probably has something to do with the island. But then why would he and Xiang be so keen to delay any possible change in the island's sovereignty? Of what possible interest could this island be? Is there anything that suggests a Japanese involvement on the island?"

"They occupied it during the war, but that was all."

"Maybe that is the reason for his interest. I wonder if Muramori was involved in the occupation and if so if he did something there that he does not want anyone to find out."

"Such as?"

"A massacre leading to a mass burial. Remember, such burial places have been found in Nanjing and other formerly occupied territories. Let's see if we can discover what our Japanese neighbours did on that island."

"Muramori might want to hide a mass burial site, but I can't see Xiang doing so. But I think there might be something both would want and compete for."

"Such as treasure!" Fang Wei exclaimed.

"Exactly. I will notify Beijing. But my next task will be to encourage Miss Liu to reveal more on how I can find Xiang."

Just then a policeman informed them that Holroyd was back. Fang Wei ordered Holroyd be brought to the office.

"Well, Doctor Holroyd," Fang Wei said once Holroyd had arrived, "do you know Brugge and why he was interested in you?"

Unbidden, Holroyd collapsed wearily into one of the chairs and tried to regain a measure of composure.

"Yes, I do know the man but not as Brugge. He was introduced to me as Harrison. I met him in Singapore as an American government official when I was asked to abandon my research."

Li became very attentive. "The American government wanted you to abandon your research? Why was that?"

"I don't know, but I suspect the Americans do not want the island's sovereignty to change."

"What did this man, Brugge or Harrison, have to do with you?"

"I can only guess but maybe he was to follow and watch me or even to stop me."

Li looked at him. *The leaders in Beijing will be most interested to learn that the Americans have interfered in this matter. They suspected they might,*

"Doctor Holroyd, you will be asked to write down everything you have told us. Now you will return to your cell." Holroyd was taken back to his cell. When food was offered again, hunger overcame his caution, but he feared his troubles might have increased.

He spent the rest of the day writing down everything that he thought he could safely pass on to the Chinese. After handing in the document, he was taken to his hotel and allowed to clean himself up and relax, pending his release.

His task was done, and now under virtual house arrest, Holroyd was left to amuse himself in the hotel. The front desk let him know he had a visitor. *Probably a police visit or perhaps someone from the embassy. If it's the embassy, they left it rather late.* Morosely he went to the lobby where, to his delight, he saw Pearl.

"Doctor Holroyd!" She smiled. "I hope I'm not intruding, but I wanted to make sure you are alright."

"No, no! Not intruding at all. I'm delighted to see you." He stopped, unsure what to say or do next.

"Shall we have coffee?" Pearl led him to the small roped-off area opposite the bar. "Please sit while I arrange for someone to bring us coffee, or would you prefer tea?" With that, she went over to the concierge who, after some discussion, removed the rope and disappeared to arrange service. Once settled, Pearl looked at Holroyd.

"I'm so sorry you were treated badly. I may have put you in jail, and I came over to apologize."

"Oh, Pearl, you did nothing wrong. In fact, I'd say you have done your country a great service. With your help I managed to finish my task, and the police caught a thief, not to mention recover a great treasure."

"Yes, but—"

"No buts." Holroyd smiled.

"What will you do now?"

"I'm not sure I will be given much choice. I expect to be escorted out of the country quite soon, and I don't know if I will ever be allowed to return."

Pearl processed the news in silence.

"I had hoped I could ask you to show me the sights and maybe have dinner, but I'm not sure that will be allowed."

"That would be nice if you come back."

"Then let's hope it will be possible."

From then on, the conversation became awkward as neither one seemed to want to end it, though neither knew quite what to say. Finally, Pearl took her leave, wishing him a safe journey.

The next day, Fang Wei escorted Holroyd to the airport and, with none of the usual exit procedures, put him on a flight that would connect to one leaving for London. Luckily, Holroyd had originally purchased a return ticket and relaxed again in first class.

****

"I say! You, there! Who in hell are you? Stop what you're doing! Stop at once, I say!" Mrs. Hardcastle looked down into the pit where half a dozen Japanese workmen were lifting a heavy box out of a hole. Frowning, she continued indignantly. "You've just ruined my flower garden. Look at those Birds of Paradise and Manihots! Damned cheek! Do you have a permit to dig here?"

"No, Mrs. Hardcastle, I don't believe they do." George Wilson stepped forward and looked at the site. "In fact, I'm certain they do not." He stepped into the pit. "You're from the Japanese freighter that docked last night. You're supposed to be unloading fruit, not digging up respectable peoples' gardens."

None of the Japanese seemed to understand English, but as some workmen moved threateningly toward him, he pulled out and flourished his pistol. Undeterred by this show of force, one man pulled out a dagger, gave a loud yell, and rushed at George. A shot rang out.

The man stopped his rush and fell back into the pit, blood gushing from a wound in his leg. Nobody moved, but a moment later, the man plunged the dagger into his stomach and pulled it horizontally across his abdomen. He groaned once before twitching convulsively and dying. No one moved.

Then the other men advanced on George, shifting the shovels in their hands with every sign they wanted to harm the policeman. Calmly, George aimed his pistol at them. One of the men reached the edge of the pit and, with a yell, tried to clamber out while raising the shovel to use as a club. A shot rang out, and he, too, subsided into the pit.

"Now let's not be hasty. Come on down, boys!" Three more armed policemen appeared.

The remaining workmen dropped their tools and resignedly stood around.

Wilson went over to the boxes; each stencilled with Japanese writing. "Now, what do we have here?"

37

"Holroyd! I say, Holroyd!"

Holroyd turned to see Sanderson running down Whitehall after him, waving frantically. "Holroyd, can you stop for a minute?"

Curious about what Sanderson wanted, Holroyd obliged by stopping until Sanderson caught up with him, panting. His mouth worked frantically, but nothing came out. Looking at him with a frantically moving mouth and bulbous eyes, Holroyd thought Sanderson looked like a fish in an aquarium.

"You cad!" Sanderson spat. "You, you..." He stopped, perhaps at a loss for words or unable to think coherently. Holroyd could not imagine what he had done to make him so upset. Given Sanderson's recent triumph with funding, it should have been Holroyd who was expressing anger. But even though he despised Sanderson, the effort was not worthwhile.

"Look, what do you think you're doing? I thought it was clear I was to get more funding, and they would cut back on your department. Now I find out I'm not getting more funding because they're not cutting back in your department."

"Oh? How decent of you to let me know. I was unaware."

"Oh, don't act so damn innocent." Sanderson was frothing at the mouth, and Holroyd almost instinctively reached for a handkerchief to wipe it away.

Oddly, Sanderson had mismatched the buttons on his shirt with the proper buttonholes, and his loosely knotted tie was off to the side. He might be a brilliant scientist, but he was a rather pitiable specimen outside his laboratory. Holroyd felt sorry for Sanderson.

"The bloody fools reversed their funding decision not realizing the importance of what I'm doing." His bitterness was almost palpable, and Holroyd couldn't help feeling mildly sympathetic.

"Really? How short-sighted of them." Sanderson turned a shade of purple, perhaps puce, and gave him a look of horror.

Holroyd was relishing every second of his discomfort. But suddenly, he worried that Sanderson might succumb to a heart attack right in front of him. Sanderson did not seem to be in any hurry to leave, nervously clenching and unclenching his right hand. "I say, calm down, will you? There's no need to get violent," Holroyd said, adopting his most soothing tone.

"Oh! Go to hell!" Sanderson snarled and then stalked off.

No, Holroyd thought, not a fish in an aquarium, but a rabid hyena perhaps? He watched Sanderson weave through the crowd in an unsteady gait. Had the man been drinking his anger away? If so, Holroyd had not detected it. Poor fellow!

Holroyd felt a little sympathy for him, recognizing that the day might come when his funding could disappear. On recollection, that had happened recently, but he told himself, not today.

He wondered, however, what had caused the reversal because he had neither a network of supporting colleagues nor enough influence to lobby in the circles that made such decisions. With that, Holroyd went on his way.

He sauntered down Whitehall to the large office building to which he was admitted after thorough security checks. A liveried footman led him upstairs to a room with high double wooden doors. Once inside, he found the room was large and expensively finished in the opulent style of a Regency-era gentleman's gambling club.

A large polished wooden table exquisitely inlaid with different woods on which were three crystal decanters, and several cut-crystal goblets occupied the centre of the room. Files on the table served as seating maps.

Several people were standing around and chatting quietly with each other, but he only knew Merry. Conversation stopped while they scrutinized him, but apparently, no one saw anything untoward because the hum of conversation resumed.

"Ah, good morning, Peter." Merry moved over to him. Holroyd felt a rush of anger as he experienced an urge to punch Merry's face. This was the man who had betrayed him and cost Rostwick his life.

"You and I need to talk." Holroyd saw a puzzled look cross Merry's face,

"About what, old boy?"

"I don't think you should play that game with me. Not after what you did."

Merry looked at him with concern. "I say, Peter, what on earth are you talking about?"

"Thirty pieces of silver."

Merry turned white before stepping back and, turning from Holroyd, addressed the room.

"Gentlemen," he said, "let me introduce Doctor Peter Holroyd. He's the fellow who's been researching for us about our little problem. Just come back from China, Peter has, and he has news for us."

There were nods and a few introductions from men Holroyd later discovered represented different ministries. All he heard were a few insincere "Nice to meet you" before people turned back to whatever conversations they had had before his arrival.

"Tea, sir?" A footman approached with a cup of tea, milk, and sugar on a silver salver.

"Thanks. Milk and two lumps, please."

Merry turned back. "I really don't know what you're talking about, Peter, and whatever it may be, now is not the time or the place to discuss it. Until we do, let's keep our attention on the business at hand. Got your report, I did. Good job. Thanks very much for all your help. Just sorry it didn't quite work out."

"Any news about what happened after I left?" Holroyd asked.

"People over there got very excited about the nice things you found. Off the record, they asked if next time we could please keep our noses out of their internal affairs. Seems they think of you as a wolf in sheep's clothing or, to put it bluntly, a spy, and they aren't sure whether they should like you very much. Told them not to be so suspicious of a revered academic like you." He stopped to give Holroyd a chance to reply, which he didn't. "Told them you're harmless."

"Thanks, that's very reassuring." He took a sip of tea. "What about your friend, Xiang?"

"Hardly a friend, old boy. A nasty piece of work."

"But that didn't stop you from helping him. Sold me right down the drain, you did." Merry flinched but said nothing.

"Oh, come off it! Don't look as if you have no idea what I'm talking about." Merry looked as if he had just bit into a lemon but went on as if he had not heard Holroyd.

"Once I thought he might be useful in helping you, but then events took a wrong turn for him. They accused his son of distributing Class A substances and making untoward advances on his fellow students of both sexes at Oxford. Got sent down, the scion of the family was. All very embarrassing, and we had a devil of a time pushing it under the rug. Tabloids would have had a field day about allowing sons of criminals to enter Oxford. Anyway, we got him out without too much fuss." He paused and shook his head.

"The Chinese weren't too happy. Seems they wanted young Deng to answer a few questions. Apologized profusely, we did. Told them that if we had only known of their interest, we would have cooperated fully. As it is, all we can tell them is he left the country and is now in parts unknown. Don't want to do all their work for them without some return.

"As for the father, seems certain people got to know more about his whereabouts than was healthy for him. Left his office in Hong Kong one morning and disappeared. A little birdie tells me he's on the Mainland somewhere enjoying 'official hospitality.' Seems you stirred up quite a wasp's nest."

"I don't follow you at all. I think others helped."

"Oh, you mean that young assistant of yours? Wendy Liu or something like that?"

"Yes."

"That's an odd case. I had heard the Chinese had arrested her, but then her body washed up off one of the Japanese Islands." Holroyd was silent. *Wendy dead? Perhaps Muramori was not satisfied with her services and punished her. I wonder if Merry had anything to do with that. Given what she knew about him, her departure would be a relief for him.*

Holroyd decided to wait until the others had left the room before confronting Merry about his treachery.

"Talking of the Japanese, the Island's Governor called me about some Japanese digging up an old biddy's garden. A Mrs. Hardcastle. You met her, I believe?" Holroyd nodded.

"Yes, well! It turned out the Japs had hidden part of their wartime loot on the island. Went to get it back before the island changed hands. Got caught with their hands holding spades while digging it up. One of them had the document you asked Rostwick to look at. Turns out it was a coded treasure map. Looks to have been quite a haul. We'll probably get to keep it because we can't trace any of it back to its original owners, and they found it on British soil. Treasury will thank you for that."

Holroyd nodded and fleetingly wondered if he had any claim to a share. Probably not!

"To change the subject," he said. "I submitted my expenses and got a call from someone who said she was in accounts. She pointed out that, for overseas flights over eleven hours, the regulations allow stopping overnight or travelling business class. Because I stopped overnight on the island, I may only claim for economy class. They won't reimburse first class because I was not of sufficient rank and did not get prior approval."

"Oh! Bad luck, old boy. Regulations, you know."

Holroyd felt a wave of resentment wash over him. "Dammit, Merry, I risked everything for you, life and limb, even went to jail, and in return, the Treasury is richer by several tons of gold, the Chinese catch a whole nest of criminals, and all your lot does is quibble and refuse to reimburse me for my expenses?"

"You could always ask the Chinese! I'm sure they would be receptive to hear from you." This response did not please Holroyd.

"I suppose I can forget about the rest of my contract," he said ruefully.

"Oh, don't be too sure of that. I think we can find a way, what? Anyway, lots of pleased people out there, so well done. Your university chancellor was very pleased with our expression of gratitude. Asked his advice on how to thank you. Jolly sporting of him, I thought."

Holroyd felt a glow of pleasure as he understood he was back in the university's good graces. So that's what Sanderson was all worked up about. He smiled inwardly as Merry continued.

"Seems the Chinese noted our efforts. Perhaps they found the proofs they told us they had. Could it be they have a copy of the destroyed document?" He looked at Holroyd. "D'ye think we could ask them for such a copy or even the original, what?"

"The only copy you might get would be if it's manufactured in Zhu Ma Dian!" Holroyd could not resist a scornful response.

"What's that?"

"That's a town in Henan Province that has the reputation of being able to supply you with a genuine Ming vase manufactured yesterday."

"Are you serious?" To Holroyd's satisfaction, Merry put on a pained expression.

The sound of muted conversation stilled, and the green baize door at the end of the room opened. The permanent secretary entered with a thin file folder under his arm. In appearance, looks, and demeanour, he reminded Holroyd of Sir Humphrey Appleby in the British television comedy series, *Yes Minister*.

Appearances, however, were deceiving. Both politicians and his colleagues respected the man for straight talk, not suffering fools gladly, and for getting things done.

"Good morning, everyone." He took his place in the table's middle, opened his file, then looked up and around at the others. "Can we start?"

Holroyd gave his report and listened to the discussions that followed. When things looked to be wrapping up, the permanent secretary looked around again. "It seems that we are not much closer to an agreement. Is there a consensus that we advise our masters that we do not have enough evidence or a strong enough hand to recommend opening negotiations with the Chinese?" The permanent secretary waited. As usual, Merry had to have the last word.

"Oh, my hat. That'll cause Auntie to have a conniption. She might even get annoyed." Holroyd was amused.

"That is all, I think. Thank you for coming. Oh! Merry, a word, if you please," the permanent secretary called out as the meeting dispersed. Merry went over to him, and the permanent secretary spoke to him in a quiet voice. "A couple of questions. The American ambassador is furious that the Chinese have accused them of interfering in a purely Chinese and British matter. Did we whisper in anyone's ear?"

"I don't think so, but I'll ask around,"

"Do so. We also got a communique from Beijing asking whether we could provide any information on the recovery of treasure the Japanese had hidden on Dejection Island during their occupation. Beijing seems to be under the impression someone connected with its discovery might have failed to pass on relevant information that would have assisted in repatriating the trove. I think it's a curious question. Is there anything I need to know?"

"I say! Can't think why Beijing wants to barge in. I think it's a bit of a forlorn hope. But I'll make a few calls and see if we can make soothing noises."

"Thank you, Merry, I think that would be very helpful." He left the room, and Merry turned to Holroyd, who was about to leave.

"Peter, thanks for coming. Sorry it was wasted but good try."

"Well, I'm relieved to be back and that it's over. But I want to know more about your role. I know you were asked to provide information that led to Rostwick's murder."

"That's despicable of you! How do you come to that outrageous charge?"

"Let's say I was told about your gambling debts and your preference for beautiful young Asian boys. Hardly something that would reflect credit on you if it became public knowledge."

Merry went white. "Are you trying to blackmail me, you little twerp?"

"Not at all! This remains between us. Anyway, it would be very hard to prove in a court of law. But I want you to know that I know you behaved abominably!" Merry looked at Holroyd in silence.

"And, by the way, I overheard the permanent secretary just now. Since the government retrieved the treasure, your friends might not be able to pay you your pieces of silver after all."

The look on Merry's face as he digested what Holroyd had just said gave Holroyd enormous satisfaction.

38

The phone rang, and after a long wait and several forwarding switches, the caller got through to Miller.

"Mr. Miller, how kind of you to take the time out of your busy schedule to take my call."

"Not at all, Director Hsien. Thank you for leaving your other pressing business to call me. How may I be of service?"

"You remember we discussed my government's interest in Britain's position on the future of Dejection Island?"

"Yes, yes, I do."

"My government has become aware of the activities of your Doctor Holroyd, and it seems that he was almost successful in finding a document that would have helped resolve the issue of the island's ownership. My government is grateful for the British efforts that, but for the actions of a Chinese... how do you put it so quaintly? Ah, yes! A Chinese harpy. But for her actions, it would have provided a solution satisfactory to both governments. My government wishes not to dismiss the British efforts and recognizes China's actions in frustrating the outcome. Accordingly, my government offers a suggestion that could serve the interests of Her

Majesty and the people of China. I have taken the liberty of sending the pertinent documents over for your perusal. When you can respond, perhaps we should talk again."

"Oh, indeed, Mr. Hsien. I will do my best to get back to you quickly."

"That would be most helpful. We can arrange a time, but meanwhile, I'm sure you will be happy to know we consider Doctor Peter Holroyd to be innocent of any misbehaviour while in China."

"That is marvellous, and I will pass the information back to London."

"That is good of you. However, I have some more news. With the cooperation of your Doctor Holroyd, we have apprehended criminals engaged in criminal activities and recovered a large trove of valuable Chinese artifacts. I have to say that the size and value of what we recovered exceeds by far any previous finds. As you might think, achieving such a happy event with the assistance of a foreign guest is an unusual situation and requires an appropriate response. My government wishes to express its appreciation by honouring Doctor Holroyd and would appreciate your assistance in the matter."

Miller almost choked with surprise. "That is very helpful. I'm sure everyone will be most pleased." He managed to gasp out.

"Excellent. Then I will wait to hear from you. Thank you for your cooperation." With that, Hsien hung up.

Miller sat back, thinking about the call. He had not expected an initiative from the Chinese side, but there it was. Just then his secretary came in with a large folder.

"This came by hand delivery for you."

Miller opened it and found the file Hsien had mentioned. He skimmed over the first few pages before grabbing the phone and asking for a secure line to London.

"Hantington."

"Miller here, sir. We just got an amazing offer. The Chinese government is proposing that we start discussions regarding the island's future. They are offering to let the sovereignty remain with Britain under certain conditions for fifty years or until the island becomes uninhabitable because of rising waters."

"Are you sure?" Merry asked, surprised.

"Yes, sir. Got it in writing right in front of me."

"I say! Do we know just why they have become so generous all of a sudden?"

"It seems your academic friend had something to do with it."

****

Holroyd was out, so Merry left a message.

"Peter, old boy, just received a call from our Beijing chappie." Merry paused for dramatic effect. "The Chinese invite you to visit them with all bells and whistles at their cost. Want to give you a gong or something. And one other thing. Our accounting department has approved your first-class ticket. Nicely done, old boy. Knew I could rely on you. Oh, and your university will do the honourable thing and offer you tenure as well as reinstate your funding. Least they could do, I thought."

Another pause. "Free for drinks? I have an interesting problem on my desk. Right up your alley, I think. Call you next week."

Holroyd pressed the erase button.

About the Author

Peter King was born in Scotland and grew up in Switzerland and England before coming to Canada to study civil engineering at McGill University. He obtained his MBA at Western University and his doctorate from the University of Phoenix at age seventy. He spent his career as a naval officer, a public servant, a consultant to First Nations, and as a professor at the University of Hearst. For fifteen years he was a professor at the Beijing University of Technology. He has competed and coached in fencing, rowing, and cross-country skiing. He was also an international umpire refereeing at world rowing championships. He has been recognized by federal, provincial, and municipal governments in Canada and by the City of Beijing in China. He has published a history of rowing, several academic papers, and this is his first attempt at writing a mystery thriller while writing further novels, poetry, and rebuilding a model railway in his basement.

www.ingramcontent.com/pod-product-compliance
Lightning Source LLC
Chambersburg PA
CBHW070153310726

48976CB00001B/85